# PLAY ME!

Charles Harris is a best-selling and award-nominated author and a writer-director who has won international awards for his work in cinema and TV. He lives in Hampstead, London.

# Also by Charles Harris

# CHARLES HARRIS

# PLAY ME!

BLUE COAST PUBLISHING

PLAY ME!

Copyright © Charles Harris

First published in 2025 by Blue Coast Publishing

ISBN: 978-1-917936-00-2 (hardback)
978-1-917936-01-9 (paperback)
978-1-917936-02-6 (ebook)

*To E*

# Track 1

# 1 The Market Place

Freddie Forrester's problems started when they sentenced him to death. Second problem was nobody told him.

That morning he'd hightailed three hours across the island to Rodadora, the town he'd hoped never to see again, missing out on his eleven o'clock coffee and Danish, because his cousin Sid had sent a shit-scared message, saying he needed to meet, urgent. Something life-threatening, it seemed.

Freddie was up to his eyes in hustle and Sid was a klutz, but family was family. Right now though, Freddie stood in the middle of the town's market square – Sid was late – caffeine and patisserie withdrawal was kicking in – and Freddie was concluding he might happily whack Sid himself.

Thing was, for some months Freddie was growing disillusioned with his chosen career of drugs baron. He'd tried to be a good mobster, treated his clients nice and his gang nicer. He could command people as effectively by smiling as shooting them in the knee, though he'd do that also if he had to. But he was in his mid-thirties already and the long hours were getting to him.

Retiring was not something you did lightly. Not as a mobster. He'd be putting a target on his back for everyone who held a grudge, or even disagreed with his choice of beverage. He had to do it quickly. Like ditching a girlfriend. He'd take his crew for an expensive dinner, maybe, tell them it's not them, it's him. No hard feelings. And make like Houdini. Small cottage somewhere in the hills. Just him and his sister. Tending fruit trees and playing dominos with neighbours outside the village bar.

He counted to ten. Then twenty. He used to love this little town where he grew up, beaten into submission by the Caribbean sun. He hated what it had become. Hated the few shoppers meandering between the dusty trestle tables, looking with jaundiced eyes at tomatoes and avocados, tortoise-wrinkled as the farmers selling them. The freshest produce was a pile of heavy metal CDs. At the far end of the square, half a dozen layabouts in torn T-shirts bothered a football. Three workmen stood on the other side, scratching their heads over a hole in the road that seemed to astonish them by existing.

Freddie's intestines griped. Something didn't fit. His gut was an Alpine weather house: sometimes the good weather guy came out, sometimes the bad. Today was dyspepsia.

He looked to his main wingman, leaning against a palm tree, pointed at his watch. Pontiac nodded in agreement. A big man, with a small moustache and an evil glint, not the brightest star in the sky, but he liked money. Freddie trusted people most when he knew their motivations. Freddie's two other bodyguards glanced up from where they were playing Candy Crush on their mobiles.

The CD stallholder had fallen asleep on his stool, chin on his chest, like an old balloon, with the air leaked from inside him. Next to him, a dozen 7-Ups and Fantas sat tepid in a bucket. Freddie took three and tossed them to his men, who drank gratefully.

The stallholder gave a shudder, but didn't wake. Freddie pushed a large banknote into the old man's shirt pocket. Too generous, but… Four local children saw their chance and pounced, hands out. Freddie gave them a can each. They ran off giggling.

'Say thank you, you little egg-suckers,' he called, but they disappeared out the square, doubtless headed for their gang HQ. He remembered the hideouts from when he'd grown up here – one beside the broken-down bus station; another behind the school; his posse in the graveyard. Good times – until they weren't.

But still his insides griped.

The footballers stopped playing. The road-menders stopped mending. The market square went quiet. Cousin Sid the klutz, Freddie realised, wasn't coming. That was what you got for being caring.

He straightened an AxMan Flyn CD with his left hand and slid the other hand into his jacket. He caught Pontiac's eye. Pontiac was reaching for the back of his belt.

'The footballers,' Pontiac said quietly.

'And the road-menders,' Freddie said. 'Nobody cares that much about a pothole.' For a long moment, nothing moved, except a turkey vulture circling overhead.

The first bullet shot shattered a Celtic Spring disc next to Freddie's hand. Five black-clad snipers bobbed up from where they'd been hiding on the town hall roof and laid down a pattern of fire.

'Shit!' Pontiac said. Freddie could only agree.

The footballers and road-menders dropped what they weren't doing and pulled out hand guns. As bullets whipped past him, Freddie upended the CD table and dived behind it. Discs flew. Pontiac joined him, banging his knee, swearing. The stallholder opened his eyes.

'Here!' Freddie beckoned him from the ground, but the dumbass sat frozen with fear. Pontiac grabbed him by the shirt lapels and dragged him down.

The other gang members scrambled for cover. The footballers and road-menders fired as they advanced. The old man looked from side to side, dazed like he'd found himself in a movie. Next to Freddie, three Live Aid albums and the AxMan Flyn CD exploded in a shower of silver fragments. No respect for art.

He did a quick stocktake – they were outnumbered and the nearest shelter was a café, over a hundred metres away. A born pessimist, Freddie's philosophy could be summed up as: things usually get worse. But this was more worse than usual.

Instinctively, he reached out and scooped a handful of remaining CDs to safety. Then he made a decision. He pulled out his phone, speed-dialled. A woman's voice answered, but before Freddie could speak, he heard running feet and a police assault rifle pressed against the side of his head. He took a deep breath.

'One minute,' he said to the muzzle. 'I'm on the phone to the president.'

# 2 Turnip Island

Freddie loved and hated the island of his birth in equal measure. The Caribbean climate was sweet and the island generous – or at least it had been before an English privateer landed in the 1500s. Sir Roland de Fois inspected its peaceful bays and teeming jungle and christened it Benkuda, which was the islanders' word for turnip. Historians argue whether he named it for its shape or because he asked a passing hunter-gatherer where he was and the man thought he wanted lunch.

Sir Roland promptly declared his new discovery to be his favourite place in the world and proved his love by ripping up the forests in search of gold he was sure was there and whacking the locals when he didn't find it. He then died of fever, contracted from an insect bite. Ironically, the islanders could have given him the cure, but he'd just killed them.

The Englishman's tough love would be echoed over the centuries by thousands who washed ashore this vegetable-shaped smear in the ocean. Among them were Freddie Forrester's own ancestors. They'd hoped to make their fortunes, but their sole talent turned out to be growing just enough stumpy plants to survive and pass on their DNA.

Freddie and his sister Dania were born in the north of the island, which was famed at the time for its luxuriant explosion of flowers and its markets crammed with fruit. As kids they played among the laden stalls and scrumped for snacks in sweet-smelling orchards. But when Freddie was eight, the then president took over the land around the town and gave it to his nephew, a young man who believed himself to be God's gift to the world of agribusiness.

The new landowner diverted the river to water his sugar plantation and feed the lake in his gardens of his country house, which he called Versails, being crap at spelling. The town's orchards shrivelled. The fields grew brown. Many farmers gave up, took underpaid jobs spraying pesticides on the nephew's sugar cane, but the Forresters struggled on with their patch, paying higher and higher taxes to keep the nephew in the luxury he felt he deserved.

Freddie hated watching his parents grow hunched over with poverty. The landowner sat on their backs, a parasitic hippopotamus. Finally, at fifteen, Freddie slung his few belongings in a bag and headed south for the capital and what he called "real life" - promising his sister he'd send her a ticket once he could afford it.

Trouble was, real life wasn't so easy. After a long search, he found himself a discarded hut in a slum overlooking the sea. He loved that hut. The wood had rotted and it sloped to one side, but it was his own and he had to answer to no-one.

Over the days and weeks, he repaired and furnished it. When he wasn't there, he worked from five in the morning to eleven at night to earn enough to eat. Jobs in the city paid so little that most people had three. He cleaned, helped in a tobacco shop, and evenings he delivered groceries to the well-heeled.

One day, he was busy washing down toilets in one of the city centre hotels when a young man darted in. He was not much older than Freddie and came with a cloud of expensive aftershave that made Freddie gag. The man thrust a pistol and a bag into Freddie's hands, told him to keep his mouth shut, and ran off.

One minute later, armed police burst into the toilets and arrested Freddie for not being the drug dealer they were searching for. He started to say about the other man, but the nearest cop lamped him in the face and told him to keep his mouth shut. He smelt of the same aftershave.

Five years later, Freddie walked out of the city prison after serving his sentence for packing a weapon and holding a ki of cocaine. The first thing he saw was a rusty Cadillac, sitting low on bust springs. A thick aroma of aftershave drifted out of the driver's window. The young gangster beckoned him over, gave him a significant wad in gratitude and offered him a place in his crew, where he said Freddie could rise high.

Freddie was a polite young man. He thanked him, but declined. The gangster looked surprised, but Freddie had learned many things in prison. First, he'd learned how crime worked. Second, he learned he wasn't a team player. He liked bossing people around too much. Third, he'd become friends with Dr Woolworth Tensing.

A successful GP, Woolworth was an angry rake-like man, whose parents, like many Benkudans, liked to name their children after their favourite brands. He'd been banged up for failing to cure the president's sciatica and had spent his time in the pen studying the war on drugs.

'It's a fool's war,' he'd tell Freddie at night over a glass of smuggled hooch. 'Every human on the planet takes drugs, whether coke or paracetamol. Or hooch. All a fucking war does is drive up the price and kill people.'

Thinking about Tensing's words as he lay awake nights, Freddie had a vision: if he could sell his *yayo* with less violence than the others, everyone gained. The rich people of New York and London would be happy putting his merchandise up their noses.

With the money they paid, Freddie would employ the poor people he'd lived among, paying them better than they would ever make at their three jobs a day. He'd call it Forrester Income Benefit.

# 3 The Aviary

The morning after the ambush, Freddie didn't feel much benefit, hand-cuffed in the cells below the presidential palace, wondering what would become of his DNA and shivering at the sight, through the bars, of the presidential aviary.

Rearing over the trees of the palace gardens, the aviary formed a dark pyramid, a brooding shape, whose fame relied less on the exotic birds than that President Isobel Bachman liked to eliminate her inconvenient citizens there. Though it stood at least two hundred metres away, Freddie was sure he could see dried bloodstains glinting low down on the black metalwork.

The cell door rattled open and two guards shoved Freddie out into the corridor. The guards pushed him forward towards a flight of grimy stone stairs. As they went, Freddie tried not to look at more brown stains that spattered the walls and steps, giving off a sharp aroma that could have been cleaning fluid or blood.

In silence, the police guards marched them up the steps to a heavy steel door that led to the outside and the grim black aviary beyond. They stopped. Freddie stiffened himself ready for them to unlock the bolts and take him out.

But then the lead guard indicated the opposite direction, into the ground floor of the palace. Up one more flight of presidential stairs, down another presidential corridor and Freddie found him ushered into the presidential office, pushed over to stand in the freezing air-conditioned air, facing the empty presidential desk.

Two armed commandos entered, stamped, waited for the prison guards to leave and stood to attention either side of him. Expensive paintings hung on the walls, many procured by him to keep the president sweet. But of President Isobel Bachman, nothing was to be seen.

He glared at the two commandos, members of the presidential com-mando squad who'd been sent to kill him.

A minute later they were joined by two more presidential thugs and another prisoner.

He eyed Freddie. 'You?' Freddie didn't deign to reply. He hated people who stated the obvious. 'What the fuck are you doing here, Forrester?'

Lucky Strike Morton. Lucky Strike ran the Sunshine Cartel, based around the docks, the largest and most violent of the mobs. He was tall, red-faced with designer stubble, and wore a polo shirt and jeans, which strained to hold in the flesh, so business must have been good, but right now he looked like he wanted to rip out someone's heart and barbecue it with onions.

'I was going to ask the same.'

'I went to meet a man.'

'So did I.'

'About a deal. Twenty kilos of *yayo* – good price too. You?'

'A cousin being given some grief.'

Lucky laughed. 'Typical. Fucking Mother Teresa! Not even something you might make some green out of.'

Freddie felt his jaw tighten. 'Clearly we were both misled.'

'Sodding cops.' Lucky scratched parts of his anatomy. 'What's the point of paying them off if they start tricking and ambushing us? That's no way to run a country.'

Before Freddie could find a reply, the door banged open and the captain of the SWAT team entered.

'Stand up, ready for the president!' he ordered.

'I'm already standing,' Freddie said, and the police captain laughed raucously. He was six foot six, broad in the chest, with a bucket jaw and steel-blue eyes. President Bachman seemed to recruit her palace police out of Men's Vogue.

'Then get fucking taller.' He'd made the joke twenty times since the ambush and Freddie was tiring of it.

Freddie faced front. 'Today's filth have no respect for the business owner.'

Captain Bucket-Jaw raised the butt of his rifle to smack one Business Owner upside the head, but President Isobel Bachman bustled in. She stopped by her desk, laid her hand on a skyscraper of official papers and gazed at her two captives, like posing for a presidential photo-op.

'Well, well, here you are!' She smiled. Both Freddie and Lucky Strike had worked closely with her at election time, persuading rivals to consider their personal safety, but her smile was cooler than they were used to.

'Thank you for your phone call, Mr Forrester. And thank you, Mr Morton, for surrendering too–'

'I don't never surrender,' Lucky Strike broke in. 'Florence Nightingale here might have surrendered. My gun jammed.'

'Whatever. Those operations were expensive enough as it was.'

'The operations to have us killed?' Freddie asked delicately.

'The very ones,' answered the president. 'We go back a long way, the three of us, but in politics everything is come and go… You came in very useful to me once. And now it's time for you to go.'

She gave a convincing sigh. 'Anyway, Freddie, you phoned to say you had a suggestion. As I've always told you, you can call me day and night. Though, to be honest, you may not have many days or nights left.'

Freddie was about to answer when a junior aide sidled into the room and handed Bachman a note. She glared at the aide. He departed. She glared at the four armed commandos and captain, who saluted with a loud stamping of boots and marched off to stand guard outside. She glared at Freddie and Lucky Strike, who held their ground, so she smiled once more and waved them towards a sofa.

The sofa was antique, small and uncomfortable – Louis-something. Freddie had sourced it himself through a client in Miami, as a contribution to Honour-the-President Day. Lucky Strike sat, filling three-quarters of the space, leaving Freddie to wedge himself into the remaining quarter. He made a point of elbowing Lucky by accident on the way in and was rewarded with an angry grunt.

Bachman slid her eyes over the printed message she'd been given. 'The Americans!' She banged it down onto the pile of papers.

'Difficulties?' Freddie said hopefully. Solving presidential difficulties was one way he'd stayed alive.

Bachman sniffed. 'Last month I agreed to the White House's demands that I arrange free and fair elections, but now they're demanding the elections actually be free and fair.'

Freddie nodded in a gesture of support, but Lucky Strike puffed out his cheeks. 'Tell them to piss off.'

Freddie despaired of his rival's diplomatic skills. The president made a moue of disbelief, her downturned painted mouth looking like she'd been dining on raw blood, and came over to sit on a sofa facing them. 'I cannot overstate the role of your – businesses – in drumming up votes. But now we have started the Cull.'

'Of course the Cull.' Freddie tried to deflect her onto safer ground. 'As you mentioned, madam President, I did phone with a kind of proposal–'

But Bachman jabbed at a button. A servant entered nervously, pushing a trolley, like he was walking onto a firing range. 'Take a last drink, for old times' sake.'

Lucky Strike grunted again and reached for a can of President Bachman National Beer. Freddie selected a bottle of Isobel Bachman Freedom Diet Cola. On the label, the president waved at her citizens, in honour of their freedom to buy from her drinks monopoly. Meanwhile, in front of him, the real Bachman poured herself a slug of rum large enough to entertain a troupe of street musicians.

'Yes, the Cull.' She contemplated Freddie like a praying mantis eyes up a caterpillar. 'I need to have our country accepted as a place where foreign companies can invest and tourists can relax.'

'We don't target foreigners—' Lucky Strike began, but Bachman cut him off.

'Yes, yes, I know that. You just sell drugs to them. But it's not ideal when holidaymakers complain on TripAdvisor about dead bodies in their hotel pool.'

'*One* body.' Lucky Strike slapped a thigh in indignation. 'An American decided to take a midnight swim while I was sorting a deal. Who knew?'

Bachman fixed him with a cold glare. 'I'm a tolerant woman. I tolerate my husband's monthly trips to Paris to see his mistress. I tolerate the rude limericks about me, spray-painted onto walls in the barrios. You've seen them?' she asked, suddenly turning to Freddie.

Freddie hesitated. 'No, not at all—'

'Of course you have. They're not true. Mostly.' She made a fist as she spoke. 'But now we must clean up.'

'Clean up?' Freddie asked. Presidents with hygienic intentions worried him. It was one thing for politicians to talk about cleaning up, quite another to actually do something about it. 'Well, madam President, I've been thinking about getting out anyway. Buying a little farm. Doing something... legal.'

But Bachman was shaking her head. 'Too late.'

'But—'

She held up a hand. 'These are times of change. When change happens, some people move on and some get left behind. Or, in your case, executed.'

Freddie straightened himself. He wanted to look dignified in his last moments, but he'd have felt more dignified if they weren't his last.

'What about fucking justice?' Lucky Strike asked. 'We demand a fair trial—'

'Oh, you've had a trial–'

'We did?' Freddie said, surprised.

'It was held in secret.' She slid two judicial forms across the coffee table between them. 'Part of our confidential anti-corruption legislation, which was passed by parliament last year, also in secret. You'd have been impressed at the procedures, if we'd told you about them, which of course we couldn't. The evidence was weighed with care, arguments put on both sides. Your defending attorneys were persuasive. But sadly, not persuasive enough. You were both found guilty on all counts.'

Next to Freddie, Lucky Strike crushed his beer can in his hand. 'What counts?'

'We can't tell you that either.'

She beamed at them. 'But Mr Forrester, your proposal?' She checked her watch. 'We don't have much time. I've arranged for a quiet shooting, here in the palace grounds, beside the Isobel Bachman Aviary. We'd have organised something more public, but you never know. Some idiot films it with a mobile phone and suddenly I'm made to look like Cruella de Vil.'

Lucky Strike jumped up, as if to assault her. Freddie pulled on his arm. 'Sit down,' he said. Too late, he forgot you didn't give Lucky Strike Morton orders. The other man turned, eyes popping.

'Sit the fuck down,' Freddie repeated. 'It won't help. I've got an idea.'

Lucky Strike wavered for a moment, apparently torn between the possibility of something that might save their lives and the enjoyment of tearing Freddie's throat out. For the time being, curiosity won. He sat like an unexploded bomb.

Freddie took a breath. His idea had seemed so enticing when he was crouched behind an overturned table being shot at, but now he wasn't so sure. He could see the presidential aviary through the large windows behind her, a sullenly dark pyramid looming over the presidential park. He'd be joining many of the island's population who'd smoked their last cigarette there. 'You'll love it,' he said.

Bachman waited, her eyes steady. Lucky Strike gave Freddie a rude look and said, 'Go on!'

'Go on,' repeated the president. 'I hope it's good. The SWAT team were most annoyed after you phoned, when I ordered them not to shoot you.'

Freddie lubricated his vocal cords with weak cola. 'You remember the earthquake five years ago?'

Bachman nodded, arms crossed, an impatient schoolteacher, waiting to give them the strap. 'Yes, of course. Terrible, terrible…'

'All the relief funding. The profit you made. The TV coverage. You heroically pulling them stones off that buried hospital ward. We organised that film crew, remember? We helped bury the patients beforehand–'

'Of course,' she said. 'And your point is?'

'Wouldn't you like that again?'

'You can make an earthquake?' She seemed momentarily impressed, then shook her head in disbelief.

'Better,' Freddie said. 'A peace concert. Remember that Prime Minister over in Jamaica? He had a peace concert with Bob Marley. Did it to stop the gangland wars.' Both the president and Lucky Strike were looking at him like he'd farted. Freddie pushed on regardless. 'These pop singers, they love flying to poor countries to save us.'

He silently promised the Almighty that if He helped him out here, he'd go to church again, though he took care not to say when. 'You'd call for peace between mobsters, and democracy to allow you to help your starving oppressed subjects,' He was warming to his theme when he saw Bachman shift on the sofa and urgently added, 'not starving or oppressed, of course, through like any fault of your own.'

'A peace concert? But doesn't that sound bad? As if I can't control my own country?'

'It shows you're committed to cleaning up.'

'More committed than by shooting you?'

She had a point, but he was too deep in to wade back now. 'Maybe, but here's the kicker: you invite the charities.' He clapped his hands with enthusiasm, but she didn't seem to get the point.

'Charities?'

'Yeah, charities. Because with the charities comes cash. Fund-raising appeals. Save the Kids. Say No to Poverty. Get Rid of Land Mines.'

'We don't have any land mines.'

'We'll lay some. Believe me, you won't be able to keep them charities away. They can't resist putting pictures of our hungry children on their websites. Best if they're missing a leg or two. Think of the money they'll spend: first class flights on your niece's airline, top suites in your brother-in-law's hotels, tables in your friends' five-star restaurants, hire of limousines, security, Portaloos. We can provide that. And then your legacy–'

Freddie traced a headline in the air. '"*Isobel Bachman champion of peace and democracy: international stateswoman, saviour of starving children…*" The world's eyes turn to our little – sorry, great – country… And the world's chequebooks…'

'And they cancel my debts.' There was a slyness in her smile now.

'Whatever.'

'It's most important.'

'Yeah, we'll get that done too.' Freddie smiled back, proud of his new brainchild. Maybe retirement from crime wasn't going to be such a bad idea.

Bachman said nothing for a long while. Lucky Strike was tapping his leg like a countdown timer on an overweight stick of dynamite.

Bachman frowned. 'Shame Marley's dead.'

'We'll get someone else.'

'We'd need a Geldof or a Bono.'

Freddie waved airily towards the wider world outside the palace windows. 'My sister runs a music company. CDs and nightclubs.'

'I know,' Bachman said. 'Half my money goes to her when my family goes clubbing.'

'But it's not just the clubs. Her CDs are by the best in the business.' He thought it best not to mention that most of them were bootleg.

'OK, maybe.' Bachman stared thoughtfully out of the window at the aviary. 'Of course the conviction means that we'll be taking over all your assets anyway, including your sister's company and your parents' farm.'

'You can't do that!' Freddie flapped his hands. 'They're just ordinary people. What I do isn't their fault.'

'I think you'll find we did. Fruit of the poisoned tree, and all that.' She turned back to him. 'Suppose I considered your idea. It has possibilities. Why you though? I could get one of our proper music promoters.'

'If you can find one. Last I heard, they'd all pissed off to Magaluf or Miami. Anyway, you need someone you can trust not to go rogue and give all that money to the wrong people.'

'You mean like the poor?'

'Whatever. All we need is some dim rock star to front it all and bring his friends.'

'You're saying you'll both arrange this in exchange for your lives?'

Freddie hadn't planned on including Lucky Strike, but he didn't seem to have a choice. He nodded slowly. But Lucky clenched his fists. 'I'm not working with Forrester on any crap rock concert.'

Bachman smiled. 'The aviary is just over there.'

Lucky glared at Freddie.

'If I agree,' Bachman said finally, 'you will need to organise it all from jail.' She held up her hand before they could interrupt. 'Non-negotiable. Unless you want to be shot now and get it over with?' She smiled icily.

Freddie held out his hand and tried to keep it as steady as possible. 'Afterwards, everything is cancelled against us? No secret convictions, no executions. No taking my family's farm. All clean.'

'Agreed.' President Bachman pressed the button to summon the armed guards. 'I'll give you two months. Of course if there's no concert by then…'

She nodded eagerly towards the aviary, which glowered: a jet-black thundercloud beyond the trees.

# 4 How Do You Make a Rock Concert?

'You said what!' Dania Forrester was generally a woman of a calm, if negative, disposition, but sometimes her brother challenged even her ability to cope with surprise. She stared at the phone, as if it might have made the story up on its own, then put it back to her ear. Freddie was in the middle of explaining, but she didn't want an explanation. She wanted a denial.

'Do you have any idea what's involved in putting on a charity concert?' she said, interrupting his flow.

'Of course I don't. Do you?'

'Not a thing. But it's not exactly going to be like ordering a pina colada. Musicians are always trouble.'

She was standing in Freddie's office in their compound, trying to ignore the anxious shouting that came from the other side of the doorway and her own fears for her brother's fate.

Right now though, he and his bodyguards had been arrested and the offices swarmed that morning with the few remaining gang members who were still free. Three men and two women. Just enough around to protect the Forrester compound, if they stayed, but fear was infectious. They crowded around the desks; nobody knew what was going on and everyone had a loud opinion.

Dania yelled through the doorway for some peace and pushed the door shut.

'Where are you?' she asked. 'How are they treating you? Can I send you some food? Mum and Dad have been on the phone twenty times already – they've both been watching news of your arrest on TV and are thinking the worst.'

'I knew I shouldn't have given them that plasma telly. It's not good for them. They should be out mowing the fields or something.' Freddie's voice sounded distant and something in his tone made Dania shiver. In the background she could hear the awful sound of a metal door clanging shut.

'You haven't answered my questions.' She sat heavily at his desk. She needed a vodka martini, but Freddie had the only key to the chiller, while her own supply was over in her house.

'I'm doing great,' Freddie said, his voice fading and returning. 'Don't worry about me.'

'How can I not worry? Bachman's all over Facebook talking about justice and executions. I told you, enough of the drugs, enough of the crime. It was always going to end bad.'

'You know the funny thing: over recent months, I was starting to think of easing up.'

Dania felt sick. 'It's a bit late now.'

'I've got to go. The prison governor wants to see me. We're in negotiations. Send my love to the folks. They're always in my heart. Like heartburn.'

'Negotiations for what?'

'Enough! Get going on the concert. We've got two months. If Bob Marley could put one on, it can't be that hard. Try inviting him, to kick off with.'

'Marley's dead—'

'Then try Geldof.'

'How do I—?'

But he was gone. Dania would have slammed her phone on the desk, except she'd just bought the latest Samsung Galaxy. So she screamed at the display instead, straightened herself and walked to the outer office. The small group of gangsters turned to her in concern, shouting questions.

'I've spoken to Freddie,' she said, holding up a hand for silence.

'What did he say?' asked one of the younger crew members.

'He said, 'Stop bloody yelling and wait for his orders.'' She paused. 'And someone google Live Aid.'

\* \* \*

Dania banged the steering wheel in frustration. For years, she'd told Freddie to give up crime before it was too late. She parked badly and found one of the engineers, George, in the edit suite, slumped over the mixing desk, complaining of a hangover. The other, BJ, could be seen through the glass, sleeping mouth open on the floor next to a drum kit. Five polystyrene cups of Americano were lined up in front of George and he'd reached number three. He gave a grunt as she came in.

'How do you make a rock concert?' she asked.

He frowned and passed a hand over his forehead. 'Throw Stones at it?'

'This isn't a joke. A charity concert. Like Bob Geldof and Bob Marley.'

'Does it help if you're called Bob?'

'Do you want to keep your job?'

'Can you afford to sack us?'

Dania sat on the edge of the console and contemplated him coolly. George and BJ had lost their jobs in national TV, after smoking weed while editing one of Bachman's typical presidential broadcasts, in which she railed against sex outside marriage and school truancy.

The weed wasn't the problem. However, they'd decided it would be fun to reorder her speech so that she pledged to enforce sex outside marriage and ban education. Luckily, the public watched her broadcasts about as closely as they did YouTube videos of drying paint, so the two engineers were merely tortured and sacked, rather than imprisoned for life, and the TV station's loss was Dania's gain. They were mashed more often than not, but George was probably right – they knew too much about the bootleg CD operation to be safely let go.

'Come on,' Dania said, trying the soft approach, although it went against her principles. 'I need your help. How did Marley and Geldof do it?'

George downed his fourth Americano, as if taking medicine. 'Fucking hard slog. I wouldn't bother if I was you.'

'And if I was bothered.'

'I dunno. They phoned their friends?'

'What if you don't have friends like that on speed-dial? At least not the kind that play Madison Square Gardens every other Thursday.'

'I suppose you find someone who has.'

She crossed her arms and waited for George to realise he was supposed to suggest a way of doing this. He half-opened his eyes and gave a deep belch. 'Hack their social media accounts. That kind of thing.'

'You could do that for me?'

'Hacking?' George squinted at her warily. 'I'm not sure it's in my contract.'

He went to take his fifth Americano, but Dania snatched it out of his reach. 'You just rewrote it.'

# 5 Mr Positivity

'Think positive,' Micky Slapstone yelled at a huddle of roadies trying to pull an equipment trailer out of a swamp in the backstage car park. Rain sluiced over them and AxMan Flyn did his best to think positive too, watching from the open door of their tour bus.

'Pull north.' Micky stuck out an imperious hand and the roadies pulled north. 'Push south.' He stuck out the other hand and they pushed south. But the trailer wasn't listening, wheels jammed deeper into the mud than wheels had a right to go.

It was mid-afternoon at Midlands Metal Hell. Armageddon was coming on as apocalyptic clouds emptied themselves over acres of misshapen tents. Nearby, in the glare of the main festival stage, two thousand sleep-deprived fans bounced to an obscure Canadian death metal band. The farmyard smell of mud reminded AxMan of afternoons spent many years ago on school soccer fields, trying to avoid the ball.

'Any calls?' he shouted to Micky, but his PA didn't seem to hear.

Micky was a bullet – short, snub-nosed and shaven-headed. What he lacked in height AxMan's personal assistant and guitar tech made up for in persuasive force. But the trailer wasn't to be persuaded.

AxMan gave up on positive thinking. He was waiting for a phone call that never arrived. Couldn't concentrate on anything else. He took out his mobile, but it showed no messages or missed calls. He put it back in his gilet pocket. Then took it out again. What if it rang and the ringtone got lost in the wind and rain?

He spotted a movement on the ground. A snail had stopped in the middle of the car park, trusting its shell would protect it from all dangers. But a van lumbered towards it, headlamps glinting off the puddles. AxMan hesitated. He believed in saving nature. However, he had his limits. The rain was growing heavier – and there was no sign of the umbrella the festival had promised to bring. The snail turned its head towards him, its tentacles wavering. If a mollusc could implore, it was imploring.

'Oh, shit!' AxMan said. He plunged into the storm as the truck splashed towards them, grabbed the snail between two fingers, returned to the tour bus seconds before the van barrelled past. He positioned the little animal carefully on the top step.

'OK, mate?' he said to the snail, which had retreated into its shell. He took that as a thank-you.

Shaking the rainwater off his Lenin cap, he picked up his phone again. Today the judge would give her verdict on his four-year lawsuit against Pissoff Entertainment for cheating him of decades' worth of dosh. It had *taken* him decades to work out why his royalties and tour earnings had been so low. A trickle, virtually, despite his early hits still selling well. Right now, he should have been at the lawyers' office, waiting, but couldn't have stood the tension.

Instead, he re-read an email he'd got two days before. This puzzled him in itself. He never gave out his address.

*Dear Mr Flyn,* it began.

*I am the chief executive of Forrester Music which sells your records among others here in on Benkuda. My brother Freddie greatly admires your singing about rebels and street fighters, which is similar to his job here.*

*We're working with President Isobel Bachman to produce a Peace and Democracy Concert, just like Bob Marley in Jamaica, and would like to propose you as the front man to this concert.*

*You will help us bring social harmony and food for the starving, as well as rock star friends, international charities and a stop to the president's debt repayments, which President Bachman wants you to know are very close to her heart.*

*You would also be much better than Bono or Geldof, who sadly didn't have time to reply.*

*Yours in hope*

*Dania Forrester, Ms.*

He'd googled Benkuda and found a largish, vaguely oval, island in the east Caribbean, like someone had trampled on a potato. The national emblem was a misshapen blue-green fruit that everyone apparently agreed was inedible. The national flag – the same lumpy fruit against a night sky. Forrester Music's website flaunted an impressive list of top rockers, although strangely not the brother, Freddie. Maybe he laid tracks for a different label.

A charity concert was tempting – a fresh chance to broadcast the AxMan Flyn message against oppression and injustice. Plus better weather.

But he didn't have headspace to think about it now. Too tangled up in plans for his next album. He'd send this Forrester woman a polite refusal and a box of signed T-shirts. Shit, he didn't want to be Scrooge. Make it two boxes. Micky could set it up.

Still, AxMan's phone didn't ring. How long could it take a judge to see the obvious? Micky had said only fools went to law. But Cla-Rice, his muse and soulmate of five years, had told him to contact his inner truth and fight. So he had.

A young festival volunteer ran up, holding a festival programme over his head to shield himself from the downpour.

'Wow! Ax,' the youngster said. 'Hey, it's an honour. I've dug your work since I first heard *Slut on the Slide*.'

'Not enough of an honour to bring a fucking umbrella.'

'Umbrellas are most definitely on the way. Stay cool.'

AxMan moved the snail to one side and told the volunteer to come under the shelter of the doorway, but he seemed too in awe of him to accept. Instead, he reached inside his waterproof and for a weird moment AxMan thought he was going to pull a gun. Instead, he produced his phone. 'Is this OK? It would be cool.'

AxMan posed for a selfie with him and gave a double devil's horns for good measure.

'Wow!' said the volunteer. 'Cool.' He started to pocket his phone. 'Shit, I almost forgot. You're not on the main stage at ten any more. You're on the Meg Richardson Stage at six.'

He turned to go, but AxMan grabbed his arm. 'What the fuck?'

The volunteer paled. 'Not my call. It's the festival director. What can I say, man?'

AxMan shouted to Micky, but he was still ordering around the roadies, so he called to Cla-Rice for back-up, but right now, his muse and soulmate was sitting at the back of the bus, bent over The Font, lead guitarist of Kremlin, who were headlining the festival at eleven. The Font had dropped in to "say hi" and was now saying hi to Cla-Rice at length, legs hooked over the seats in front of him, picking his teeth with a plectrum. 'Bitch' and 'fucking-A' floated across. Their heads almost touched, as did other body parts. Clearly, what he had to tell her was important. Maybe he too was contacting his inner truth.

AxMan turned back to the volunteer. 'The Meg Richardson Stage!'

'You should feel privileged. Meg was a local celebrity.'

'She was a fictional character in a soap that's not even been on for years!'

'People loved her.'

'Phone the festival director.'

The volunteer trembled in his grip. 'I don't have her number.'

'Fuck off and get it!'

The volunteer fucked off. AxMan sat again and rolled himself a joint. It was always the same. He tried to think positive. Then they slapped you in the face. Six o'clock on the smallest stage? It was the last album. He was sure. Nobody liked innovation any more. Plus, he'd always had doubts about the festival director. She used to do PR for S-club 7.

The snail brought out its head again. Waggled its horns. AxMan placed a spare flake of bud next to its mouth. Even a mollusc had a right to experiment.

# 6 Stick it to The Man

Umbrellas arrived and AxMan watched them surround the bus, a cluster of damp tortoises. Volunteers built a pathway across the mud with sawn-up beer crates. As a headliner, The Font made sure he disembarked first, while reminding everyone he didn't really care about status. He'd opted to wear a white Elvis suit, and AxMan was delighted to see him slip off a crate and get spattered with mud. Who said there was no such thing as karma?

AxMan had opted for his signature blue leather jeans and studded leather gilet, being more Armageddon-proof. He looked round for Cla-Rice, but she dodged past, mouthing something inaudible. AxMan took a deep breath and started after them, inhaling a lungful of generator fuel and weed.

The same rain that thundered off his umbrella drenched a small crowd of fans huddled the other side of the backstage fence, like they were being hosed down by a satanic water-cannon. They waved and shouted AxMan's name. He recognised most of them – hardcore Axers, turning up all over the country, just for him. Some he'd known for over thirty years. Seeing his Axers always gave him bounce.

He sent them his AxMan registered-trademark glare, shook his Ax-Man-registered-trademark pigtail, then made AxMan-registered-trademark gun-shapes with his fingers. They whooped and shot finger-bullets back. Nothing enthused his fans more than miming an exchange of fire.

AxMan paused. His volunteer looked at him anxiously. 'I was told to get you to the interview tent in five minutes.'

'Have you got me the director's number?'

'I don't have the authority–'

'Then you don't have shit to say about it.' AxMan strode off into the rain towards his sodden fans, while the kid chased after him, brandishing his umbrella like a desperate samurai.

As young Benjamin Goldstein, AxMan had been brought up to fix things. His folks fixed teeth. So Benjamin set out to fix the world. He wrote political songs in his bedroom, practised power guitar chords on the knock-off Strat his father had bought him for his bar mitzvah, dreamt of world revolution to the backing track of drilling from his parents' orthodontist surgeries below.

But the world wasn't interested in being fixed. It might have helped if Bennie had grown up in New Jersey or Chicago, rather than a middle-class road in north London. He was cursed to have a violence-free childhood, deprived of the deprivation an artist so greatly needs. Then, still in his teens, he astonished himself and everyone else.

The song's intro arrived like from nowhere, descending from a mystical cloud one Friday evening, while his mother shouted the kosher meat-balls were getting cold already. It wasn't complicated, a simple seven-note riff, but it seemed to hold a special magic and the rest of the song came in minutes, fully formed.

*Stick It To The Man (Wiv a gun in your han')* was picked up by a tiny failing company called Pissoff Records.

'Don't expect too much,' the A&R man said over beers after a gig which only Benjamin's friends and Micky had turned up to. Micky promptly appointed himself as Benjamin's guitar tech and personal assistant and told him to Think and Grow Rich.

To everyone's amazement, Micky was right. Not knowing any better, Benjamin had fused punk, heavy metal and anti-establishment rap into rebel metal, a genre nobody had thought of before. The song went platinum, saved Pissoff from insolvency. *Kerrang!* called him the new Motörhead, *Sounds* produced a give-away poster of him, and The Guardian compared the opening chords to Verdi's *La forza del destino*. Eighteen-year-old Bennie Goldstein – singing under the name AxMan Flyn – had his first hit. It helped that he looked older and nastier than his years, tall for his age, sporting impressive stubble, long hair and chains. And if he was still a little gangly, he'd fill out later.

A few smaller hits followed, along with a concept album about the failings of capitalism. The month it appeared, the Soviet Union chose to collapse and nobody was ready to diss capitalism. Micky told AxMan he was ahead of his time. He was Van Gogh, without the missing ear.

Meanwhile, Pissoff Records expanded into Pissoff Media and Events, then Pissoff International plc. With each expansion, AxMan slid down the priority list for marketing spend. Each January, a new AxMan album appeared. Each January, he was sure it would be the one. Each January, the new album sold fewer than the one the year before. He knew the songs were better each time. His friends said they were better each time. The critics said it. Everyone said it, except the public.

AxMan's stellar rise turned into an astronomical sink. Less rocket-man than leaking balloon. It didn't help that the phrase "Stick it to The Man" felt more and more dated. He wished he could change the chorus, but his fans still chanted it.

He'd tried for thirty-four years to repeat the miracle of that moment in his bedroom and sometimes came close, but never close enough. Sales slumped. The fans grew older. Gigs got smaller until he was playing to fifty ageing men and women (and their dogs) in Hartlepool. It was a cruel joke played on him by the universe.

But he still could hold a crowd with his old hits, still dreamed of fixing the world through music. Just as he had when he was mere Bennie Goldstein, practising alone on a second-hand Strat knock-off made in Taiwan.

The Axers hollered and whistled, rainwater dripping from their leathers and tattoos.

'AxMan. Hey, man! Yo, big man! Shoot me dead, innit!'

Ahead of the chasing umbrella, AxMan was soaked. He began to regret his impulsiveness. He performed his number two snarl. Invigorated, the Axers waved wet CDs and posters. 'My people!' he called. 'My merch!'

Discs pushed through the wire fence. AxMan took the nearest and began signing. 'Keep up the fight,' he growled.

'Yo, AxMan! Tell it how it is.' A plump red-haired man thrust an early CD at him. 'When's the next one?'

AxMan scribbled his name. 'The best things are worth waiting for.'

'But what about your song *Fight the fight now! Don' delay?*'

'Well, sometimes, hey, the fight needs a recording studio in Mustique.' The man looked confused and withdrew, clutching the disc to his chest.

One middle-aged woman asked AxMan to autograph a pair of sodden knickers. He squinted at the label. 'Marks and Spencer? Helping The Man, yeah?'

She nodded uncertainly. For a moment he felt bad. He'd told her Santa Claus didn't exist. But no, truth was truth.

'Smell the coffee, girl. All them companies are The Man, man. The Man runs the world. Do you want to change the world?'

'I want to change the world.'

'Change where you buy your knickers. The journey of a hundred miles starts with the first piece of lingerie.'

'A thousand…'

'What?'

She blinked, but stood her ground bravely. 'I think the saying is "A journey of a *thousand* miles…"'

'Who's counting? Stick it to The Man and all his underwear.'

He gave a double devil's horns and strode away under the volunteer's umbrella, as best anyone could stride in thick mud. His bounce was back. Micky joined him, wiping dirt from round his eyes, looking like a determined owl. He handed AxMan a thermos.

'Thought you might need something.'

'Spot on.' AxMan twisted the top, taking a swig of Laphroaig. 'But you look knackered.' He went to pass it back.

Micky shook his head. 'What doesn't kill you makes you stronger.'

AxMan thought about this. 'What about dementia? My dad had it for six years and it didn't make him stronger.'

'Did he die in the end?'

'Yeah, in the end.'

'Well then, it killed him. Proves my point.'

AxMan pondered for another twenty-five yards. Sometimes he felt there was a flaw in Micky's logic, but he could never quite pin it down.

Micky's mobile rang. He mouthed, 'Lawyers!'

AxMan's bounce disappeared again. Why were they phoning Micky and not him?

'Yeah,' Micky said to his phone, his expression annoyingly unreadable. 'Yeah,' he repeated. 'Yeah.' And for variety, 'Yep.'

He rang off.

'Well?' AxMan was unable to stop his voice going up an octave.

Micky contemplated the mud in front of them for another ten paces. Finally, he said, 'You won.'

'We won!' AxMan punched the air and only narrowly missed braining the umbrella-volunteer. 'Everything?'

'Outstanding royalties, overcharged fees, withheld tour receipts, fraudulent accounting, the lot.'

'Wow!' AxMan hugged him, then hugged the surprised volunteer. 'Not that money is important. But… wow! When do I get the luka?'

'Never.'

AxMan took another three steps before the answer hit. 'Say that again.'

'No dosh. We signed with a subsidiary. Pissoff Metal. Pissoff International closed down Pissoff Metal ten minutes before the hearing. There's no assets. Even their electric SUVs are in their wives' names. There's not enough in their bank account to pay your legal costs.'

'But, fuck, man, my costs are…' AxMan tried in vain to do the arithmetic. There were too many noughts. 'Get me the lawyers.'

Micky got the lawyers back, but before he could speak AxMan snatched his phone. 'What the fuck is this, Russell?' he shouted. 'I win, but I don't get shit?'

His solicitor's voice came over with the calm sorrow of a well-paid undertaker. 'Yes. Dreadful. The subsidiary's in liquidation.'

'Dreadful?' AxMan shot up an octave more. 'What about my costs?'

'We asked for them, but if the well runs dry…'

'It didn't run dry; they hid the fucking water.'

'Life's a bitch.' His lawyer gave a sad chuckle. 'As you happen to say in one of your own songs. No matter, we'll email you our final invoice. Payment in the usual thirty days.'

'I can't afford another invoice.'

'Then we'll need an inventory of what you own… house, car–'

'I've never had a car and I mortgaged the house to record my last album.'

'Guitars?'

'I can't sell my guitars! How am I going to live? The fee for this festival will hardly cover my–'

'You're getting paid for the festival? We'll need that money as well.'

'Russell. I'm bankrupt.'

'No problem, Bennie. We handle bankruptcies too.'

# 7 In the Media

In the media tent, no Cla-Rice. AxMan was dismayed. His soulmate always sat in on his interviews and gave him notes afterwards – such as how he needed more gravitas like Elton or Bono. Instead, he was greeted by a lank young Indian PR assistant, who flopped from side to side like a festival brochure in the wind, said, 'Cool,' and led AxMan over to the journalist from *Kerrang!* who was briskly fixing a camera to a tripod.

They shook hands and she said 'Awesome!' with an air of on-demand excitement and a spiky blue mullet. As she flickered around her equipment she looked like a Bunsen burner.

'Cool,' the Indian said.

'I love your work,' the Bunsen burner cooed. 'Awesome!' And they probably would have continued like this for some time but AxMan suggested they might like to start soon.

He tried to concentrate on what he was going to say, while she finished setting up, but he couldn't stop thinking about the money. Though it wasn't just the money, it was everything he'd created. He'd hate losing the house that he loved. And his guitars… the Gibson Flying V had been played once by Hendrix. And his career… He'd have to cancel the studio he'd booked for his new album.

Every few months, he had the same nightmare: he was back in his bedroom in Grove Gardens, Golders Green, plain Benjamin Goldstein, forgotten, no more hits to his name, playing his second-hand knock-off Strat to an audience of none. He shuddered and beckoned to Micky. 'You know, I won't be able to pay you.'

'We'll talk about it later.'

'No, I mean it. You'll have to find some other guitars to tune.'

Micky muttered something about the sound check and disappeared back into the rain.

'Awesome.' The journalist turned the camera on.

Normally cameras settled AxMan's nerves, not this afternoon, as he squeezed himself into a plastic chair and gave his number three snarl.

'Cool,' said the PR assistant.

'Brilliant,' said the journalist, catching everyone by surprise.

She asked the usual questions about his old songs. He tried his best to sound as if they were the most original questions he'd ever heard.

Then she asked about his past life as an anti-establishment rebel. In truth, the young Benjamin Goldstein's life of insurrection constituted shoplifting two packets of Smarties, shortly before his eleventh birthday – followed a few years later by a caution for possessing a quarter of an ounce of weed. But, without actually lying, AxMan contrived to make his rap sheet sound substantial and scary. At least this was partially true – it was scarily lacking in substance.

The *Kerrang!* journalist hesitated, then enquired about the lawsuit. He'd been hoping she hadn't remembered.

'I just heard I won,' he said, trying to sound triumphant.

'You won?' She squinted at him. 'That must come to millions.'

He shrugged, unable to bear telling her the truth. She pulled out her phone. 'I have to put this on Twitter.'

'No, really, don't feel–' But her thumbs were already working. She twisted in her seat and reached up to turn off the camera.

Afterwards, AxMan stood in AxMan pose as she busied herself taking photos and saying 'awesome' again, but with less enthusiasm. He made devil's horns. The journalist snapped him from different angles. She said 'awesome' one last time, picked up her bags, camera and tripod and departed for her next appointment.

The PR person remained. 'Cool,' he said.

'I need a drink,' AxMan moaned.

'Yes, of course. No problemo.'

'Now.'

The PR assistant paused, as if searching for the right word then gave up the struggle. 'Cool,' he pronounced with finality and left in search of alcohol.

AxMan stood in the empty media tent. Micky had disappeared. Cla-Rice was still nowhere to be seen. Congratulatory messages began to arrive on his phone from friends who'd seen the news of his lawsuit on Twitter. His musicians could be heard laughing nearby in the hospitality tent. Everything smelt of stale cigarettes and stewed coffee.

# 8 Seven-note Riff

Sometimes a performance slips out of your hands, like a fumbled wine glass. The crowd cheered AxMan onto the Meg Richardson stage, but grew quiet when he opened with a new song – *Global Gobble*.

He missed Cla-Rice standing in the wings, dancing to the beat in a bra and hot-pants, smoking his scag and flirting with the roadies. Where was she? She had style. She inspired him. She'd been the one he'd been thinking of when he wrote his most romantic numbers, *Gagging for It* and *Hoes and Bitches*. With lyrics such as *"Down in the street/sucking meat."* And *"wait/for the cash injection/of my heart/with your legs apart."* And he'd meant it.

For a second he caught a movement off-stage where she used to be… But it was just a punk stage-hand stubbing out a fag.

He was late for his cue at the start of his second number, *Entrails in the Street*. He swore at the kid on lead guitar – though it wasn't the kid's fault – strode around the stage, pummelling chords on his Les Paul Junior, but felt strangely empty. A vampire had drained his blood.

The Midlands Metal Hell crowd received AxMan's two new songs with polite applause. He ended the second and stared out at the mosh pit. The mosh pit fell silent. This was horrible. A voice called out, '*Stick it!*' Others took up the cry. The band looked at him uncertainly. Something had to be done.

He tapped his right foot four times, nodded to the band. He played *Stick It To The Man*'s famous opening riff:

*BLAM BAM*

*BAM BAM-KRAM*

*BAM BLAM*

The seven notes ran an electric shock through the crowd. This was the song that had made his name. He stood taller. The mosh pit woke up. The lead guitarist repeated the riff. The seven beats reverberated. Hammer blows around the arena. A giant dancing in Doc Martens. A rebel army on the march.

'*Stick it to The Man,*' AxMan sang.

'*Stick it,*' the crowd sang back happily.

'*Wiv' a gun in your han'.*'

'*Stick it! Stick it!*'

The crowd roared. Their maverick hero was back. The band picked up the rhythm. A circle formed in the mosh pit, bouncing wildly. AxMan marched across the stage. He felt good again. Duelled with the young guitarist, face to face. Renegade mobs stampeding through bloodstained alleys.

AxMan hit heavy chords. the guitarist replied with a series of powerful runs up and down the scale, wailing and screeching. AxMan felt proud of the kid. He'd found him gigging in pubs in Camden – a kid of eighteen, called Zane Vyper, with his head shaved on one side and an attitude. Now Zane took the riff. Turned it upside down. Played it backwards. AxMan held his own. The crowd cheered.

AxMan knew how to command an audience once he had caught them. He loved the feeling. It was like driving a Formula One car. Once you had control, you could take them anywhere at any speed.

He punched the air, every inch the rebel leader, took off his guitar and climbed the scaffolding at the side of the stage, reaching at least three feet off the ground. Pretended to karate-chop the security guards. Threatened the mosh pit with personal violence. They adored it. He jumped off the stage and stalked towards his fans, as if to do real damage, and was held back by two minders, who'd been warned in advance not to fight too strongly. The crowd adored it even more. He felt great.

Doctor Stage was working his healing magic. AxMan was back.

\* \* \*

As he came off stage, people surrounded him, high-fiving with insane excitement. VIP pass-holders he didn't know clapped him on the back. Men and women in black leather and chains thrust programmes and other artifacts at him to sign. Middle-aged women pushed cleavages towards him.

Then Doctor Stage's brief medicine wore off. Under the lights, AxMan had forgotten his anxieties, but they hadn't forgotten him and returned in a swarm, wasps at a picnic.

Micky disappeared to organise the de-rig. The rain eased into a depressing drizzle. AxMan went looking for Cla-Rice in the band's dressing room, but she wasn't there. Only the band bitching to each other about who got in whose way and who'd played in F instead of G.

Once he'd changed, he swung by the hospitality tent, but she wasn't there either. He high-fived someone he was sure he knew, then wondered if he'd got him wrong. He tossed back a couple of beers and greeted mates from other bands, but the place teemed with loud hangers-on one-third his age.

In the end, he cut back to the tour bus. As he entered, an urgent rustling came from the back and Micky's bullet-head emerged from behind a seat, to be joined a moment later by one of the stage-hands.

'Man,' AxMan said, 'this is not a good time.'

Micky muttered a few words to his new best friend, who stood up and apologised, adjusting the zip on her jeans. Micky ushered her outside.

The bus stank of too many weeks on the road. AxMan flung himself full length on a bench seat and looked up. A red thong dangled from a luggage rack, like a pennant. The matching bra lay on the seat opposite. He recognised Cla-Rice's size. She'd once spent a day on page three of the *Star* ("Cla-Rice Levy, 18, wants to study social economics – enjoys reading Dostoevsky and buying clothes.")

Next to the bra lay a pair of mud-spattered white boxer shorts with *The Font* embroidered in purple on the crotch. AxMan contemplated them. Then he picked up the shorts between a thumb and forefinger and flung them as far out of the door as he could. They fell onto the mud and got run over by a passing tech truck.

Micky returned, wiping rain from his scalp, and saw the bra and thong. 'Don't give her the pleasure of thinking about her,' he said, clearing them away. 'She's not worth it. I'll get one of the roadies to bring over the rider from the dressing room.'

'Forget the rider.' For the rider, AxMan had asked for beer, vegan black pudding and a dish of Smarties, green only. Yet that night, he didn't have the energy to care. He shuddered and beckoned to Micky. 'This money thing is awful.'

'We'll talk about it later. Just chill.'

Micky trotted back into the night like a determined terrier. AxMan lay back again, staring at the lager-spattered roof, trying to chill. But chilling wasn't a strength of his. And now he found himself thinking about that peace concert in Benkuda. The email hadn't said they were going to pay him, but then again, it hadn't said they weren't. Maybe something could be negotiated.

Over in Benkuda it seemed there were people who wanted him, needed him. He pictured himself comforting children dying of drive-by shootings and disease. He saw himself visiting the ghettos, bringing peace and vaccines. The Bono of rebel metal. He imagined Cla-Rice gazing up at him in admiration, along with other attractive young women (but most importantly Cla-Rice). The more he thought, the more excited he grew.

He dug out his phone to tap out a reply to Dania Forrester.

Fuck the lawyers, fuck The Font, fuck Pissoff. AxMan hadn't felt so positive for years.

# 9 A Typeface

AxMan still felt the buzz when he walked onto a plane and turned left – even though it was three decades since he'd last turned right (on an educational weekend trip with his parents to Auschwitz – they believed in holidays with a purpose).

First class had become a badge of honour. He'd told Micky to insist on it when talking terms with Dania Forrester a week before. Micky sounded insulted at having to be reminded: second class wasn't in his dictionary. And after they settled on a surprisingly large appearance fee, two first-class tickets with BenkudAir had duly turned up by email a day later.

It was only then that the agonising reality hit him. AxMan lying awake for hours in the Mongolian yurt Cla-Rice had had installed in his master bedroom. Constructed of air-dried wood and hand-dyed felt, the structure squatted in the centre of the room like a multi-coloured toad and was supposed to promote sleep. But that week sleep didn't come.

It was one thing slagging off 'The Man' at the Mercury Awards, but now AxMan would have to meet real politicians face to face. And make speeches. This charity stuff looked so easy when Geldof or Bono did it. Proper speeches required knowledge, didn't they? Micky would have to find a way for him to back out.

He'd informed Micky over coffee in his basement cinema, three days after Midlands Metal Hell. Micky nodded sympathetically, but reminded AxMan how much money he owed. Anyway, this Forrester woman wouldn't have invited him if she thought he needed to know anything. If she'd wanted Geldof or Bono, she'd have asked them.

'She did. She says they turned her down.'

'Well, more fool them.' He tapped AxMan's hand. 'If anyone's capable of leading a charity peace concert on a small island, it's AxMan Flyn.'

'Yeah, you're right,' AxMan said, with growing conviction. 'I can do this

– whatever it is. I'm AxMan Flyn. What could be so difficult?' And indeed, he felt a new energy once he'd decided properly. There was something good about making decisions. He resolved to make more of them.

Dania Forrester had asked him to bring his rock star friends. He began by phoning the names he'd bumped into at festivals: Kylie, Paul, Ringo, Madge, Phil, KT, Dave, Annie, Bruce, Roger and Mick... His calls went through to their assistants, who promised wholeheartedly that Kylie, Paul, Ringo, Madge, Phil, KT, Dave, Annie, Bruce, Roger or Mick would be in touch as soon as they had finished their rehearsals / yoga / photo shoot / vacation / spliff.

AxMan did wonder briefly about the risk of violence on the island. Despite his songs, he'd actually seen almost no fighting. His childhood in Golders Green had been quiet and content. The streets were not so much mean as pleasantly tree-lined. His greatest risk to life was eating gefiltefish after the sell-by date. To reassure himself, he'd told Micky to send him everything he could find on this turnip-shaped country they were going to save.

What he learned, lying in the yurt with his iPad, was just how dreadful life was for the average Benkudans. There was food, but few could afford it. He saw clips of children searching for food on refuse dumps. Gangs fought in the cities and rebel militias roamed the jungle. Despite all this, the people remained mostly decent, fun-loving and unrealistically optimistic. AxMan's heart went out to these brave people and to the wonderful altruistic Forrester family who–

His thoughts were interrupted by the sound of the Nigerian maid, bustling into the bedroom to clean.

'Oxfam?' she called into the yurt. 'Or rubbish bin?'

AxMan put his head out of the curtained doorway and saw the woman eyeing Cla-Rice's ra-ra skirts and seven-inch heels, still scattered where she'd left them two weeks earlier.

'When my bastard husband played around, I threw him clothes in the road.'

'No, no. Not just yet. Give it time.'

'You say same every day. She not coming back, you bet yourself. You have no money. That Font, he well endowed. He young. I've seen on TV his tight jeans bulging and–'

'Enough,' interrupted AxMan. 'I'll sort it. Meanwhile...'

'Meanwhile?' The maid waited, scratching her chin. AxMan was almost man enough to face up to the truth – but not man enough to do anything about it yet.

'Store room,' he said, ignoring the maid's pout.

He tried to distract himself with a few minutes' exercise in the tai chi dojo on the second floor but strangely, since Cla-Rice had left, their tai chi teacher hadn't shown up either, so AxMan retreated to his first-floor studio for a jam session.

As he picked up his favourite 1958 Les Paul Tiger Stripe to tune, he found another of Cla-Rice's pieces of lacy underwear underneath. She managed to leave them in all kinds of places. It was almost as if she did it on purpose.

It was time for another decision. Manfully, he sent her a text: *I've got your clothes. Chuck or send?*

To his alarm, she rang back immediately. He hesitated before taking the call. What does a poet say to his errant muse? AxMan had no precedent to draw on. His diet of TV cop shows and Black Sabbath was no use to him. He finally swiped the green button, remembered Micky's advice and tried to think positive. But Cla-Rice spoke first, 'It's not personal, babes.'

AxMan had promised himself he'd remain aloof but failed. 'How exactly is it not personal, Cla? And now that I think of it, were you cheating with the tai chi teacher too?'

'Babes, no way. I'm working on improving myself.'

He heard The Font's fake drawl in the background, 'Fucking A.'

'*He's* there? You're calling to talk to me with him listening!' AxMan stood up clutching his phone. He felt exposed. Made to look a fool.

'Ax, there's nothing between us. We're just working on an album together. Like you always promised me, remember?'

'And we're going to. As soon as—'

'You said that last month. And the month before.'

'And now, man, I'm doing this big island thing for peace—'

'And the starving children, yeah,' she said. 'Micky told me. But you don't actually have to go there, do you?'

He told her, like, Geldof didn't feed the children by posting from his bedroom on Twitter, but she wasn't listening. 'The Font understands me. He probes me deeper than I've ever been—'

'Enough with the probing.'

'He's a true artist—'

'An artist? A man who names himself after a computer typeface?!'

'It's nothing to do with typing…'

'"The Font." That's what he calls himself. A typeface.'

'Hey!' The Font's voice came over louder. He must have grabbed her mobile. 'It's not a bloody typeface.'

'A font is a typeface. I go onto my computer and you know what? It tells me what *font* I'm using. Times New Roman. Comic Sans. That's what a font is.'

'It's not a typeface. It's about wisdom.'

'Wisdom…?'

'Man, it stands for The Font of All Wisdom.'

'That's the *Fount*!' AxMan cried triumphantly. 'It's been pissing me off since you first joined Kremlin. It's not The Font. It's The *Fount*. The Font is a typeface or a baby bath in church. You've named yourself after a typeface or a baby bath.'

'I think you're wrong,' The Font said, though with a trace of nervousness. 'I checked on Wikipedia.'

'Well, check again, Wise Man!' AxMan stabbed his thumb on the red icon to end the call and threw the phone into the corner of the room, where it landed on Cla-Rice's wispy suspender belt. Together, they'd looked like a symbol of something, but whether it was hope or despair he wasn't able to tell.

* * *

As he clipped on his seat-belt, AxMan tried to distract himself with more positive thoughts. He was on his way to make a difference in the world. Forrester Music waited only hours away.

He hardly noticed someone rush onto the plane at the last minute and slip into the first class pod next to him.

# 10 Dunkirk Spirit

Meredith Heel settled next to AxMan and steadied her breathing. Only three hours earlier, she'd been up before dawn in her West London flat, polishing a report on making money from Third World sewage, when her boss messaged her to get straight onto Teams.

'Who's this Flyn guy then?' The old man hovered on Meredith's laptop screen, tapping the desk in front of him with a wrinkled forefinger. 'Is he going to sour the cream?'

'Don't worry, we can deal with him.' Surreptitiously, Meredith checked her makeup in the smaller window. Appearance was important. Her parents had drummed this into her before she was old enough to march out of the door of their semi-detached in Alpine Crescent, Braintree, and not look back.

'I never worry when everything's under control, Heel. I've always believed in you. I've handed you a shitload of responsibility, given your lack of years. I hope you're going to prove I was right.' Martin Plante sounded firm yet calm. He liked a slower pace, preferred conifers to concrete and Berkshire to Bank. Yet his quiet tone was scarier than any shouty boss. He gazed at her through the screen, the folds under his eyes and chin like tree-rings, earned over uncountable ruthless years. 'How is Benkuda these days?'

Officially, Meredith's job for Gropius-Plante plc involved advising governments of small countries on projects to develop their economy by arranging massive loans. Loans from Gropius-Plante. The money came into the country and promptly went out again to pay for the projects. Projects built by Gropius-Plante.

Take her proudest scheme on the island, Three Mountains A – the first of four proposed state-of-the-art nuclear power stations. The island didn't need them and they didn't actually improve anyone's living conditions, but

Meredith was good at making figures show what she wanted. The loan was one of the largest the company had ever handled.

Martin Plante had personally authorised a large bonus for her and the power station was opened by President Bachman on Honor-The-President Day. It was a shame that fish began dying in the local rivers, but a year later Meredith was able to persuade Bachman to take out another large loan to decommission it.

After all that hard work, some people had the gall to complain that the island was still poor. This annoyed her. They simply didn't understand the Trickle-Down effect. Trickle Down meant a large fee flowed to Gropius-Plante, as a reward for the highly stressful job it performed providing the loan. Most of the rest of the money gushed to the country's leader to be placed in a Cayman Islands account in anticipation of Depose-the-President Day.

After this, a small percentage flowed down to the president's family, heads of industry and party donors. Finally, any change left over trickled down to everyone else. That way, everyone gained. Those at the top were rewarded for their crucial responsibilities and less important people, such as doctors, nurses, farmers and teachers, received just enough to eat. If they were lucky.

'The island's economy has much improved, sir–'

'What–?' Plante froze then unfroze. 'Beetroot? Did you say 'beetroot'?'

Meredith instinctively spoke louder, even though her volume made no difference to her flat's WiFi, which was as reliable as two tin cans and a piece of string. 'No, sir. Much improved, sir. Odd spots of rebel activity, but the government has dismissed them as unimportant.'

'Well, what's this about cancelling their debt?'

'Cancelling the debt?' Meredith searched her mind for some info she might have missed. She hated not being in the know.

'We have intel that Bachman is planning to use this Love-In gig to cancel the country's debts and the rest of the power stations.'

'Shit – sorry, sir. I mean–'

'Shit, indeed. You know how much they still owe us?'

'I do.'

'And how much we stand to lose if they blow out the next stage of Three Mountains?'

'No problem, sir,' Meredith said. 'I have contingency plans. We may just need to speed things up.'

'And stop this pop singer – AxMad, FatAxs… He's up to his neck in it with that gangster Forster, Forager, whoever. They're behind this charity shit. Deal with him.'

'I'm onto it, sir.'

Over in Newbury, Martin Plante stroked his dewlap. 'Whatever it takes.'

# 11 The Scorecard

Meredith always kept a small suitcase packed ready for emergencies. In the Uber to Heathrow, she made two calls. Ten minutes later, she received an e-boarding card on her phone. At the same time, Dr Vijay Bhat, professor of maritime law, arrived at check-in to be told that the computer had no record of his first-class booking and the plane was full. As for the second call Meredith made, she simply received a text saying: Done.

During take-off, she observed AxMan from her pod next to his. The singer was taller than he'd looked in the photos on his Wikipedia page, but also wider around the midriff. With him was a smaller shaven-headed man who promptly nodded off.

From time to time, AxMan poked the man with his copy of the inflight magazine, complete with pictures of President Bachman trying to smile while eating one of the island's repulsive misshapen fruits. Failing to get a result, AxMan seemed almost angry. He called out 'Micky,' first quietly, then louder, but the other man just turned in his sleep.

Meredith sighed. These D-list celebrities. They thought they could fly out, sing some songs and change the world. She wondered if they'd feel so happy if the money they despised stopped flowing. If they had to do without their luxury homes and high-end cars. Exhausted by her attempt at empathy, she closed her eyes and only opened them when the trolley-pusher came round with glasses of chilled prosecco. It was a crap prosecco and normally she would have sent it back. But, given her new charitable frame of mind, she opted to let the matter pass.

Instead, she decided it was time and caught AxMan's eye. AxMan winced slightly and Meredith realised that – in her neat bob, lightweight Escada suit and Louboutin shoes – she must look like everything the singer hated.

'You have to be AxMan Flyn,' she said regardless. 'I love your music.'

AxMan straightened slightly and made a tentative devil's horns. She handed over a business card. 'Meredith Heel, Economic Analyst, Gropius-Plante. Which you won't have heard of.'

AxMan held the card by the edges as if it was sprayed with Novichok.

'We're in very much the same business,' she added.

AxMan raised his eyebrows. 'You make music?'

'We try to improve humanity. I help countries build airports, power stations, roads, that kind of thing.'

AxMan gave a non-committal grunt.

Meredith felt she wasn't getting far in penetrating the AxMan defences from the front and shifted to a flank attack. 'I was blown away by your last album.'

That one breached the walls. 'You've heard it?'

'Heard it. Bought it. *Wankers?* Amazing. *Bankers' Funeral* was for me the best track of the year. Thought-provoking. You know, I think you really nailed the hypocrisy at the heart of the financial sector. I mean—' She stopped herself before she went seriously over the top and hoped that AxMan wouldn't ask her about individual lyrics or stuff. She needn't have worried. AxMan had melted and was responding so eagerly that she had only to nod and shake her head at appropriate moments.

'It's not often,' AxMan said, after a detailed summary of every track on the album, 'that I find someone who's so self-aware. And open. Most of my fans listen to the first hits and just don't get what I've been doing since then.'

'Too true,' Meredith added, to remind herself she was still alive.

'Look at this!' AxMan jabbed at the screen of the in-flight entertainment centre in front of him. 'I always check out my songs when I go on a flight. For some guys this might look like vanity, yeah, but for a professional performer this is important market research. You understand?'

'I certainly do.'

'So...' He tapped again. 'My name's here – but only the early hits. It's not that I'm, like, annoyed – but where's the adventure? What about the concept album about pesticides, for Christ's sake?' He snorted in frustration. 'At least they've got my Christmas song *My Ho Bitch Santa*. The music mafia on Radio Six totally ignored it. But then, that's the BBC – no sense of adventure.' He turned off the entertainment centre with a deep sigh.

'A spiritual desert,' Meredith said.

AxMan glanced sharply at her and again she feared she'd overdone it, but the singer just smiled wryly. 'They won't be able to ignore me soon.'

Meredith tried not to look too interested. 'No?'

AxMan leant over the low partition between their pods. 'It's not being made public yet, but I'm preparing a major charity concert in Benkuda. I've been invited by one of their stars, Freddie Forrester, and his sister. She runs a major record label.'

'Freddie Forrester?'

'Yeah, she says he's like me. He's all about rebels and streetfighters. Some kind of rap artist, I think.'

'You think?'

'We're planning a great line-up… Paul, Ringo, Kylie, Madge, Mick, Phil, KT… They're all due to call back… Poverty. Peace. Everything. You know half the kids don't even have clean water, but they have guns?'

'Awful. If I can do anything to help…'

This seemed to take AxMan by surprise. He looked her up and down again. 'Well, my assistant Micky says the universe is always listening. Like some kind of karma-based surveillance operation. Heaven-CCTV. I could put that in a song—'

Meredith waited for him to get back to the point then the cabin crew interrupted with pre-lunch amuses-bouches. Despite the wine, she felt restless. Plante was right to be worried about Bachman's plans to cancel the country's debts and the new power stations. The loss of the interest payments alone would dig a dangerous hole in Gropius-Plante's annual turnover.

Meredith Heel respected money. Money was like a scorecard. There was so much in life that was fuzzy. For example, how could anyone tell if a film was any good simply by watching it? Luckily, God gave us a way. The weekly box-office was a scorecard. If a movie sold tickets, if people spent hard cash on it, this was solid evidence that Meredith could understand.

The numbers were handed down by the Lord to help mankind make sense of the world. You measured your health by how much your doctor earned. You audited your thirty-five years of life by how much you paid for your flats in Chiswick and Manhattan, along with the house in Leicester your bone-idle ex and two kids now lived in, while he created art installations that nobody would ever buy. God, she hated artists!

Love was more difficult to measure, which was why Meredith never quite understood it. Everyone sang about it, rapped about it, told the world how great a force love was. The thing was, she didn't believe them. If love was such a force, why was she divorced?

Right now, her scorecard showed the amount she paid in child support to maintain little Nantucket and Indigo. There it was, in black and white, with many zeroes at the end. Well, maybe love was a force after all. Helped along by divorce lawyers. She hated them too.

When the cabin crew had moved past, she took out her ear-buds and leant over to AxMan again. 'I'm sure you know to be careful.'

'Careful?' AxMan swallowed the remains of his wine.

'There's violent gangs who don't want you to save sick children.'

AxMan looked appropriately anxious. 'They don't?'

'People who'll try to use you for their own agendas, and others who'll do their best to stop you.'

'They will?'

Meredith toyed thoughtfully with her Rolex Pearlmaster. 'But as I say, I'm sure you know how to watch out for yourself and it will all be fine. Nothing to worry about.'

The crew were starting to serve lunch. AxMan checked they'd received his request for Ayurvedic salad, then ran a hand across his stubble. 'Yeah. Sure.'

'No problem then.'

* * *

Her glass refilled, Meredith settled back in her pod, unfolded a copy of The Washington Post and started annotating an article about how to sell more pesticides in Africa. She sensed AxMan would have liked to continue the conversation, but she kept her head in the paper and heard the singer call the nearest flight attendant over for more prosecco. Then AxMan told the attendant to make up his lie-flat bed and not wake him for meals, even Ayurvedic.

Once she was certain AxMan had closed his eyes, Meredith folded away her paper. His glass of wine was still on his table. It would be easy to reach across. Meredith always kept the appropriate powders with her, in case of emergencies. She took her handbag from her overhead locker and chose a small plastic container with a red label.

But no. She dropped it back and told herself to be patient. Her second phone call should have done the job. Instead she took a sleeping pill for herself and strapped on her eye-mask as she waited for it to take effect.

* * *

She woke to find the crew handing out landing cards. Her legs ached and her head felt like an inflatable Swiss ball.

She heard AxMan call anxiously to Micky to fill in the form for him, but Micky must have gone back to sleep, surrounded by trays of half-eaten food. AxMan caught Meredith's eye and said, 'More complicated bureaucratic bollocks created by The Man to stop the free movement of ordinary people.'

Meredith nodded briefly. She actually liked stopping the free movement of ordinary people. It was much easier to hold down wages if the workers couldn't go anywhere else.

'Micky usually does this for me. But...' AxMan turned back to his landing card and slipped on a pair of reading glasses. 'I mean, like, if I'm going to save children's lives, I can't be beaten by a little piece of card.'

'Go for it,' Meredith said quietly. 'The Dunkirk spirit.'

'Yeah,' AxMan said, sipping left-over prosecco. 'How hard can it be?'

# 12 VIP Treatment

The arrivals hall of Isobel Bachman International throbbed with heat, like someone had turned up a thermostat on the sun. The terminal building was open on two sides and in the distance AxMan could see palm trees. A musky tropical aroma wafted in. Forget Midland Metal Hell!

He and Micky found their suitcases already waiting at a VIP desk, next to a grey-haired police officer.

'Welcome to our country, Mr AxMan.' The officer inspected AxMan's landing card through steel-rimmed glasses. He appeared very different from the British kind of cop, his jacket military, a gun at his hip. But he smiled. 'I understand you are the guest of our president.'

'Yeah.' AxMan despised uniforms, but gave the man the benefit of the doubt, along with an AxMan snarl.

The cop tapped the landing card with a pen. 'You filled this in yourself, sir?'

'Too right,' AxMan said, with a meaningful glance at Micky. 'Though not by choice.'

'Do you mind if I confirm some things?' the cop said in a friendly manner.

'Whatever you like.'

'Under the flight number you have written 'Two'.'

'That's right. One here and one back.'

'For Passport, you have written "Yes".'

'Correct.'

'For Purpose of Visit, you have written "Peace" and for where you are staying, you have written "A good hotel, I hope."'

AxMan nodded, proud of his own efficiency. To his surprise, the passport officer pressed a red button, ripped the landing card in two and began filling in a fresh one.

A pale-faced cop headed over with a large German Shepherd. 'Is this them?'

'What's going on, man?' AxMan asked, as Micky shifted nervously away.

'Routine inspection,' said the handler. AxMan decided not to give this one the benefit of any doubt. Beelzebub with epaulettes. The dog snarled at Micky, who turned pale.

'Is he tame?' Micky asked Beelzebub.

'Completely. Just don't make any sudden movements.'

AxMan put an arm round Micky's shoulders. 'He wants to be friends, yeah.'

The handler pointed to the bags. 'Did you pack these yourself?'

'Of course not.' AxMan recoiled, affronted. 'That's Micky's job.'

A female customs inspector arrived dressed in plastic overalls and latex gloves.

'Keys,' she demanded. AxMan noticed that each new person showed less politeness than the one before. In a few minutes, they'd be treating him like cabin class.

'Hold on,' he said. 'We're VIPs, invited for a peace concert. You've heard of Freddie Forrester? And President Bachman.'

The customs inspector snapped her fingers and three more cops came over with machine guns. 'He wants VIP treatment.'

'Here's VIP treatment,' said the first policeman. He tapped AxMan on the head with the butt of his gun.

AxMan leapt back, his hands in the air. 'What's that for?'

'If you wasn't a VIP, I'd have hit you properly. The keys.'

'Micky, give him the bloody keys.'

Micky handed over the keys. AxMan turned to the inspector, but she waved him away. 'Stand at a distance.'

'Is this how you respect the arts?' He tugged out his phone. 'Look, I'm recording this for posterity and social media.'

The customs inspector shrugged and unlocked the first case. She pulled out AxMan's spare ripped leather jeans and Calvin Klein underwear.

'See – nothing,' AxMan said.

The inspector opened the second bag.

'I'm going to make a complaint directly to the President.' AxMan panned the phone. 'I'm recording your name badge. Happy now?'

The customs inspector took out AxMan's back-up gilets. Underneath lay a huddle of small sachets. 'Much happier,' she said.

'Hey!' AxMan said. 'I've never seen those before!'

'They appear to be in your suitcase, which you said your valet packed.'

'Personal assistant,' Micky mumbled. The dog growled and he shifted further away. The inspector teased open the first sachet. It contained white powder. She dabbed a small amount onto her finger, tasted and smiled.

The air in the hall grew more humid. AxMan found it difficult to breathe. 'This is a stitch-up,' he managed.

'Bringing drugs into our country?' she said. 'Are you an idiot? Everyone else is smuggling them out.'

'There you are, yeah, that proves it. Someone planted them. Why would we bring our own in if we could buy gear here?'

'Interesting.' The inspector peered into another sachet, filled with leaves. 'So, you've already set up a source of supply on the island?'

'No!' said AxMan, in alarm. 'Dude, you're twisting my words. We're being framed.'

'Exactly,' Micky said. 'The Man!' He waved an imperious hand. The dog took a bite of it. Micky leapt backwards. 'Fuck!'

AxMan inspected Micky's bleeding palm with horror. 'Assault! Police abuse. What kind of country is this?' He appealed desperately to the other passengers standing around. 'We're being attacked, framed, drugs planted on us, bitten by dogs.' Nobody moved. 'Is there a doctor in the hall? Or a lawyer?'

He pointed his phone at the nearest two cops, who took this as an attack and pinned him to the floor. The third seized Micky and pushed him against the VIP desk.

'More abuse!' shouted AxMan from underneath the first two.

The customs inspector bent down and took AxMan's mobile. 'Thank you for filming, sir. All this will be useful in court. Our judges don't like people who criticise our justice system.'

From his position, head jammed under the cops, AxMan caught sight of Meredith Heel striding through the arrivals hall, pulling a Valextra calfskin cabin bag and fanning herself in the heat.

'Hey, help,' he called. 'Look, that's the woman who warned me. Hey, Ms Heel…? You were right. They're trying to stop me. Just like you said.'

But Meredith can't have heard him, because she kept going straight to the exit without a pause.

# Track 2

# 13 Waiting for Axx-Mann

Outside the arrivals exit of the terminal, Freddie also felt the heat, along with a dozen hardcore Axers. The fans had been standing in the sun for two hours, singing their favourite AxMan Flyn lyrics.

Freddie waited impatiently nearby, cuffed to a screw, as was Lucky Strike. Between them stood, or rather fidgeted, Freddie's sister Dania, a Forrester Music tote bag slung impatiently over her shoulder, like a holster.

Every time the automatic doors slid open, the Axers cheered. But every time, instead of AxMan, they were faced by a party of startled golfers from Miami or a cluster of returning au pairs. The fans took out their frustrations by commenting loudly on each arrival.

'Hey, sir, you come to buy our country?'

'Buy my sister instead.'

'Forget his sister, have that one behind you with the bad hair extensions.'

'Hey, he dissing your hair, woman. You going to take that lying down?'

'For sure she'll take him lying down.'

Lucky Strike toyed angrily with a white card, on which he'd scrawled *Axx-Mann* in green. 'Where is he?' he said, for the tenth time, jerking at his handcuffs. 'He don't respect us. I tell you from the start this is a mistake.'

Freddie felt his jaw tighten. 'He's coming.'

'If this is one more of your scams. I'll grind up your penis and feed it to your wife.'

'He's sodding coming,' Freddie repeated, hoping he was. 'And I don't have a wife.'

'You think I care who you poke at nights?' Lucky Strike molested the corners of his sign. 'No show, after all the green we put in for tickets.'

'What would you have done instead?' Dania asked. 'Have him swim here? With your business sense, you probably would.' She snatched the card from him, corrected it and handed it back. 'And while you're in jail, learn to spell.'

Dania would have made a good gang leader herself, Freddie always said – she hated incompetence and made sure everyone knew it. She shared with him his light brown eyes and thick hair. She also shared his deep and abiding belief that the universe would function much better if it did what it was told. But not his love of committing violence when it didn't.

She had a business head though. Forrester Music had been her idea.

For some months, she'd been saying how guilty she felt, seeing that her lifestyle was paid for by drug deals.

'What are *you* feeling guilty for?' Freddie retorted, after she said it yet again on her way out one evening, dressed in the most stylish skirt and top that his money could buy. 'I should be the one to feel guilty and I don't. I employ men and women who couldn't feed their families before. Now all paid for by rich lawyers and hedge-fund managers in London and New York, an ounce at a time. Nobody forces them to buy our *yayo*. They get what they want. Our families get fed. Everyone gains. It's Forrester Unemployment Benefit. Guilt is in your imagination.'

By chance, he'd just inherited a derelict nightclub from someone who owed him. He thought Dania could do with something to occupy her, so next day he asked her to sell it for him. To his surprise, she refused. He was about to tell her she was a hypocrite, complaining she felt guilty for taking his money, then refusing to do any work herself, when she interrupted and said she didn't want to sell it, she wanted to run it.

After a long silence, he couldn't think why not. Anything she tried would be good for laundering cash, before it inevitably sank like a dead crocodile.

But Dania took to her new enterprise with an energy nobody knew she had. She reopened the club and set up a music studio in the attic. She replaced the mildewed chairs and tables, bought second-hand recording equipment and hired a pair of out-of-work recording engineers to make rip-off CDs of hit albums.

In a year, Forrester Music was making a profit. The islanders loved good music. The CDs sold well and the nightclub was rammed. It became the go-to place to see local celebrity singers, soap actors and members of the president's family.

That year Freddie presented her with her first Christmas bonus.

'Conscience money?' she'd said with a sniff and donated the cash to a refuge for abandoned cats. But he noticed she held herself straighter than before.

Right now, Dania was distracting herself by loudly rehearsing the reasons why Freddie's concert was going to fail. Freddie's dyspepsia returned. 'Give me your phone.'

'Use your own.'

'Prisoners aren't allowed phones.' Truth was, his phone was stashed in his cell, where the screws could be bribed not to find it. Dania sighed and passed hers over.

With no sign of AxMan, the fans were organising running battles among themselves to pass the time. Freddie dialled his contact in customs. The man didn't answer. Lucky Strike looked so red in the face it could be a traffic light. 'Can't you organise anything? Like maybe a whores' party in a brothel?'

'Elegant image,' Dania said. 'Do you have any more like it? Maybe you could write poetry.'

'Stuff your poetry in your—'

'He got on the plane,' Freddie said quickly, wondering if his pacifist sister was about to pick a fight with the most violent gangster on the island. 'I checked.'

He sent his customs contact a message, involving what he'd do to his two pet schnauzers if he didn't call back within one minute.

'Maybe he jumped out the plane on the way here,' Lucky Strike said. 'At the thought of working with the Forrester family. Did you check that?'

'You know, Lucky Strike,' Freddie said, 'you're like an itching bite on the arse. You never stop. No wonder your wife hates you and sleeps with that teenager who cleans your pool.'

Lucky Strike grew even redder and his eyes turned small. But then the customs contact called back.

# 14 Everyone is Innocent

It was dusk by the time AxMan and Micky arrived at the state prison in a rusty police van, along with six other men of various sizes. They were unloaded brusquely into a hot courtyard. Armed guards lounged on the surrounding walls. Warehouse-like buildings stood around, their windows glassless but barred.

'I demand a lawyer,' AxMan said to the nearest guard.

'And a doctor for where the dog bit me,' Micky added.

The screw didn't answer, but shoved the prisoners through the nearest doorway.

As the heavy metal door locked behind them, AxMan realised the guards hadn't followed them in. Instead, he and Micky found themselves standing in a sweltering entrance hall.

Prisoners curled up in alcoves while others leant against paint-peeled walls, watching the new arrivals with bored aggression. Flies flew in thick black squadrons, settling then rising as they were flapped away. The other newcomers seemed to know what to do and had already disappeared down dank corridors.

'You're looking negative,' Micky whispered.

AxMan felt he had every right to look negative. He'd set out from home with a dream of making a difference. Now he'd been flung behind bars, with no more respect than he'd give a used spliff.

'OK. Where do we go?' he asked.

Micky inspected the dog bite on his hand. 'I thought there'd be a warder or something to show us round.'

'No warders,' said a young convict who'd been squatting in a corner. Like most of the prisoners, he wore a grubby T-shirt and denim shorts. 'Austerity cuts. What's your name?'

'AxMan.'

'You're a hard man? I'm scared.'

AxMan shrugged modestly. 'I've kicked some butt in my time. I once got caught in Golders Green with this stash of—'

'Good,' the man said. 'You're gonna need to be to stay alive here.' He stood. A deep scar ran down his cheek. AxMan tried not to recoil.

The young con saw AxMan's expression, then laughed and held out a grimy, but well-manicured hand. 'Jamie J Jameson of Jamie's Prison Advice Service. 'Our mission is to serve.' I can get you an alcove to sleep in, a TV, a woman. Ten per cent commission. Twenty if I have to negotiate with anyone violent. You want a lawyer? No problem. There are loads in here.'

'No need.' AxMan shook the hand. 'We're here to help save starving children. As soon as the British ambassador hears about us, we'll be out in no time.'

'Now, if you'll just show us to the nearest phone,' Micky said.

'And you are?'

'Micky Slapstone. I'm Ax's personal assistant.'

'No problem. Take a seat.'

AxMan's heart swelled with hope. Jamie J Jameson showed them to a relatively clean patch of floor. 'So, how much cash have you got, sir?'

AxMan scratched his beard awkwardly. 'Yeah, well, they took all our money off us at the airport. They left me my credit cards though.'

He brought them out, but Jamie's smile vanished. He stood up. 'Does this look like a place that takes plastic?'

'You have to help us.' AxMan scrabbled up after him. 'It's all I've got.'

Micky followed him. 'We're innocent.'

'Everyone's innocent here. Except for the gangsters, drug dealers, rapists, wife-beaters and thieves.' Jamie was already looking past them for better clients. 'On the outside, I had a business – Jamie's Limos – though to be honest it was Jamie's Limo. I borrowed the car from my uncle. But I was building my brand.

'This is a country where anyone can do well, unless they have bad luck. I had the bad luck to meet a traffic cop who wanted more funds than I had on me. Now I'm here. This is an important lesson.' He hesitated. 'There is one possibility. There's a guy who's been saying he's interested in hearing about new arrivals.'

AxMan flinched. 'Interested, how exactly?'

'Not in that way. At least, I don't think so. I'd take the chance.'

AxMan wasn't confident, but Jamie wouldn't hear any objection. 'Developing business relationships is very important. They've been teaching me this at the online course I enrolled in at the Harvvard Business School. I suspect it's not the same as Harvard University. For one thing, it's based in Bend, Oregon. For another, it's spelt with two "v"s. Nevertheless, it's very good value for money. Don't move from here.'

Before AxMan or Micky could reply, Jamie hammered on the outer door. It opened. He hurried off across the yard.

After ten long minutes, he returned with a man who was tall enough to have to duck as he came through the doorway, the possessor of a substantial girth, unshaved chin and an angry red complexion.

'These are the newcomers,' Jamie announced.

The man inspected them like they were yoghurts that had gone off. 'You're a pop singer?'

'Rock singer.' AxMan spread his hands to show that he forgave the mistake. But there was something about the way the man's eyes popped that made AxMan feel he didn't like being corrected. 'I was invited by Freddie and Dania Forrester. Forrester Music?'

'Nah, never heard of them,' he said quickly.

'Freddie Forrester is a singer, like me.'

'A singer?' The other man looked amused at this. 'Freddie Forrester? Really? I must look out for his gigs. Listen to how he sings.'

AxMan wasn't sure what to say, but he didn't have to say anything. The convict seemed more interested in his own voice than anyone else's.

'So, you want a phone and you got no green.' The man leant in close. He was clearly no friend of breath fresheners. AxMan tried not to inhale. 'I'm a generous man. Tomorrow morning.'

Micky said in a small voice, 'You couldn't manage today?'

The man grabbed him by the throat. 'It don't fit with my plans, exactly. Is that a problem for you?'

'Well, since you–'

'Of course you could go to some other guys here who'd be happy to lend you some paper and break your fingers one by one if you're late coming up with the refunding, but I wouldn't recommend it.'

'If you say–'

'I do say.' He let go, smiled and patted him on the arm. 'Trust me. Here's the deal. You two keep your heads down. Don't start telling every-one who you are. *Incoggito*, like. There's people in here who doesn't like pop singers–'

'Rock–' AxMan started.

'They might decide to break a few limbs just for the razz. Got it?'

'Well–'

'That's settled then. Say thank you to J for the contact.' He slipped a bank note into Jamie's hand and thumped on the door. 'I'll find you tomorrow. Now sod off.'

'One thing?' AxMan said nervously.

The other man turned back. 'Yes?'

'Could I have your name?' AxMan hesitated as the man glared at him. 'You know, kind of, in case we need it.'

The prisoner thought this over, then smiled again. 'Lucky Strike,' he said. 'Lucky Strike Morton. But believe it, I'll be here to see you tomorrow. No sweat.'

# 15 Martial Arts

Micky massaged his throat. 'Well,' he said, '"a fish that doesn't swim is a dead fish," as Tom Toggler has it.'

AxMan opted not to try to puzzle out any meaning, but Jamie clapped his hands. 'You read Tom Toggler?'

'Daily.'

'"*The deeper the crevasse, the higher the mountain.*"'

'"*Big goals have big goalposts!*"'

Fearing that they might go on for some time, AxMan quickly thanked Jamie for the introduction to Lucky Strike Morton, but Jamie shook his head. 'It's my pleasure. And he's paying me for the intro anyway.'

'Lucky Strike? Is that really his name? Or just a nickname?'

'No, that's his real name. Many of my compatriots love to name their children after their favourite brands. It's part of our passion for the capitalist system. I myself only narrowly avoided being called Corona, until my mother threatened to pour all my father's beer over his head. Now, if you'll excuse me, there'll be a new intake of prisoners in the next half hour. Jamie's Prison Advice Service needs to be ready.'

Talking of beer, Micky tentatively mentioned that it felt close to dinner time and his stomach was calling for attention. Jamie told them to go down the nearest corridor and they'd find some chow. They set off the way he pointed.

By now, it was growing dark. Few of the lights seemed to work and the place became gloomier and more frightening as they walked. On the floor lay deep puddles that AxMan didn't want to investigate. Micky was still rubbing his throat and AxMan asked if he was OK.

'Don't worry about me,' Micky said. 'It's just that Lucky bloke had a strong grip and I went and hit my head before, when they threw us in the prison van, and the dog bite is feeling a bit infected. But I'll be fine.'

They rounded a corner to find a queue of prisoners. When they reached the front, a trusty handed them both a metal bowl containing something greenish-brown. AxMan chose a place to sit. He avoided a worrying stain on the floor and examined the contents of his bowl. 'Are the drains blocked, or is it the man lying the other side of you?'

Micky didn't answer, as he was busy scooping up the gruel and chewing on a few pieces of gristle. 'There's not very much,' he said after a minute.

Despite his own hunger, AxMan passed his dinner over to Micky.

Night fell. Convicts shuffled past, sizing up the two newcomers like shabby vultures. The cells had no doors, but were filling with men settling down for the night. Others had personalised shelters in the corridor, with wooden walls and light bulbs hanging from electric cables. They reminded AxMan nostalgically of his bedroom yurt.

At that moment, the power cut out and the prison was plunged into darkness. A few torches came on, but their faint glimmering made the gloom even gloomier. Home seemed very far away.

'Where are we going to stay?' Micky asked.

'I suppose here is as good as anywhere.' AxMan gave a profound sigh.

Micky promptly settled back, leaning against him. A moment later, Micky was snoring.

'Are you awake?' AxMan asked, feeling the weight of Micky's head on his shoulder, but his personal assistant and guitar tech didn't respond. He hadn't the heart to move him.

AxMan closed his eyes in the hope of sleep, but immediately opened them. He could just make out the shape of a burly inmate by the opposite wall. The convict hunched, motionless as a cat, ready to pounce.

Despite his fears, AxMan closed his eyes once more, but snapped them open again. The man hadn't shifted. AxMan stared him out. The prisoner still didn't back down.

So AxMan carefully removed Micky from his shoulder and stood up. He threw some taekwondo chops he'd learned for use on stage, followed by a series of sharp kicks, just to show the inmate what he could do if pushed. But still the convict crouched, unmoved.

Puffing at the unaccustomed exertion, AxMan decided there was nothing for it. He had to face the man down. He sauntered over, throwing two or three air punches for good measure, and discovered that the shape he'd been impressing was in fact a large man-shaped patch of mould on the wall.

He returned to his corner, cracking his knuckles and muttering – to anyone who might be watching – about how good it was to work out from time to time. But soon his mood descended again. Did anyone know where they were – the British Consulate, his lawyers, or even those Forrester people? His stomach rumbled and he thought nostalgically about the Ayurvedic salad he'd left untouched on the plane. At least they had that Lucky Strike man on their side.

AxMan curled up in the corner, his arm round his friend, guitar tech and personal assistant, waiting for sleep, which he was sure would never come.

# 16 No Sweat

Thing was, while AxMan was trying to sleep, Freddie was only a hundred yards away in the same prison, slumped in his cell, in a stolen ergonomic desk chair, worrying where his rock star had got to. Lucky Strike stood in the cell doorway, rhythmically clicking his fingers. He seemed remarkably upbeat about losing the man who was supposed to save their lives.

'You know,' Freddie said, contemplating a glass of vodka he'd paid too much for, 'it's almost as if you're pleased it's all gone ape-shit.'

'Not at all,' said Lucky Strike, though he couldn't stop grinning.

Freddie's cell was relatively well-appointed, with glass in the windows and carpet. Indeed, it had once been the governor's own office. Over the years, the governor had been running a good business leasing out spaces in the prison blocks. However, before long all the cells had been let, so he renamed the admin block the High Security Wing, shoved all his staff into portakabins and rented the rooms to the richer gangs.

Lucky Strike's cell next door had been the governor's secretary's office and was smaller, which pleased Freddie and – as a bonus – annoyed Lucky Strike. Freddie had also spent copiously to get a reliable supply of electricity, a comfortable double bed and the ergonomic chair, as his back went regularly. Luckily, there were many osteopaths in jail for not paying enough bribes to the Ministry of Health.

Freddie spun his chair and mulled over what he knew. Frustratingly little. All he'd heard from his contact in customs was that drugs had been found in AxMan's bags. However, Freddie's bribes should have been more than enough to get the singer through without a search.

'It does my head in that nobody seems to have seen the guy. You've heard nothing?'

'Not a sniff of his arse.' Lucky Strike hummed a few bars of a tune to himself. 'It's just I never expect nothing to go right when you're involved,

Forrester. I should have shot you years ago when we were fighting over who ran the docks.'

Freddie sighed. 'But shit, we ended up sharing. We both won.'

Lucky Strike gave a sour shake of the head. 'Don't like sharing. Never have. When I was a kid, my brothers kept telling me to share our toys, share the one bicycle, share our food. I refused. Sharing's for girls.'

'What did they do about it?'

'Not much, because I beat their heads in.'

'You're all heart, aren't you? You probably spent your childhood skinning live kittens.'

'Didn't everyone?'

Freddie decided he himself must have had a misspent youth. He should have been torturing animals rather than helping his father and mother protect their farm from bent land officials. He drained his vodka.

'You're empty,' Lucky Strike said. He whistled. A young gang member in a sleeveless T-shirt sprinted up. Freddie gave him his order and watched thoughtfully as he ran off again.

'Why do you care so much about this AxMan guy?' asked Lucky Strike. 'We'll leave him to be raped by convicts and we'll find another pop singer. I've never seen the point of them anyway. Except for buying our yayo, what good do they do the world?'

'Something in all this makes my nose itch.'

The young gang member returned with a six-pack for Lucky Strike and a new bottle of vodka for Freddie. Freddie slipped him a tip.

'Don't spoil them,' Lucky said, opening one of his beers. 'Better if they shit themselves when they see you.'

Freddie decided not to comment on the mobster's philosophy of leadership. Instead, he twisted open the vodka and poured. 'Some high-up gave the shout to have those bags searched.'

'And found fucking drugs. I mean, what dickhead smuggles narcotics onto this island? We're busy busting a gut trying to smuggle them *out*. He's either very stupid or very clever. Either way I don't like it.'

'Exactly. It don't make sense.' Freddie lay down carefully on his settee. His lumbar vertebrae felt tight. He might book himself an appointment with that attractive little Filipina who was doing two years in the women's section for refusing to give a hand-job to the mayor.

'Stop trying to mate spiders,' said Lucky Strike. 'You're overthinking things as usual. Let him rot.'

After Lucky Strike had gone back to his room, Freddie phoned his sister on the iPhone the governor had rented him.

'Do you think I'm overthinking this?' he asked, keeping his voice low. 'Lucky Strike says so.'

'Lucky Strike?' Dania said. She was at the club. Freddie could hear dance music. 'I wouldn't believe him if he told me my own name.'

The signal kept breaking up, so he stood and moved to the window. Below, he could make out the few guards, cigarette ends glowing, red stoplights in the night.

'He's got an angle somewhere,' she was saying as her voice came back. 'I can't prove it – but looking at him at the airport today – he's got those horrible little piggy eyes.'

'What's this, woman's instinct?'

'Yes, that and the fact he's as trustworthy as a hyena.'

'What would Lucky Strike gain by stiffing the concert? If it don't take place, he's going to get shot by Bachman too. He's not that mad, is he?'

'I don't know, but if he invites you to dinner, go with a food-taster.'

Freddie rang off uneasily and sniffed his vodka, just in case. Then he heard a sound, a scuff of a shoe outside his room. He walked over, put his ear to the door.

'No sweat,' said a woman with a nasal British accent.

Lucky Strike muttered something darkly in return. The woman said, 'Whatever it takes.'

Freddie stayed with his ear pressed to the woodwork, but all he heard after that was Lucky Strike's door closing and high heels walking away, ticking over the stone floor like a count-down timer. But counting down to what?

# 17 What Doesn't Kill You...

Having decided he'd never sleep, AxMan was astonished to open his eyes and find it was daylight. He was further surprised to discover he was being punched in the ribs.

'Mr AxMan? Mr AxMan?'

He closed his eyes again. He'd been dreading violence and now it was here.

The voice and the fist continued. 'Hey, you, Mr AxMan.'

What next? he wondered fearfully. A boot in the face? A steel rod up the anus? He tried to protect his ribs, his backside and his head in turn but ran out of arms.

'Wake up, Mr AxMan...'

This was getting stupid. He knew moves, didn't he? AxMan braced himself then sprang up in one of the taekwondo postures he used in gigs. At least he tried to spring, but his legs gave way under the unexpected early morning strain and he wobbled back down to sitting, clutching his left thigh. 'Shit!'

'Mr AxMan...?' Jamie J Johnson peered anxiously down at him. 'It's just me. Mr Lucky Strike Morton is on his way. He's got your phone.'

'Great.' AxMan felt his ribs and limbs to see if they'd survived the night. Most of them indicated they'd have preferred to stay asleep. Micky lay rumpled on the floor next to him, a frog, eyes tightly shut, mouth opening and closing. AxMan felt strangely protective towards him. However, Jamie looked full of pep. Far fuller of pep than a young prisoner had a right to be. He handed AxMan a bundle wrapped in newspaper. 'Breakfast.'

AxMan handed it back. 'I still don't have any dosh for you.'

'No problem,' Jamie said. 'I checked you out on the internet. Turns out you really are a big international star and you have a ton of fans.'

AxMan shrugged modestly. 'Well, not so big–'

Jamie's face fell. 'Oh.'

'I mean,' AxMan corrected, 'not that small either, in fact—'

'Anyway,' Jamie interrupted, 'we've no time to lose before the autographs.'

AxMan struggled painfully to his feet. 'Autographs?'

'Apologies for taking the liberty,' Jamie said. 'There was no time for contractual discussions. But we can do this on a handshake, yes?' He shook AxMan's hand vigorously.

'Do what?' AxMan asked.

Jamie turned to beckon down the corridor and AxMan noticed 'AXMAN' scribbled on the back of his T-shirt in red marker pen. 'Jamie's Prison Advice Service has launched a new subsidiary just for Mr AxMan – Jamie's Media Appearances. This is your advance on royalties.' He shoved the bundle at him again. AxMan opened it and found two fresh croissants, two hot egg and bacon sandwiches and a small thermos of coffee.

'For you, I bent my rule of a lifetime. I borrowed from the money-lenders. It is a risk, but I used your name, not mine. If we make a profit, you get more food. If we make a loss, they break your legs. This is how business goes.'

'Break my legs?'

'"No pain, no gain." Isn't that what your friend Micky would say, if he wasn't busy doing the zeds? Eat up. We have five minutes.'

'Five minutes?' But Jamie had moved away again.

The smell of fresh food reminded AxMan that, legs or no legs, he was ravenous. He bit into the first sandwich and roused Micky with a gentle foot to his backside. Micky opened his eyes cautiously, saw the breakfast and declared he didn't feel well.

'You ate the supper they gave you last night?' Jamie asked, returning. 'Not to worry. It normally passes in three days.'

Micky groaned, stood, ran to the nearest glassless window.

'Maybe more than three days,' Jamie said thoughtfully.

'What doesn't kill you makes you stronger.' Micky was hunched over the window sill.

Jamie frowned. 'You know, I've never understood that expression.'

'Me neither.' AxMan was beginning to like this young man.

'If someone breaks your legs, it makes you weaker, don't it?'

AxMan didn't welcome being reminded of this possibility and Micky was too busy getting stronger to reply.

A moment later, two prisoners walked up, holding leaflets with AxMan's name and photo. 'AxMan! Hey, AxMan,' they both called. 'AxMan, you come to sort us out?'

AxMan looked at the leaflets in amazement. 'You printed fliers? You know there's intellectual property rights. My branding to think about. I can't just have my name everywhere.'

Jamie smiled proudly. 'Jamie's Media always goes that extra mile. And I was owed a favour by a serial killer with an HP printer.'

'But no, man–'

'AxMan!' came from the corridor as more men arrived.

'No time,' Jamie said. 'I don't think you want to piss off these fans.' AxMan noticed for the first time Jamie had brought a trestle table, made of mismatched wooden pallets, which he opened up. 'Queue here for AxMan's autograph! Special offer today!'

'My fans?' AxMan said, feeling that perhaps life wasn't so bad after all.

'You're one bad-ass,' shouted a new arrival. 'Sing us a song, yes?'

'Now if I had my Les Paul, I could play some riffs…'

'Make do with this.' Jamie handed him a chewed ball-point pen. AxMan made an AxMan-brand snarl, pointed the pen like a gun.

'Wass he done to be in here?' came from the right. 'He kill someone? He beat up his woman?'

The first inmate handed Jamie a dog-eared bank note. He was a large man with a shaven head and muscles. He lunged aggressively at AxMan. AxMan jumped back in fear, but then realised the man simply wanted to shake his hand.

'My name Odalis,' the man said. 'I'm big fan since boy.' He leant in, forehead to forehead. 'AxMan! Big star! Great records. Even the latest.'

'Thank you.' AxMan signed the back of his flier and passed it back. He turned to Jamie. 'Some of these prisoners are very astute.'

More cons arrived and Jamie made like a sergeant major to get them in line. Some waved fliers for AxMan to sign. Others brought scraps of cardboard.

'*Stick it to The Man!*' said the next in line.

'*Wiv a gun in your han*',' AxMan sang automatically.

A loud cheer went up, which encouraged him to continue for a few verses. He signed autographs on the scraps. His lyrics echoed round the crowd, like he was back at Midlands Metal Hell, only without the rain.

'*Screw de rich…*'

'*Screw de pigs…*'

'*I'm not humble, time to rumble…*'

'You see! Axers!' AxMan said. 'They're everywhere.'

'Not all are fans.' Jamie gave the latest man his change. 'Some just want your signature to sell.'

However, AxMan noticed a rise in tension. A few scuffles started among those watching from the sides.

*'You sell me a lie/Prepare to die…'*

*'Revolution's coming/First against the wall…'*

'They do know these are just songs, don't they?' he said to Jamie, as the fighting escalated.

'Go with the flow,' said Micky, who'd finished getting stronger and returned to inspect the breakfast bag.

'It's good if they're excited.' Jamie looked up from counting the money. One of the autograph hunters sprinted away down a corridor, chased by another, while three men kicked a fourth on the ground. 'Well, maybe not too excited.'

'If this is what they look like when they're not too excited, I'd hate to meet them at a Guns N' Roses gig.'

As AxMan spoke, a strange shimmer went through the prisoners. The crowd divided and Lucky Strike walked through, with three other men, tall and unsmiling. The gangster held up an ancient Nokia with a cracked screen, looked like someone had been using it as a football.

'This is your Lucky day.' He chuckled at his own joke and looked around at the convicts, who all found it enormously amusing. He raised his hand and the convicts fell silent again.

'This is great, man. I owe you,' AxMan said, taking the phone. 'What do I have to do for you?' he added warily.

'Forget it,' Lucky Strike said with a strange smile. 'I love to help. Just one thing,' he went, like an afterthought. He reached into his pocket and the prisoners flinched, but all he brought out was his own mobile. 'A video. To remind me of this moment.'

Lucky aimed the phone and AxMan gave his trademark devil's horns.

'Maybe one of your lyrics?' Lucky said. '*You sell me a lie—*'

*'Prepare to die!'* AxMan replied instinctively.

'Spot on! And I'll show to that Freddie Frogface if I ever meet him.'

'Forrester…'

'Yeah, of course,' Lucky said with that odd smile again, as he left.

# 18 Death to The Man/Time to Rumble

After the signing, AxMan watched Jamie separate the banknotes he'd collected into two unequal piles.

'Wow, man, impressive.' AxMan reached for the larger wad of money, but Jamie took it first.

'This is my fee and repayment of loan at the standard rate.'

'Ah.' AxMan put his hand out to take the smaller bundle, but Jamie scooped that pile too.

'And this is for expenses. You have the phone and can phone your ambassador, who I'm sure will want to assist two of his most prominent citizens.'

AxMan rubbed his chin as he watched his income disappear into Jamie's pockets. 'You know, you're beginning to remind me of my record company.'

'You flatter me.' Jamie folded the trestle. 'I am only a beginner, but with your help I'll learn more.'

'Ah.' AxMan had turned on the Nokia and was staring at the cracked screen.

'Not good enough for you?'

'No SIM card.'

'Did you ask for a SIM card?'

'I thought normally–'

'Nothing's normal here in Benkuda.' Jamie took out some of the cash. 'I must do more shopping. No worry, I'll put it on account.'

In the distance, AxMan could still hear prisoners shouting his lyrics and fighting.

'And I don't think we should delay,' AxMan said.

Micky nodded. 'As Ricki Steele says in *Climb the Mountain of You,* "You can be either the cause of things or the result of things."'

'Please,' AxMan said. 'I know you mean well, but can we not have mountains and causes so early in the morning? My head hurts already.'

'I'm just trying to help. You can give a mouse to the snake, but–' Micky caught AxMan's eye and stopped.

Telling AxMan and Micky to remain exactly where they were, Jamie ran off and returned fifteen minutes later with a SIM card, saying he'd already put the phone number of the British Embassy in the contacts.

He looked particularly nervous and as AxMan stuck the card in the Nokia, they heard a distant rumbling from the other side of the prison, a rushing tide, a surf wave of voices and the breaking of things. Micky started to speak, till AxMan glared at him, so he stayed silent.

Soon you could make out individual phrases, such as *'Death to The Man!'* and *'Prepare to die.'*

'Ah, maybe we should kind of move,' AxMan said.

'I suggest the exercise yard,' Jamie agreed. 'People who shout about death and dying are often not great for business or indeed personal survival.'

'That sounds a positive idea,' Micky said.

The three of them sprinted down the nearest corridor, followed by more men who had the same idea, but as they reached the door to the yard, they found themselves blocked by prisoners with equally positive ideas, trying to come in.

They shoved forwards. The convicts outside didn't like to be opposed. They pressed back.

The prisoners behind shouted, *'Stick it to The Man! Wiv a gun in my han'!'*

The ones in front yelled, *'I'm not humble, time to rumble!'*

Nobody budged, but tempers got heated.

AxMan turned to Micky. 'Do you think…?'

'Nah, it's not your fault.'

*'Screw de pigs. Screw de rich.'*

Jamie sniffed. 'I can smell smoke.'

AxMan put his weight into pressing forwards and they burst through the doorway, like a champagne cork.

The exercise yard was filling up with hundreds of prisoners – they were pouring out of all the cell-blocks. On the other side of a barbed-wire fence swirled a horde of women prisoners, who soon broke through the fence to join the men. A brick hit Micky on the head. He grunted.

'Are you OK?' Jamie shouted over the tumult.

'Never finer.' Micky wiped blood off his forehead. 'Thinking positively, this brick reminds me to watch out for danger.'

AxMan looked round for danger. The armed guards had gone from the walls. The convicts milled around, chanting. A large group ran for the main gates, began pushing against them. The gates were large, but creaked and groaned. Then smashed and fell. Prisoners spilled out into the street beyond.

A man in a smart suit appeared on top of one of the walls, clutching a megaphone. 'This is your governor,' the megaphone said. 'Escaping the prison grounds is a criminal offence. Any convicts or remand prisoners will be automatically sentenced for a year for every hour outside.'

Someone threw a piece of gate at him and he disappeared rapidly from view.

'We're innocent.' Micky tried to push back towards the prison building, but the tide of convicts was too great. 'I don't want to escape and be sentenced!'

AxMan was a pinball, battered from side to side. He paddled his feet desperately, trying to stay close to Micky. He could see him nearby, bobbing up and down, like he was swimming in a flooded river, but they drifted apart and the stream of rioters carried AxMan through the broken entrance.

'No!' he shouted. 'Stop. I'm not a criminal. I don't want to be sentenced for a year for every hour outside. I want to go back.'

But nobody listened. They filled the narrow road and pressed him on, away from the jail. Worried, he tried to turn, but the mass of bodies forced him irresistibly forwards like toothpaste through a tube.

'Excuse me,' he said to the prisoners behind him. 'I'm innocent. I need to be back there.'

They didn't seem to care. Jammed against his left side was an older man in a torn Black Sabbath T-shirt, who bared a gap-toothed smile and said, '*Screw de rich.*'

With an enormous effort, AxMan twisted his body round, but he was being carried along facing backwards. The noise grew louder and AxMan trotted backwards faster, trying not to fall, his arms jammed against his ribs. The rioters flooded down street after street and AxMan jogged backwards with them, knees up like a demented riverdancer.

He forced himself to the edge of the road, where the people were less compressed, and managed to turn himself forwards again. He hoped he might be able to escape the crowd, but to his dismay running fights were taking place on both sides. The aggression shocked him. Savage and elemental. Men and women hurled paving stones into shop windows, fought over what they stole.

The mob slowed and AxMan slowed with them, out of breath, trembling with fear. He'd not exercised so much since Cla-Rice had entered him into a charity marathon for Chechen dissidents. They stopped at a line of tall railings in front of a grand building, gleaming with white paint, like an enormous iceberg.

'Palace,' said the Black Sabbath fan gleefully. 'President's home.' And he ran his right hand across his throat. '*Stick to The Man!*'

'No,' AxMan said. 'Not stick it to the president. She's a good person. She's not The Man… I mean, Woman…'

'*Ready to rumble.*' sang Black Sabbath, his grin widening.

The guard posts were strangely deserted. The convicts broke through the iron gates, rushing up long steps into the palace, still chanting. AxMan found himself inside a marbled hallway, smelling of fresh polish. Portraits of Bachman lined the walls. She must have had a busy schedule, ordering soldiers about, helping surgeons, being thanked by smiling families. AxMan was impressed. The rioters spread around, unsure what to do, until Lucky Strike marched in, flanked by his hard-faced entourage.

'Big Man.' AxMan's new best friend pointed at Lucky Strike. 'Make our island great again.' And indeed, Lucky Strike climbed a wide stone staircase and turned to address them.

AxMan was awed by the man's confidence – and his frightening sidemen. They'd go down well at Hammerfest.

'The system is shit!' Lucky shouted. 'The prisons are riotous. Stirred up by the foul songs of a criminal pop singer.'

AxMan froze in shock. Did he mean him? He never told people to riot. He noticed some of the nearby convicts looking at him and tried to shrink down, not to be so visible.

'The people demand law and order.'

It seemed an odd speech for a gangster to be giving to a mob of convicts, but Lucky Strike's gang moved around the audience, waving placards and hitting people who didn't applaud in the right places. There was a loud cheer and his voice was drowned out again.

'What did he say?' AxMan asked, crouched over next to Black Sabbath. 'Was he saying more stuff about that rock singer, whoever he is?'

'No. He said not to take expensive valuables,' shouted Black Sabbath.

The convicts clapped again, grateful for this reminder. They ran off in different directions and left the palace carrying antique vases, marble busts, tables and computers. Black Sabbath himself reappeared with a large oil painting of a sea battle AxMan was sure he'd seen on a TV arts documentary.

Lucky Strike led a group of his men further into the palace. But where was Micky? Had he managed to stay in the prison? At that moment, AxMan thought he glimpsed his personal assistant among the looters on the first-floor landing. He forced his way up the packed stairs. When he reached the top, he caught sight of the little man's back, disappearing at the far end of a long hallway.

He chased after him and found himself in a maze of corridors. Few rioters had reached this far. He kept on, past empty offices with chairs knocked over, like they'd been abandoned in a rush. Soon he was alone.

Then in the distance he heard the unmistakable words, 'Think positive!'

# 19 Make Our Island Great Again

Freddie had first heard the riot from his room that used to be the governor's. He was sitting in his ergonomic chair, having his nails manicured by an attractive young woman called Champagne, currently serving five years for embezzlement. She was one of the more intelligent convicts, and he was shocked to find himself having romantic thoughts. It'd be nice for a change to have sex with someone who could spell.

Champagne asked what was going on. He said to hang back while he peered through the window. Smoke floated out of the main prison building opposite. Prisoners ran into the exercise yard.

Normally Freddie was warned of riots before they happened and he hated not being in control. Usually such negative feelings resulted in him inflicting pain on someone, but in this case, there was no-one available except Champagne. This annoyed him even more.

He told her to get the hell out. Lucky Strike's door was open and all the thug's possessions had gone. Freddie's stomach was sending warning signals like a fire alarm. Pontiac ran up from the floor below with another member of Freddie's gang, arguing.

'I saw Lucky talking to the chief of prison guards earlier,' said his number two, rubbing his ear. 'Didn't make nothing of it at the time.'

'Then the guards buggered off,' said the other.

A third gang member sprinted up the stairs with news that Lucky Strike's Sunshine Crew had been attacking Freddie's men. One had been knifed and was in a crap condition.

'What's he getting up to?' Freddie asked. Pontiac puffed and shook his head.

'Shit.' Freddie slapped Pontiac urgently on the shoulder. 'Take everyone and guard the ground floor.'

'With what weapons, boss?'

'How the fuck do I know? Whatever you can find. Sharpened forks. Pictures of the Madonna. Use your fucking imagination.'

He walked to one of the further windows for a better view. No sooner had he arrived than the crowd in the exercise yard broke through the main gates into the street beyond. Someone had provided them with placards. He recognised Lucky Strike's gang stirring up the mob.

Freddie could feel his dyspepsia rising higher. Lucky Strike was as thick as a dunce's hat, but not so brainless as to believe that a jailbreak would solve his problems. There was something else going on. Freddie was angry with himself for not being able to work out what it was.

He was about to turn away when he caught sight of a taller man in a leather gilet, being awkwardly swept along by the crowd. It was AxMan. Freddie rarely felt guilty about anything, but he felt guilty about dragging the singer into all this.

He could hear fighting coming from the floor below. He looked urgently for some dirt, but the admin block had had its annual clean the week before. So he wiped rust from the window bars, spreading it over his face and – it pained him – his favourite cargo pants and shirt. The smell was metallic and mouldy, like his own body was putrefying.

As he finished, one of Lucky's gangsters reached the top of the stairs and thrust a knife towards Freddie's throat.

Freddie batted it aside. 'Wrong man, egg-sucker!' He pointed to his own room at the far end. 'Forrester's that way. Corner cell.'

The man hesitated.

'What are you sodding waiting for?' Freddie thumped him on the chest. 'You want me to jerk you off first?'

The gangster sprinted down the corridor, followed by three others who'd piled up the stairs after him. Freddie avoided eye contact, pushed his way down the stairs as yet more of the Sunshine Cartel ran up. On the ground floor, he found half his men badly wounded. Blood everywhere. The rest had disappeared.

'Get out!' Freddie yelled to anyone who could walk. 'Get lost. Hide in the crowd.'

The injured he could do nothing about and that pissed him off. Outside, he grabbed a fallen placard that read "Bugger-off Bachman!" This, at least, was something he could agree with. He chanted lyrics of AxMan songs that he could hear being repeated all around him and added any other slogans that came to mind: 'Death to democracy!' 'You're shit and you know you are!' and 'The referee's a wanker!'

In this manner, he made his way through to the main gate and joined the rioters outside. Many had already marched off towards the city centre. Others, discovering themselves free, ran about mindlessly, like a drunk crowd at a pitch invasion.

Despite the chaos, a pattern began to appear. As each fresh surge of prisoners came out of the jail, men ran between them, forming them into units and sending them off to town, like herding over-excited schoolchildren on a day trip. These unofficial stewards took their orders from someone he couldn't see, hidden in the doorway to a small bar. He shifted further forward and a tall heavyset man came into view – Lucky Strike.

Freddie didn't like this. He ducked for cover beside an abandoned street vendor cart, crammed with spiced sardines, soap, watermelons and ice pops. Leaning over, he took a strawberry pop from the ice box to calm his stomach. As he did, a white BMW drove up. It stopped next to Lucky Strike, who opened the passenger door and climbed in, still yelling commands.

What was the big shit up to? Freddie needed wheels. He could take the rainbow-coloured bicycle attached to the vendor cart, but he'd be as visible as an erection on a nudist beach. However, further ahead he could see a farm pickup. A farmer's son himself, Freddie knew how painful its loss would be to its owner, but he ran over and tested the door, which was unlocked as he expected.

A strong smell of goat wafted out. Bobbing under the steering wheel, he hot-wired the ignition. This always worked so easy in movies, but this was real life. Freddie wondered what kind of cars those movie producers were used to stealing. In the event, it took a good two minutes to get the engine to fire.

Fortunately, Lucky Strike's car was still just visible up ahead, pushing through the marching rioters. So Freddie engaged gear with a grinding crunch and followed at a sedate pace, chewing on the stick from his ice pop, trying to look agricultural.

After a quarter of an hour they reached the presidential palace.

'The hell!' Freddie muttered.

He watched the BMW park and stopped a safe distance away. Watched the leader of the Sunshine Cartel stride towards the entrance. Freddie tossed the pop-stick into the gutter and followed. To his dismay, the smell of goat came with him, but the rioters didn't seem to care. Most of them smelt worse. By the time Freddie got inside, Lucky Strike had already positioned himself on the marble stairs with four of his heavies and was in the middle of a speech.

Freddie stayed out of their line of sight while Lucky Strike finished –
or rather stopped abruptly, having seemingly forgotten whatever else he
had to say – and disappeared into the back of the palace. Something was
starting to make sense to Freddie and it scared him.

# 20 My Voters Love Me

Isobel Bachman was in her office, feeding her two cats, Churchill and Mandela, when she first heard the noise. Her cabinet was gathering for the week's meeting in the room next door, but now distant shouting came from the front. Like a football match being played in the palace square.

She shuddered – it reminded her of all those awful internationals she'd had to sit through, watching Benkuda thrashed six or seven-nil by a scratch team from Haiti or Dominica. It got even worse after FIFA stopped them bribing the referees.

The Minister for Justice came in from the cabinet room, looking concerned. But he always looked concerned. He was an overweight middle-aged man with a pasty face and a permanently raised eyebrow that people mistook for amused detachment, but was in fact the result of Botox gone wrong.

'We're getting reports of a major jail-break,' he said breathlessly.

'Get onto the police commissioner.'

'He's not answering.'

If she didn't know better, she would have thought the minister was behind this. But Quentin Treadle didn't have the guts to organise a coup.

'I've been told the prisoners are chanting revolutionary slogans written by a British singer you invited to the country.'

'I invited?'

'Some kind of charity pop concert.'

'Ah, that.'

'I recommend you leave the palace,' he added.

'Bollocks. We've got work to do in cabinet. I asked Ahmed to bring forward my plans for children's health, Manuela to finalise cancelling the debt and the remaining two nuclear power stations, Norman to stop having affairs and promote my Green Jobs bill, and you're supposed to be working on legal aid. Have you done your homework, Quentin?'

'We don't know if we can guarantee safety, Isobel.'

'My safety or yours?'

She opened the cabinet room door. The room was packed. Everyone was talking over each other and checking their phones.

'OK,' she said, holding up her hand for silence. 'Whoever doesn't want to stay and work on improving our country can leave now.'

After fifteen seconds of scraping chairs, she found herself alone in the empty cabinet room, with only the two cats and a terrified junior aide. She scowled at him and he stayed put.

'Fine,' she said, suppressing a tremor in her voice.

The justice minister opened the door again. 'It seems the palace guards have deserted their posts.'

'Well, I'm not a quitter, Quentin, even if they are. My people won't harm me. They love me. They voted for me. Some of them.'

The Minister didn't look convinced.

'You go, Quentin, if you don't have the balls.'

The Minister hesitated then left. Bachman beckoned to the aide and strode back to her personal office. Through the window, she could see the Isobel Bachman Aviary, a shadowy metal and glass pyramid where she'd had her predecessor executed. She began to have second thoughts, but no. She wasn't a quitter.

* * *

'Think positive.' The voice came from one of the presidential offices.

'Micky!' AxMan called happily. He opened a door and found himself in a large meeting room, chairs pushed aside. No-one was there except for two black and white cats licking themselves furiously. He loved cats and went to pet them, but they snarled at him, so he stepped back at speed.

At the far end, a door stood fractionally ajar and he heard the words again: 'Think positive.' Closer, he realised with dismay it wasn't Micky speaking at all; it was smoother and younger.

'—all is under control, but the president says that some support could be useful,' the man was saying, 'such as from one of your military bases on neighbouring islands. As in immediately.'

AxMan went to peer through the crack in the door. An official stood by an antique desk, speaking on a landline, while next to him fussed a stout middle-aged woman in a pink suit. Losing patience, she snatched the receiver for herself.

'Listen, pal. You lot were happy enough to go into Panama and Afghanistan. Now when I... Hello?'

She must have been cut off, because she slammed the phone down.

A door flew open on the other side and Lucky Strike entered with his four henchmen.

'Madam President,' Lucky Strike said with a small bow.

'Madam President,' said another voice, and to AxMan's astonishment the economist from the plane followed them in. She'd changed into a crisp sky-blue summer skirt and blouse.

'Miss Heel,' the president said. 'My aide has just been trying to talk to the British and American ambassadors, who won't do anything to help.'

'We asked him not to.'

Bachman stared at her.

'Everything will become clear.'

The president sat heavily at her desk, pale despite her makeup. 'My staff tell me all this was started by some singer.'

Peering through the narrow gap, AxMan felt a flood of guilt. He'd been invited to help make peace and in just a single day his songs had made things worse. In one day. Not even Michael Bublé could have managed that.

He was about to step out to apologise when Meredith spoke.

'Not at all, Madam President. It was planned. In fact, it started when we heard you were planning a speech about Three Mountains. The pop singer was a convenient bonus.'

Again with the pop singer! Why did everyone call him a *pop singer*? He was a *rock star*. But then the meaning of Meredith's words sank in. The riot wasn't his fault after all.

Tentatively, he put his eye to the crack in the door again. Bachman was tapping her fingers on her desk. 'I don't understand.'

AxMan believed her. He didn't understand either. He tried to pay attention, but real-life politics was so complicated.

'It will all be sorted out in a moment, Madam President.' Meredith smiled thinly.

'Where are the palace guards? And the police?' Bachman pointed at Lucky Strike. 'And that gangster. What's he doing here?'

'We're working with the police. Mr Morton is going to be a hero of the people. His men are to bring peace and stability.'

'I don't hear much peace and stability. I hear people looting my palace.'

'The peace and stability come next,' Meredith said.

'It had better come soon,' muttered the aide.

'As you say.' Meredith clicked her fingers at Lucky Strike.

Lucky Strike pulled out a gun and shot the aide in the chest.

The president screamed and tried to scramble out of her chair, but the aide's body had fallen across her lap. His blood spattered her face. Desperately, she pushed the man's body off and grabbed her desk phone.

Meredith Heel pulled out the cord. Bachman reached for an emergency button under her chair.

But before she could press it, Lucky Strike shot her between the eyes.

# 21 A Wanted Man

'Shit!' AxMan said. He covered his mouth. Too late. They'd heard him. In panic, he jammed the anteroom door shut.

Someone thumped the other side.

'Mr AxMan?' Meredith called. 'Open up.'

'Shit, shit, shit!' AxMan said, holding the door closed. It pushed hard against him. Began to inch open. He got a glimpse of the two bodies and shiny dark pools of blood before he forced it closed again. A key stood in the lock. With difficulty, he held the door shut for long enough to turn the key. As he did, something crashed against it, and the wood started to split.

He yelped and sprinted for the far exit. The corridor beyond was empty. Behind him, he heard Meredith call. 'Mr AxMan, there's no need to run. Come back and let us explain.'

He dodged into an office. Looters had finally reached this part of the palace and were busy dismantling computers and unscrewing original Van Gogh sunflower paintings from the walls. They swore at him as he got in their way.

In desperation, he ran through an open doorway and cannoned into a small man who fell back, smashing an antique table. The man swore in a very British way.

'Micky!'

'Ax!' Micky held his ribs as he got up. 'This only proves–'

'No time for proving.' AxMan tugged his friend through another doorway into a massive library. Slamming the door behind them, AxMan shunted a stand with a bust of Donald Trump across to block it.

'Help us,' shouted AxMan to the dozen thieves and pilferers around them. But, instead of helping, the rioters snatched up their paintings and vases and ran off through a small door at the back.

'Fire exit!' AxMan shouted. As Lucky Strike's men pushed the bust of

Trump aside to shatter on the floor, he dragged Micky through the fire exit at the other, clattering after the convicts, down bare concrete stairs, through a fire door to the outside.

Here they found themselves in a wide avenue that ran along one side of the presidential palace. Looters were tossing the less portable contents of the building from the windows above and AxMan narrowly avoided being brained by a Louis XV escritoire which smashed on the ground beside him, a flurry of snapped pieces, like a walnut-veneer firework. Cars had been overturned and set alight, black smoke rolling up in curlicues.

AxMan was riveted. He'd never seen anything like it. But he could also hear the gangsters clattering down the stairs behind. Then he had an idea and thrust one of the broken legs of the escritoire through the handles of the fire door. Loud hammering came from inside, but the escritoire leg held fast.

'You see,' said Micky. 'The universe provides—'

'Absolutely,' said AxMan. 'But let's move away from under these windows, before the universe provides anything more substantial.'

'Ax.' Micky pointed. A mud-covered farm pickup seemed to have been left untouched, perhaps because the rioters felt it was beneath them, or most likely because, even from twenty metres, it radiated a strong odour of farmyard. The rear platform was empty except for a filthy tarpaulin.

'Are you sure? What's the smell?'

'Largely goat, I think, Ax. With a powerful undertow of pig. I'm guessing it belongs to a farmer.'

'I think the goat actually died.'

'I suspect you're right. Then again, maybe it died here so that the universe could save us.'

'Yeah, well, I appreciate your faith,' replied AxMan. 'Still, I'm not sure the universe would have sacrificed a goat for us.'

Nevertheless, they sprinted to the pickup, scrambled over the tailgate and dived under the tarp, pulling it over themselves as best they could. Then they stayed as still as possible, trying not to inhale.

'This is dreadful,' AxMan hissed. 'Horrible. Awful. I just saw… the president…then the economist from the plane… and that gangster with the phone… and he … and she… and I … and blood… oh, God…!'

Micky squinted at him in the gloom under the tarpaulin. 'Run that past me again. I don't think I caught all the details.'

'I saw the president shot.'

'Bugger me!'

AxMan grabbed Micky by the shoulder. 'And they're trying to kill me too! I'm a witness, aren't I?'

'You must tell the police.'

'Shit, no. The police are like in on it too, they said.'

Micky contemplated this and admitted that, for once, he didn't know what AxMan should do. Nothing in the self-improvement books he'd read seemed to apply to being chased by presidential assassins.

AxMan sighed. 'I don't know. Maybe if we lie here and keep quiet, one of us might have an idea. Or at least not get shot.'

So they lay as still as they could. After five minutes, they heard men shouting AxMan's name. The voices came closer and he gripped Micky's arm. There was a thump as someone banged the side of the pickup. AxMan held his breath, but whoever it was just swore and ran on.

'You know,' Micky said, 'do you still have that phone?'

AxMan searched his jeans pockets and pulled out the ancient Nokia Lucky Strike had loaned him. 'Yeah.'

'So we could phone for help.'

'Who? That rapper Freddie Forrester and his sister? I wouldn't want to drag innocent music producers into trouble.'

'The British Embassy. Didn't Jamie say he'd put the number in the contacts?'

AxMan inspected the handset and after fumbling around with the buttons he managed to dial the embassy.

'Well?' Micky whispered.

'It says there's no-one in over the weekend,' he hissed back.

'Shit.'

'But they've got an emergency number. Have you got something to write on?'

'No, but I learned this great memory technique in–'

'One-eight–'

'You start by finding a rhyme. What was that?'

AxMan tried to hear. 'One-eight-oh-nine–'

'Just a sec. One. That rhymes with gun.' Micky counted with his fingers and thumb. 'Eight? What the hell is eight? Mate? Slate? So something slate, something…' He frowned. 'What was the first again?'

AxMan held up his hand for silence. 'Fuck, I've missed the next numbers… hang on. Four-six–'

'Four… door. Six? Six? Wait… sticks. Or maybe bricks, fix… Something, slate, something, something about fixing a door–'

'Two,' AxMan finished. He looked at Micky. 'So what have you got?'

'Something, slate, something-something, fixing a door with a shoe… give me the number again?'

'Now it's asking me to leave a message … Hey,' he whispered to the phone. 'My name is AxMan and like I'm being chased by gangsters and–'

As he spoke, they heard the door to the driver's compartment open. He cut the call in panic. 'Sod it. We've got to get out before–'

But before he could say what it was they should get out before, the engine started and the pickup began to move.

# 22 Two Murders to Report

'I saw a movie once,' Micky said, as they gathered speed, 'where this man jumped from a train as it started and rolled over in this special way so as not to get hurt.'

AxMan peered out uncertainly from under the tarpaulin. 'The roads here look rather hard.'

The pickup rattled over potholes like a badly maintained dodgem car.

'It's too late now,' Micky grunted.

The truck shivered and creaked down a succession of streets and, to AxMan's relief, the sounds of rioting faded.

After twenty minutes, the truck shuddered to a halt. They held their breath. The driver climbed out, thumped the door closed and walked away.

'How long before it's safe to get out?' Micky whispered in the semi-darkness. 'Not that I'm afraid.'

'It depends on where we are… And I *am* afraid.' AxMan lifted the edge of the tarp. 'It looks like a suburban street. Quite attractive. Nice houses. Trees. A bit like where I grew up in North London, but kind of less leylandii and more palm trees. It makes me feel nostalgic–'

'Great,' Micky said. 'I'm pleased for you, but can you see anyone?'

'Not at the moment. I'd say to get out, man, but I can't tell where the farmer's got to.'

'And farmers often have shotguns.'

AxMan contemplated this possibility. 'We wait. Not that I'm not used to guns. But I have to think of you too.' They waited a long while. Then: 'You know, Micky, on consideration, perhaps we should get out sooner rather than later. Last time we left it too long. And it's getting very hot under here.'

'Timing is everything,' Micky said nervously next to him.

AxMan started to raise the tarpaulin again. 'Totally.'

There was a burst of police sirens. Cars raced past then screeched to a halt.

'Shit!' AxMan pulled the cover back over their heads. Cops could be heard running past and shouting.

'It's a good thing we didn't get out sooner,' Micky said.

After many more minutes, the shouting lessened and AxMan squinted through a tear in the covering. He could just make out a man ducking and weaving in an odd way between parked cars. He seemed young, mid-thirties, and pleasant-faced, but if he was the farmer he wore remarkably hip, if grubby, clothes – designer cargo pants and trainers. AxMan dropped back as the man scuttled up and slid into the driver's seat.

Before the truck could move, new footsteps ran up. Doors flung open and angry talk. AxMan wriggled closer to the front to listen.

'What are they saying?' whispered Micky.

'Shh!' AxMan hissed. 'They're not speaking clearly. Oh!'

'What?'

'Someone hit someone.'

There were more words. Then they heard the men get out. Three pairs of feet started to walk away. AxMan let out his breath in relief.

This was the moment that the consulate chose to call back.

The Nokia's ring echoed around the back of the pickup. AxMan snatched the phone from his pocket and poked it frantically to turn it off, then lay motionless, hoping it hadn't been heard.

But the footsteps stopped, and after a pause returned. The tarpaulin slowly lifted.

Two policemen and the farmer looked down at them. One cop was holding the farmer, who was in cuffs.

'Hi,' AxMan said brightly. 'Am I pleased to see you! I have two murders to report.'

The second policeman nodded. Then hit him on the head with his night-stick and the world disappeared.

# Track 3

# 23 The Voice of the People

After Lucky Strike finished his speech on the staircase of the presidential palace, Freddie wasted ten minutes shoving through the crowds, trying to find where he'd gone. Then he returned to the farm truck, angry with himself for pissing away so much time.

Luckily, the pickup stood untouched among the vandalised cars and vans. Any case, there was nothing to smash or steal other than a greasy big oilcloth, crumpled up in the back. He hot-wired the engine again and set off for home.

Home for Freddie and Dania Forrester was a gated complex overlooking the sea in a western suburb of the city, a neighbourhood where everyone was too polite – or scared – to ask how Freddie earned his living.

In the compound stood three modest houses. The largest was normally occupied by Freddie, along with whatever gold-digger had temporarily attached herself to his genitals – position currently vacant. Dania lived in the smallest, overlooking their private beach, and Forrester Public Relations had its HQ in the third.

Forrester PR never actually carried out any public relations. Freddie held that PR firms did very little anyway: mostly they charged a lot for writing pretty words. The closest he ever came to PR was when a politician needed help convincing a rival not to stand against him. Freddie enjoyed that kind of PR. It paid well and didn't involve many words at all.

He approached the compound with care. Everything looked quiet. One of the younger gang members, Austin, sat sleepily by the gate, an AK47 across his lap. Just to be sure, Freddie drove past and parked fifty yards away. The kid didn't look up as Freddie approached quietly from the side.

He kicked the boy's chair from under him. Austin fell back onto the ground and snatched at his gun in panic. Then he saw who it was and gave a lazy smile. 'Boss. When did they let you out?'

'Shit, if I'd had a knife, you'd be dead right now.' Freddie booted him in the ribs. To his credit, the youngster didn't complain and simply climbed back into position, holding his side. He was a good kid.

Freddie found his sister in the back room of his villa. None of the other soldiers could be seen, which annoyed him. He shouted until one of the younger grunts turned up then yelled at him to go round up whichever gang members he could find.

Once the grunt had run off, he turned to Dania, who stared gloomily out the picture window at the beach. The morning had turned grey and the sea stirred uncertainly beyond the rocks. Next to her, a computer played videos of rioters at the presidential palace.

'What the hell's going on?' she asked.

'I need my indigestion tablets.'

'Forget tablets, look at this.' Dania clicked the mouse and brought up a news headline – the single word *Assassin!* 'Our pop singer just shot the president.'

'He did what?'

'And they say you paid him to do it.' A news report played. It showed President Bachman lying in a pool of blood and a wobbly shot of AxMan running away. Then blurred footage of Freddie pushing through the crowds downstairs, caught on someone's mobile. Probably one of Lucky's thugs.

The video cut to the president's husband, floating dead in the presidential swimming pool. Then Lucky Strike, standing outside the presidential palace, telling a news reporter that his men were working with police to restore calm.

'I have evidence that notorious mobster Freddie Forrester conspiracied with the pop singer AxMan to make a riot and personally assassinate our wonderful President Bachman!' Lucky held up his phone and showed a clip of AxMan in the jail, saying *'Prepare to die…'*

'It's time for a strong man,' Lucky continued, striking a serious pose for the camera, 'to clean up this cesspit of a country, rid ourselves of establishment toadies, and bring criminal AxMan and his accomplice Forrester to justice. We have already handed police enough evidence to arrest Forrester and his entire family. It's what the people want.'

'Shit! Have you checked the folks?' Freddie asked, dialling his father.

'There's been no answer all morning.' Dania kept brushing her hair off her face, without seeming to be aware of what she was doing. 'We should get out.'

'Lucky Strike wouldn't dare come at us here.' Freddie got his father's voicemail. 'Dad,' he said, 'pick up your bloody messages. I showed you how to use the phone a hundred times. I'm sending a car for you and Mum.'

He rang off, poured himself a vodka. It was mid-morning, but his doctor would forgive him. Special circumstances.

'No-one will believe that crap from Lucky about the family,' he said, more to convince himself than anything.

Dania thrust her hands in her jeans pockets, but then took them out again to gesticulate. 'Who knows? Myself, I wouldn't believe that man if he told me milk came out of cows. I told you on the phone last night–'

'Women's instinct? You get one thing right by guessing and now you're a genius.'

'I'll give it five minutes before he declares himself president then we'll all get cleaned up for good. I'm not staying here one more minute.'

'You're off your cake. Where are you going to go?'

'I don't know. Anywhere is better than here.'

'More women's instinct? This is the safest place to be, Dania. Still, to make you happy…' He went to a drawer, took out two pistols and handed one to her.

She pushed it back at him. 'No guns.'

'Take. Afterwards, you can be against violence again. And stop waving it in my face.'

Dania thrust the pistol reluctantly into her belt. 'I probably can't even remember how to use the thing.' She left with a sniff.

Freddie shrugged. His sister's political views were always getting in the way. He needed time to think. What had happened to his spies inside the Sunshine Cartel? Why hadn't they warned him?

He yelled again for his soldiers. Five men and three women turned up. Austin was still on guard outside. Freddie told one of the women to go make sure his parents were safe and bring them back. He sent everyone else to get their guns and guard the compound.

After they'd left, he threw his glass across the room. He was pissed with Lucky Strike, pissed with himself. Same time, he couldn't help admire his rival for chutzpah. Freddie would have never thought of anything like starting a prison riot. It had a certain brazen balls to it.

He took another glass and poured a fresh slug. At least he was back home. There was something reassuring about the familiar view. The shark-grey waves rolling onto the shore. The turkey vultures circling overhead. He could hear his men and women getting ready to mount guard front and back, when he heard a car stop outside in the street.

There was nothing unusual in that, except it braked heavily. Freddie walked through to the front room for a better view. He could see Austin hunched forwards in his seat. Freddie smiled. He liked the boy. He was studying for a degree in mechanical engineering. Freddie hated that students today were so desperate for money they needed to work for a gang like his, but the kid tried hard. Freddie waited for him to take out his phone to warn the house about the car, but Austin didn't move. Then he saw the dark red exit wound in the teenager's head.

That second, Freddie heard the front door smash open and cops shouting.

There was nowhere to hide in the front room except behind the door. He could hear cops running into the hall, splitting up, taking different rooms. More cars, sirens blaring. Blue lights flashed through the windows.

The SWAT team headed first to the back, so he waited till they'd charged past, then doubled round to the kitchen at the side. But another team was breaking down the side door. No fucking respect for property. He dived into a gap beside the fridge. The door smashed in and they fanned out, yelling like mad and firing at random. An innocent espresso machine got it along with a bowl of fruit. Nobody checked by the fridge.

Freddie waited for the last of the cops to run through, then peered beyond the broken door. It seemed quiet in the yard. He pushed the pieces of wood out of the way and slipped through, tensed against a shot. It didn't come.

Next he peered around the corner of the building to see if he could get to Dania's house: but police were already there, kicking down her door.

Fuck it. He thought about shooting his way through, but he'd get two or three at most before they turned and whacked him. It would just give them a good excuse. There was nothing he could do and he hated it.

He sprinted to the compound wall and scrambled over, landing in the next-door garden. This was an unkept mess of gravel and jungle plants. He had regular rows with his neighbour about cutting the taller weeds to stop them spreading into his own back garden, but now he thanked them for the cover. He zigzagged across and pushed through a gap in the fence on the other side, reached the street, a hundred yards down from his home.

He yearned to go back, to lead his crew, to rescue Dania. While honour and bravery were lovely ideas, he was too rational not to know it was impossible.

Luckily, he'd thought to park the pickup away from the compound. He stooped to scuttle over, opened the passenger door and slid to the driver's side, reaching down to hot-wire the ignition.

The engine refused to fire. He swore and tried again, but as he did footsteps ran up. Both the truck's doors slammed open and two guns cocked.

'Freddie Forrester!'

Freddie straightened up. 'Hey, Bruno!'

Bruno was one of Lucky Strike's most loyal payroll cops.

'Chief of Police Bruno.' Bruno smiled widely. He was stout, squat and loved waterboarding people. 'Just appointed by President Lucky Strike Morton.'

'Well,' Freddie said. 'Never let it be said your boss ever paused for thought. Shouldn't you be busy with your new job, restoring law and order and all?'

'Ah, well, you see, I'm doing exactly that, mate.' Bruno snapped cuffs on him while the other cop reached over and took Freddie's pistol from his belt. 'Catching assassins.'

Freddie chuckled. 'Still going with that fairy tale?'

'Simply following orders,' Bruno said. 'Now, where's that pop singer?'

'Who do you mean?'

Bruno hit Freddie in the stomach so he lurched chin-forwards into the steering wheel. 'The one with the stupid name – AxGuy... ManAx... AxHole... ... whatever he's egg-sucking called...'

'Try asking your boss. He filmed him this morning while framing him as a ruthless assassin. Other than that, I've no idea.'

Bruno tapped his pistol against Freddie's temple. 'Still don't know, egg-sucker?'

'Actually, no.'

Bruno whacked him three times on the back of the head. 'You're lying.'

Freddie grunted in pain. 'Still no idea. But keep hitting me, I might discover a psychic skill I didn't know I had.'

'Sod it,' Bruno said, thumping him on the skull one more time. Bruno looked at the other man. 'To Three Mountains.' He jerked the gun for Freddie to get out.

'Pretty please?' Freddie climbed painfully from the driver's seat and the two thugs pushed him towards a white van nearby.

Then they stopped.

Under the tarp in the back of the pickup, a phone had started to ring.

# 24 Killed While Resisting Arrest

'What the hell's going on over there?' Martin Plante was on Teams again. 'How did you manage to kill the gangster and the pop singer? It's all over social media.'

Meredith composed herself. It was late in the evening and she was sitting at the desk in her hotel room, in what had until that morning had been the President Isobel Bachman Ocean View and had now become the President Lucky Strike Morton Continental Deluxe. The renaming had changed nothing. The service was still surly, the carpet still had that strange green stain next to the bed, and the electricity still failed every few hours.

Over in Berkshire, Plante could be seen blowing his nose noisily on a maroon handkerchief. Meredith was impressed. It was two in the morning in the UK and he looked fresher than she did.

'I told the board you could handle this,' he said. 'I always said I believed in you. Remember?'

She remembered. On her first day, he'd placed a liver-spotted hand on her shoulder and said she could be destined for great things in Gropius-Plante. Meredith's heart had swollen. (She'd never discovered what happened to Gropius, though dark rumours circulated round the Newbury offices). Right now, she felt herself grow hotter and hoped the sweat on her forehead wasn't visible.

'You were supposed to keep it all under control,' he said, dewlap flapping, 'neutralise the gangster and ship the pop singer back home to his miserable little one-hit career before they had a chance to screw everything up for Three Mountains. No headlines. Now it's all over Twitter, both killed while resisting arrest.'

'One-and-a-half-hit career,' Meredith said without thinking.

'What?'

'Nothing, sir.'

'You're not getting leftie on me over there, are you, Heel? Not going native? Not going to start agitating for trans rights and a minimum wage?'

'Sir, no, sir.' She tried to flap herself cool. The aircon gurgled ineffectually in the night-time heat. 'I took the opportunity to press ahead with our plans for Lucky Strike Morton.'

'Ah, President Morton. At least something went well. Put a stop to all that debt and power station cancelling and helping-the-poor rubbish. Does Morton do what he's told?'

'Absolutely.'

'Thank God for small mercies.' The lights blipped. Martin Plante's face froze on Meredith's laptop then reassembled. 'What?'

'I didn't say anything, sir.' Meredith's spirits descended further – the nightly power cut was on its way.

'Downing Street is all lined up to support the new regime. The spine of a jellyfish. Promise of a large party donation sealed the deal. The US president doesn't like the coup. Feels it goes against his membership of the presidents' self-preservation club. But I can sort him out. Keep a sharp eye on Morton.'

'Sir?'

Plante's face froze again, then restarted. 'Watch out for when he starts getting ideas. You put them in charge of the country and they think they can run the place.'

'Sir.' The lights blipped again. 'There is one thing,' Meredith began, hoping the power might go before she could give Plante the bad news. To her annoyance, the Teams screen remained stable. 'They're not actually dead, sir. The singer AxMan and the gangster Forrester.'

The old man stared at her for what seemed a long while. 'Not dead?'

'No, not exactly, no. The local police put it out prematurely. We haven't in fact killed them. We've just removed them to somewhere safe.'

'Do they know anything?'

'Only,' Meredith couldn't stop herself flinching a little in her chair as she steeled herself to say it, 'the singer did witness the assassination, accidentally, as it were…'

Plante glared at her through the screen. 'How the hell do you let him witness the assassination accidentally?'

'It seems he was in the presidential cabinet room at the time. Think of it like Zapruder, only without the camera. Or the grassy knoll.'

Martin Plante scratched his dewlap. 'There seem to have been a shitload of accidents, Heel.'

'Just the two, sir.'

'Has he told anyone else what he saw?'

Meredith shook her head vehemently. 'Not so far as I believe. Only possibly Forrester.'

Plante reached over to turn off the call. 'Then eliminate both of them. This time for real.'

# 25 Continuous Realistic and Positive Improvement

Kidnapping was not an issue for AxMan. Rock stars who'd not had a hit since the late eighties tended to be low on the abduction priority list. On the one hand, this hurt his pride. On the other, it gave him one less thing to worry about.

When he regained consciousness in a place that was dark and stank of sweat, he didn't first realise what had happened. Instead, he assumed he'd taken too much of something the night before and had passed out in bed with someone nubile. That he had his arm around another breathing body made this quite likely. So he fondled the nearest body parts he could reach.

'Piss off!' said Micky and thumped him on the nose.

'Sorry,' AxMan said, rubbing said nose. 'Mistaken identity. No offence.'

'None taken.' Micky moved away. AxMan tried to do the same, but everywhere hurt, from one end of him to the other.

As his eyes adjusted, he found he was in a round hut made of bamboo slats, through which filtered a dim early dawn light. The floor was packed earth, strewn with straw and bundles of leaves. A cock crowed nearby and birds and large insects could be heard waking and making their own personal noises. Other than that, there was nothing, no traffic, no people talking, no radios playing. He was alive, but the lack of civilised sounds was as worrying as the semi-darkness. Wherever they were, the word "remote" came strongly to mind.

'Shit,' he said. 'Where are we, man?'

Micky owned to knowing relatively little. 'After the cop knocked you out, they shoved us into a van, drove for hours, stopped, drove some more down some very rough roads, then dumped us with some other guys who weren't police.'

'What happened to the farmer?'

'Lost track of him. We arrived in the middle of the night. It was all very dark and confusing. Then they pushed us in here. Oh, and they took the phone. But we can still think positive.'

'I don't see,' AxMan said, checking out one bruised limb at a time, 'how even *you* can find something to feel positive about here, mate.'

'CAPI,' said Micky. 'Continuous Realistic and Positive Improvement.'

'Run that by me again.'

'Even a small improvement is an improvement, OK? For example, back in that jail, there was chaos. And here there is order... That's an improvement. For another example, I've now moved away from you. And given you haven't washed for two days that's a most definite improvement. What we have to do is, we keep looking for ways to make things better. Big or small. That way we Continually Realistically and Positively Improve. CAPI for short.'

'It should be CRAPI.'

'I know. But it don't sound so good.'

'And you haven't washed either.'

They fell silent. The first rays of sunlight crept shily through the slatted walls. AxMan stood up despite the pain and went to squint through one of the gaps. He seemed to be in some kind of village. He could see rainforest, a barbed wire fence, other huts and the remains of a smoking fire but no people. He'd thought country people rose with the sun, but clearly this lot liked a lie-in.

Thinking CAPI, Micky suggested they work out methods of escape. There was no window, so that was out. The wooden laths that made up the walls seemed solid and the door strong. However, the floor was nothing but compacted earth.

'Remember *The Great Escape?*'

'Something about prisoners of war?' ·

'A tunnel wouldn't take long to dig.' Micky began scraping at it with his hands. 'A month or two.'

However, the earth was hard and in ten minutes he only achieved a small dent. 'Maybe we should wait until the rains come and soften it.'

'Would that be soon? Just asking.'

'I don't know, Ax.'

AxMan gave a sigh that was less than positive and surveyed the door a little longer. Then after a while he pronounced, 'I can't see a lock.'

Micky peered over and agreed no lock was visible.

'Do you suppose…?' AxMan pressed the door gently and it opened an inch. He pushed it further.

Micky jumped up. 'Bloody hell! All this time–!'

Beyond the open doorway, the village lay quiet in the low beams of the early sun. AxMan held a finger to his lips and took a first step tentatively towards freedom.

At that moment, a man in torn boxer shorts stepped out of a nearby hut, yawned and stretched his arms wide. AxMan and Micky halted, trying not to be seen. The man finished stretching, sneezed and was about to go back inside when he spotted the open door and AxMan and Micky, frozen like statues. The man frowned. Squinted at them. Then called loudly. He disappeared into his hut, still shouting, and ran out with an assault rifle. AxMan gave a yelp.

Other men emerged from other huts in their underwear and with guns. They converged on AxMan and Micky.

'Look, dude,' AxMan said. 'I think there's been some mistake.'

'Get your motherfucking hands up,' said the first. He was a lean wiry man, endowed with a large pistol, facial scars and an accent that AxMan recognised from too many war movies.

AxMan raised his hands at speed. 'German?'

'That's no business of yours.' The lead kidnapper tensed, finger on the trigger.

'Hey, I've nothing against Germans. I voted no to Brexit.'

'We know Brexit and we know gangsters. You're the rebel pop star who killed the president.'

'*Rock* star, *rock* star! Not *pop* star.' AxMan forgot himself and lurched forwards. The kidnappers cocked their guns. He lurched rapidly back.

'I wouldn't get them too edgy,' Micky said.

'They think I'm a pop star!'

'I don't think genre is the issue here, Ax.'

'Listen,' AxMan said to the kidnappers. 'I didn't kill the president. Why would I? She invited me to run a peace concert. With one of your own singers, Freddie Forrester. I'm like him.'

'Freddie Forrester!' The leader advanced a pace, waving his gun in AxMan's face. 'You're like him?'

'Yeah! Now we're getting somewhere.'

'He kills people. Breaks knee-caps, cuts off fingers – You're like him? Hard man. Leading the rebellion.'

'No, no, you got it all wrong. Not hard men. We're both singers, me and Freddie… Look–'

But they weren't listening. The armed men dragged AxMan and Micky back into the hut. Shackled them together with chains, back-to-back. On their way out, the men roped and padlocked the door.

AxMan and Micky stood in the middle of the hut, forced to face in opposite directions. They could hear the kidnappers talking as they made breakfast in the middle of the village. An enticing aroma of coffee floated in.

'That door was unlocked all the time,' Micky said.

'Seems so.'

'Tom Toggler says—'

'I don't give a monkey's testicle what Tom Toggler says.'

Micky grunted. 'At least now we know where we stand.'

AxMan fell into a depression. He wanted to believe Micky, but in truth whenever things seemed to be getting slightly better, they then got enormously worse. The kidnappers didn't understand he was here for a good cause. And it sounded like this Freddie Forrester singer guy had the same problem – wherever he was. Everyone thought he was a killer too.

'Fuck,' AxMan said, kicking with frustration at a bundle of wood and clothing on the floor.

'Shit!' said the bundle.

AxMan jumped back in alarm. A face emerged from the mess on the floor, like a witch in a cartoon. 'All this noise. Can't you let a man sleep?'

# 26 Confinement Issues

AxMan peered down as the man pushed aside the leaves and branches and looked up with irritation.

'Dude, you're the farmer from the pickup.'

'I was driving the truck, but I'm no farmer.' The other man held out his hand as best he could, given he was wearing cuffs. 'Freddie Forrester.'

'Freddie Forrester?' Micky said from behind AxMan.

'That must be Mr Slapstone.'

AxMan turned and Micky swung round, chained to his back. 'Man, are we happy to see you!'

AxMan swung back again. 'You can tell these guys out there who we really are. Like, they seem to think we're all gangsters.'

'But I *am* a gangster.'

'You're a singer. I saw the email. Forrester Music.'

'Fuck off!' Freddie said, rubbing his wrists. 'I can't sing to save my life.'

'Shit... Are you sure?'

'I think I know my own CV.' Freddie squinted through the slats. 'And you? You flatlined Bachman?'

AxMan flinched. 'No, no, no!' He waved his arms and stepped back to bat away the thought, which destabilised Micky behind him, and they almost tumbled to the ground.

'Listen,' Freddie said, 'I've seen your CV. You fight The Man.'

'Shit, no. That's what they think out there. I just sing about it.'

Freddie gave him the eye. 'You putting me on?'

'That's the truth. I've played Glastonbury. Four times. That's more than Oasis or Ed Sheeran... But I was there in the palace. I saw him do it, man.'

'Who? Ed Sheeran?'

'The Morton guy.' AxMan fanned himself. 'He put a bullet... right between the... shit! I still see it every time I close my eyes.'

'Did it himself?' Freddie brushed bits of twig from his cargo pants. 'That figures.'

'I thought there was something odd about him when he lent me a phone.'

'Lucky Strike lent you a phone? Don't tell me, he took a video of you at the time? Saying a line from one of your songs like *Get ready to die?*' Freddie shook his head sadly. 'It's so unfair. A bloke sings about killing people and people jump to illogical conclusions—'

AxMan came towards him again, with enthusiasm, pulling Micky rattling behind hm. 'Totally. Totally. The critics, they always get the wrong end of the lollipop. There's a deeper meaning—'

He would have continued, but the padlock clattered outside the door and four kidnappers entered, dressed now in brown jackets, with the initials GP on the epaulettes. Two stayed back, covering them with rifles, while the other two nervously laid tin mugs of coffee and plates of sliced bread on the ground.

Freddie held out his wrists. 'Hey, what about undoing the cop-locks so we can eat?'

'Sodding manage,' said the nearest of the guards in a very British accent.

AxMan contemplated his plate. 'I'm not supposed to have white bread. I don't suppose…'

He caught the guard's eye and trailed off. As the kidnappers backed away, Freddie exchanged a few quiet words with one, before they slammed the door, roped and padlocked it after them.

'Chow down,' Freddie said, coming back and passing a mug and plate to Micky, who started eating.

AxMan didn't touch his. 'You know, my therapist says I have confinement issues—'

'You prefer I ask them to set up a table outdoors?'

'That could—' AxMan stopped himself. 'I get it. Gangster humour.' He toyed with his mug. 'What did they say to you just then?'

'It seems we've been reported dead. Shot, knifed, or run over by a police car, depending on who you listen to.'

AxMan felt surprised at not being alive and Micky gave an incoherent squeak.

'It's nothing to worry about.' Freddie dunked his bread in his coffee. 'Social media's just a tad in advance. They're going to kill us tonight.'

# 27 There's Nothing Like the Certainty of Being Hanged

As the sun rose higher, the heat rose with it. AxMan squatted on the dirt floor and tried to think of a way to contact the British embassy. They'd sort things, soon as they knew. Two British citizens in trouble. They just needed to get a message to them. It must be possible. People did it in movies.

'Can't you do something?' he said to Freddie. 'Bribe one of those thugs out there? Threaten to kidnap their children?'

Freddie sat with his back against the bamboo slats. 'You've been watching too much TV. It's not so easy in the real world.'

AxMan rubbed his beard. 'But you, you really whack people, yeah? Out in the real world. You've had guys killed.'

'When I had to. It's not good business to whack too many. Better just leave them thinking you can. Then, if you're nice, they behave. It helps if the rest of your crew's around. And that you're not double-cuffed.'

AxMan shuddered.

'We'll work something out,' Micky said from behind him. '"There is nothing like the certainty of being hanged to concentrate a man's mind." It's in chapter nine of Tom Toggler's "Climb the Mountain Within".'

'Samuel Johnson,' Freddie said.

'Tom Toggler. I have the book at home.'

'He stole it. Jesus, I may be the son of a peasant, but I read.' Freddie snapped a stick in half. 'Though I've found thinking about other people's deaths is generally more useful than thinking about my own.'

'Hey, man,' AxMan said. 'Micky is well read too.'

'And I believe in signs,' said Micky grumpily. 'Like that bird out there in the forest, that could be calling your names. That's a sign from the universe.'

They listened hard, but sign or no sign, the bird fell silent.

AxMan said, after a while, 'You really killed people?'

Freddie scratched his chin. 'You really played Glastonbury?'

'Four times. That's more than Ed Sheeran.'

'So you said.'

* * *

At midday, the kidnappers reappeared toting the same coffee and white bread, this time with a slice of processed cheese.

AxMan leapt towards them, dragging Micky along the floor behind him.

'Listen, you've got it all wrong. Let me talk to your chief again.'

The kidnappers conferred briefly and one of them said, 'Why?'

'I'm not a gangster like this guy here.'

'Nothing to be ashamed of,' Freddie grumbled.

One of the men went off then came back with their boss, wiping his mouth, napkin still flapping from his neck. 'You want to talk?'

'Like I told you. I'm a rock singer. Micky, behind me moaning quietly, is my personal assistant. We came to put on a peace concert, not assassinate anyone.'

'A singer, for real?'

'I'll show you what I do, dude. Anyone got a guitar?'

After a search round the village, someone returned with a battered ukulele, missing one string. AxMan handed it to Micky who tried to tune it, gave up and passed it back.

AxMan ran a few untuned riffs and chose *Blood in the Playground* – one of his more reflective songs – to show the kind of peace-loving rebel metal singer he was. He wasn't sure afterwards quite what went wrong, but around the line *Shoot 'em right-wing bastards in the balls* he felt he'd lost his audience, who promptly left, firmly padlocking the door again. AxMan dropped the ukulele into a corner.

Freddie said, 'I think you convinced them.'

AxMan lowered himself and Micky to the ground and contemplated his white bread and cheese. 'If I don't get shot, man, the constipation will kill me.'

'Eat,' Freddie said. 'Not eating will kill you.'

'You sound like my mother.' AxMan pushed his plate to one side. Freddie took it and ate. 'Hey! I might have changed my mind.'

'Too late. Like my mother would have said, it's gone to feed the starving.'

When they'd finished, Freddie talked to a guard through the slats and came back with the latest news. 'We're still officially dead. The police have fingered me as ring-leader. The British Foreign Secretary knows about you—'

'Great—'

'—and has disowned you as a terrorist—'

'What! Even the—' But Freddie waved his objections aside.

'You're confusing a politician with someone who gives a fuck. In other news, your mother's organising a memorial service for you with the support of the British Society of Licensed Orthodontists. And your ex-girlfriend has gone onto YouTube to say she's writing a song about how horribly you treated her.'

'I never…' AxMan trailed off. Had he treated Cla-Rice badly? She'd always seemed happy, except when she had her moods. He'd promised to help her with her own singing career. Could he have done more? He'd always meant to talk to Pissoff about getting her an album for herself, but the time never seemed right.

Meanwhile, Freddie had also fallen silent. What he hadn't mentioned was the guard had showed him a video of the police strong-arming his parents into police vans. He fought hard to look unaffected as they kicked his father on the legs for not moving fast enough and smack his mother's head against the doorway on the way in.

# 28 Business Ethics

At sun-drop, they heard a vehicle drive into the village. AxMan went to look through the slats, bouncing Micky painfully across the floor behind.

'You know,' Micky said. 'I'd miss it if I didn't get a few more knocks from time to time.'

AxMan apologised, but suggested Micky didn't quite realise how difficult it was, having someone chained to your back.

'Stop bitching.' Freddie peered out. 'It's our new President  Lucky Strike.'

'I've got issues with him,' AxMan said.

'I believe it.'

'That video of me. I never gave permission.'

'I'm sure his lawyers are worried.'

The commander-in-chief climbed from a silver SUV, mounted with national flags, to be greeted by the leader of the mercenaries. They disappeared together into the largest of the huts. His bodyguards went off to the other side of the village to smoke.

'That's sweet,' said Freddie.

'What on earth could be sweet?' AxMan said.

'He wants to watch us get killed. Never one to miss a good execution.'

They fell quiet.

Five minutes later, a Mercedes swept imperiously past the guards at the gate and crunched to a halt by one of the smaller village fires, knocking the evening's roast dinner off its spit. Leaping out, the uniformed driver opened the passenger door with a flourish. A smart young woman with a blonde bob and a thin smile stepped tentatively onto the muddy ground, before she too was led into the largest hut to join the others.

'Shit!' AxMan said. 'That's her.'

'You know that woman?'

'Meredith Heel. She was on my plane then she was with Lucky when Isobel Bachman was killed. Some kind of economist. She told me she was a fan of mine, but I'm starting to think she might have been lying about that.'

Freddie shook his head sadly. 'You just can't trust economists any more.'

But AxMan was staring at the chauffeur, who wore a neat white shirt with black trousers and a cap. 'Man, I know him too. It's that dude who helped us in prison.'

'He helped you? What's his name?'

'Jamie. Jamie J Johnson. He's a good guy.'

Freddie nodded urgently to where Lucky's crew were still sitting not far away, smoking, talking and taking pot-shots at passing birds. 'Call him. But keep your voice down.'

AxMan called quietly. Jamie J Johnson didn't react but continued delicately wiping smudges off the car's paintwork, like it was a Ming vase.

Freddie hissed, 'Again, quickly before those egg-sucking hoods spot us.' And the second time Jamie looked up. Beamed.

'Hey, Mr AxMan.' He bounded over with the enthusiasm of a small friendly dog. 'They said you'd been shot, knifed and run over by a car. There's been obituaries.'

He gave AxMan a high-five against the slats and AxMan raised his hand to meet it, causing a squeak of pain from behind.

'Is that Micky?' Jamie said happily. AxMan turned round so that he faced into the hut and Micky came face to face with Jamie. 'Hey Micky!' Jamie high-fived him too.

'Did they say *I* was dead?' Micky asked, in a small voice.

'No, you weren't mentioned.'

Freddie coughed.

'And this is Freddie Forrester, who invited us here.' AxMan swung back. 'I told you about him.'

'Great,' Jamie said. 'My pleasure.'

Freddie started to speak, but AxMan leant closer to the gap in the wall. 'My death? There's been a lot of coverage?'

'Some, yeah.'

'Listen, Jamie,' said Freddie. 'We need–'

'What did they say? Not that I ever read my reviews, but…'

Jamie frowned. 'Well, you know, they were pretty good, in the circumstances. 'One-and-a-half-hit wonder.' 'Also-ran.' 'Could have been a contender.' That kind of thing–'

AxMan smacked his forehead against the slats. 'One-and-a-half-hit wonder! Who wrote that? No, don't tell me, I can guess. Screw 'em! I'm definitely not subscribing to that rag any more. One-and-a-half-hit wonder… You should hear what I'm planning for a new album, that–'

Freddie jabbed AxMan in the ribs. He glanced again towards the body-guards. 'For fuck's sake, forget sodding obituaries. Jamie, they're going to ice us proper tonight.'

Jamie looked shocked. 'That's bad. Is that because you got AxMan to shoot President Bachman?'

'No, I didn't do that, man!' said AxMan. 'I was just–'

'Enough,' Freddie interrupted. 'Jamie, we need your help.'

'Help you? Anything. I have AxMan to thank for this, you know.' Jamie waved excitedly towards the car. 'Because of the riot you started, I got out of jail and relaunched Jamie's Limos. My uncle still had the car. And the orders are coming in.'

'I didn't start a riot–' AxMan protested.

Freddie pointed to the other side of the camp fire, where Lucky's goons were finishing their drags and standing up, still talking. 'Listen, Jamie, we don't have time to fuck around. Call the British Ambassador. Tell him he's wrong to disown me. We're innocent. About to be whacked without trial. Two innocent Brits.'

'Maybe just one,' Micky said hopefully.

Jamie shook his head sadly. 'Sorry, no can do.'

AxMan squinted at him through the slats. 'I thought you said you'd do anything.'

'Commercial confidentiality.'

'What the hell is that to do with anything?'

'Look, sir, I sympathise greatly,' Jamie said. 'But Ms Heel is my client. And confidentiality is king. This I was taught in my first module of the course I took at Harvvard online business school. And while it does have two "v"s–'

'Sod the two "v"s,' Freddie snapped. 'This stupid musician here didn't kill Bachman and didn't start the riot.'

'Hey, man!' AxMan said. 'What's with the "stupid"?'

Jamie took off his chauffeur's cap sympathetically, nodded empatheti-cally, waggled the cap considerately, then shook his head. 'It's a matter of trust. And business ethics. My brand is at stake here.'

'What's he saying?' Micky squeaked from the back.

'He's saying he can't help us.' Freddie punched the wall. 'You sound like a corporate brochure for designer socks.'

'Thank you. I'm flattered.'

'Listen, dude,' AxMan said, pushing closer. 'You have moral values and I respect that. But think of the PR. You'd be famous for saving our lives.'

Jamie scratched his elbow thoughtfully. 'You think?'

'I'm sure.'

'Maybe… It's true, the PR would be excellent–'

'Exactly.'

'And there's more to success than short-term profit.'

'Exactly.'

'There's long-term profit,' Jamie said firmly. 'And in the long term, I'd be known for betraying my client's trust. Sorry. No can do. Without business ethics, we're all nothing. It was nice knowing you.'

'But we're going to die!' AxMan flung himself at the slats in desperation, with Micky clanking behind him.

'I don't think he cares.' said Freddie punching a fist into the palm of his hand.

'I *do* care. I'll miss you. No man is an island. Every man's death diminishes me.' Jamie put his cap back on. 'Mr AxMan, you've helped me in my growth and clarified many things in my mind. I would look forward to doing more business with you in the future…' He added, turning away, 'Although you probably won't have one.'

# 29 Over There

After another hour, the kidnappers unchained the hut door and led Ax-
Man, Micky and Freddie down to the centre of the village, prodding with
their rifles. This was the first time they'd been out of the hut since dawn
and AxMan, for one, welcomed the thick burnt evening scent of the forest.
That and being distanced from the plastic bucket they'd been sharing as a
toilet.

Micky bumped along behind him in the darkness, insisting that he
wasn't complaining, but it would be nice if he didn't have to walk backwards. Ahead, AxMan could see three tall planks of wood being hammered
upright into the earth next to the village fire. Ready for the firing squad.

'You still thinking positive?' Freddie asked Micky, who for once didn't
have an answer.

Meredith Heel came out of the chief kidnapper's hut, strode up to them,
looking crisp in the firelight, like she'd just showered, sporting a pearl grey
tropical suit that probably cost more than AxMan had made from his last
album. Her eyes were cold and passionless, like she was supervising the
extermination of a nest of ants. 'I'm truly sorry that this is necessary,' she
said. 'I am. And you'll excuse me stepping further away. It's simply that you
all smell like dead carrion.'

'I welcome your apology,' AxMan said, 'and would welcome it even
more if your thugs weren't keeping us chained up. It's most uncomfortable.'

'Of course! My bad.' Meredith nodded to the nearest guard who un-
shackled them, while the others kept their rifles trained.

Micky cranked his neck to ensure it still worked. 'You know, there's
nothing like intense pain to make you appreciate the little things in life.
Like being in less pain.'

Next thing, Lucky Strike came out of the chief's hut, with the chief
mercenary, who marched tall and bristled with knives, a lethal porcupine.

Lucky Strike glowered at them, then shifted to a haughty detachment, more suited to a guy who was now head of state.

'OK,' AxMan said. 'First thing, we're being held against international law. Second, I want representation and a proper trial. Third, I demand to speak to the British ambassador. Fourth, you got to take down that video of me, dude.'

Lucky Strike laughed and looked at Freddie. 'Is this guy for real?'

'Seems so. Are you?'

Lucky Strike maintained his presidential hauteur for about five seconds, then spat on the ground.

Freddie shifted forwards. Lucky Strike couldn't stop himself flinching for a second, but covered it with a cough.

'Where are my parents?' Freddie asked.

'The extended Forrester family has been lawfully arrested for terrorism and anti-government agitation. Save a few odd relations who we're still searching for in the sewers.'

'Egg-sucker, you know my relatives have nothing to do with this.'

The president brushed a smut from his shoulder. 'It's what comes of being related to you.'

AxMan reached for the president's sleeve. 'Look, let's do a deal. Anything I saw in the palace, or might have seen, or might not have seen, like you shooting someone, or not shooting someone… I didn't see. Anything. At all… And you can keep that clip of me in the prison online if you want. You could make good money out of it.'

Lucky drew his arm away as if AxMan was trying to pick his pocket, and pointed for Freddie and AxMan to be taken over towards the planks by the open fire. 'Get on with it.'

'Are you sure? You're making a big mistake. This is going to look bad when it comes out.'

'I'm sodding certain,' Lucky Strike the president said, his eyes narrowing, remarkably like Lucky Strike the mobster.

'He's certain,' said Freddie. 'He's an expert in making mistakes.'

The president/mobster grew red in the face. Meredith stepped forward. 'OK, we're certain. The only question is how. First reports said that the police shot you in the head. The Times produced a diagram to show where a police car hit you, including tyre tracks, while the Daily Mail interviewed a knife expert about celebrity stabbings, from Julius Caesar to today.

'I hold up my hands – the press release went out early and could have been clearer. Someone on our side blew it. I'm looking into it and people will suffer. But that's the way the bombs drop. So, which is it to be?'

'A bullet to the head, ja!' went the chief mercenary with enthusiasm.

'Stab them in the stomach,' said another, behind him.

'Run them over with the presidential SUV,' Lucky Strike added, presidentially.

'If you can't decide,' AxMan suggested, 'we could just leave it.'

'It's not a problem,' Meredith said, with a wave of her hand. 'We'll do it all: stab you in the stomach, run you over then shoot you each in the head to finish. That way everyone's good and the press release was correct. Will be. Will have been…'

While she pondered her tenses, two of the kidnappers pushed AxMan and Freddie against two of the planks. The chief scratched his moustache, then took a large knife from his belt.

AxMan winced. 'At least you don't have to kill my PA. He didn't see anything.'

They all turned to look at Micky, who'd been sidling away into the shadows. He stopped sidling.

'He has a point,' Lucky Strike said.

'Exactly,' AxMan added generously. 'He won't tell.'

'I'd totally forgotten about the little guy.' Meredith twirled a bracelet round her wrist. 'But no. Kill him too.'

Micky was manhandled into the centre and positioned against the final plank. The fire crackled and flames licked up into the night sky. Despite the heat, AxMan felt a trickle of cold sweat dribble down his back.

'Thank you for trying, mate,' Micky said.

'I thought it was worth a go. Positive thinking and that.'

'That's OK,' Micky said. 'It's going to turn out all right. Believe me.'

'I'd *like* to believe you,' AxMan said, as the chief kidnapper stepped towards him with the knife. 'Nevertheless, things seem to be getting late.'

'Never too late,' Micky whispered. 'Look over there.'

'Why? Is there someone magically come to rescue us?'

'It's an old trick. If we all do it, then they'll have to take their eyes off us and we can run and escape.'

Freddie raised his eyebrows.

'Think positive,' Micky said.

So they all peered towards the barbed wire perimeter fence, but nobody looked round. Instead, the president snatched a knife from the chief and announced that, as president, he was going to kill them all himself. He held the blade against AxMan's throat.

'Stop!' AxMan said. 'Didn't you say shoot us first?'

Lucky Strike frowned. 'Did we?'

'Yeah, shoot, then run over, then stab.'

Meredith shook her head. 'No, for sure, stab, then shoot, then run over.'

'I was for certain it was stab, then run over, then shoot,' said the chief mercenary.

'Jesus!' Freddie smiled. 'You know the words piss-up and brewery occur.'

'Fuck you,' said the president, waving the knife irritably. 'Presidential decision. Stabbed, run over, then shot. First the pop singer.'

'*Rock* singer!' AxMan said, beside himself. 'For the last bloody time, I'm a sodding *rock* singer. If I'm going to be stabbed, run over and shot, then I'm going to be bloody stabbed, run over and shot in the right genre.'

'You tell him.' Freddie laughed and AxMan turned on him.

'How would you like it if I called you a sneak thief?'

'Woah, how about your inner anger?'

Lucky Strike was chuckling. AxMan turned to him. 'And you're a petty mobster who can't even kill someone properly.'

It was surprisingly good, being angry. He wished he'd done it more often, but it was getting a bit late for regrets. Lucky chuckled louder.

'And while we're at it,' AxMan said, 'there really is someone over by your car—'

'You actually don't think I'm going to fall for that fuckery,' Lucky said.

'Setting fire to it.'

'Guys,' Meredith said, 'he could be right.'

# 30 Flames!

Beyond the huts, small flames could be seen licking round the bonnet of the president's SUV. A dark figure sprinted away into the trees. Then doubled back, trapped by the barbed wire fence. Lucky pulled out a gun and fired. The others did the same, shot at anything they could see and much they couldn't. The figure fired back.

Lucky Strike waved at his men. 'Extinguishers! Foam! Save my fucking car!'

The kidnappers seemed less interested in saving his car than in saving themselves from getting shot. They dived behind boxes and crates. Meredith dropped behind a box of tinned burgers and called on them to act like men.

Freddie snatched a burning branch and hurled it towards the nearest gang members. The fire caught twigs and dried leaves and spread rapidly.

'The Merc!' Freddie shouted, shoving AxMan towards Jamie's Limos's limo.

AxMan froze.

'Run!' Freddie shouted to AxMan.

'Stay!' shouted Meredith Heel, snatching up one of the gangsters' guns and pointing at him.

AxMan hesitated, but right then the nearest hut went up in flames like a firework display and Meredith put her hands up to protect herself from the heat. Under cover of the distraction, he sprinted to the limo, pulled open a door and leapt into the empty driving seat, but there were no keys in the ignition. Micky piled into the driving seat on top of him.

'Shit!' AxMan said. 'That hurt.'

'Don't shoot,' came a voice.

'Why would I shoot you?' AxMan asked Micky.

'I didn't say anything,' Micky said.

AxMan turned and Jamie poked his head up from below the back seat, his hands in the air.

'Give me the keys,' AxMan said.

'I can't.'

'Client loyalty?'

'No.' Jamie lowered his hands. 'I haven't got them.'

Outside, the flames intensified, leaping from hut to hut. AxMan peered over the dashboard. He could see Freddie running from tree to tree for cover.

'Freddie!' called AxMan, sliding over to open the passenger door.

The gangster sprinted across the open ground to the limo and jumped in, landing on AxMan.

'That hurt too,' said AxMan. 'This is like a tour bus I once—'

Freddie turned to Jamie. 'Where are the keys?'

'He doesn't have them,' Micky said.

Shapes of kidnappers appeared through the smoke, running towards them. 'They're coming after us!' AxMan shouted in panic. A bullet smashed through the side window. He ducked. 'They're shooting at us!'

'So?' Freddie said, clambering into the back. He grabbed Jamie by the lapels. 'Give me the egg-sucking keys or I rip your fingers off you, one at a time.'

Trembling, Jamie handed him a key fob, which Freddie threw to Micky. 'He lied,' he said, pushing Jamie out of the car.

'Drive!' Freddie shouted at Micky.

Micky started the Mercedes. It jerked backwards and slalomed past the nearest hut. Four kidnappers jumped out of the way. 'Sorry. So, *that's* reverse.'

Flaming branches dropped onto the bonnet and roof. AxMan grabbed a door handle to stop him being flung about. Another bullet whined off the roof. Micky discovered a forward gear and headed erratically towards the entrance gate. As they approached it, the figure stood up, holding a gun.

'Stop!' Freddie shouted.

He flung open a rear door and the figure scrambled into the back seat next to him, panting for breath. 'Go!' Freddie said, reaching to slam the door shut.

Micky accelerated the limo towards the barbed wire gate. It was closed, but he didn't stop, smashed through and slalomed onto a dirt track beyond. Bullets whined past, but soon the limo was out of range.

AxMan slumped back in his seat. The anger had gone. He felt weak. His legs shook.

'AxMan, Micky–' Freddie said, as the light of the burning village dwindled behind them. He turned to the figure hunched next to him, clutching a pistol. 'Meet Dania, my pacifist sister.'

# 31 Men Have No Idea

'Oh, my god, oh my god, oh my god!' AxMan felt hot then cold then hot again. 'Shit! Oh, God! And that knife…' He felt his throat to check it was intact. 'Oh shit! Are we really alive?'

'We are indeed alive,' Freddie said from behind him.

'Woah!' AxMan yelled. He hugged Micky, who thumped the steering wheel as he drove.

'I told you,' Micky said happily.

AxMan turned in excitement. 'We survived!'

Dania Forrester shrugged. 'So far!'

AxMan searched for something intelligent to say but failed. Freddie's sister looked even more impressive than in her photo, though he told himself quickly, no comparison to his muse, Cla-Rice.

Dania adjusted her tight jeans and thigh-length boots. She spotted him watching her and raised an eyebrow. 'I'm sorry. I didn't have time to get changed for this meeting.'

Micky was speeding down the narrow dirt road, branches clapping against the sides like a standing ovation.

'Still nobody.' Freddie was squinting through the rear windscreen.

'There wouldn't be,' Dania explained. 'I emptied their petrol tanks.'

'A good thing you left this one alone,' AxMan said, as they bounced over the stones and ruts in the road.

'I didn't.'

As she spoke, the engine choked and restarted, then sputtered again. Then cut out completely. The limo glided to a halt. Silence fell, except for the buzzing of nocturnal insects.

Dania flicked leaves from her T-shirt. 'You took the wrong one. Mine's back there, hidden in the trees.'

Micky gave a low moan from the driver's seat. 'It's not that I'm not being positive. But I suspect I've been shot. More than once.'

To AxMan's horror, Micky was bleeding from a number of places, a bullet-headed raspberry ripple. 'Shit, he needs a doctor.'

'You've got one nearby?' Freddie was staring at the dark track behind them. 'I give it ten minutes before that crew finds Dania's car with the full tank and comes after us.'

Dania leant over Micky to examine his wounds. 'Grazes.'

'It's just,' Micky said thoughtfully, 'the bullets happened to graze me in exactly the same spots where I got bitten by the police dog in the airport customs hall, hit by the flying brick during the prison riot, knocked around in the van they kidnapped us in, and battered when I was chained to AxMan. Then again, thinking positively, doubling up on the painful parts is probably better than having more injuries in areas that are currently not hurting at all. If you consider it that way.'

'Ah, positive thinking again!' Freddie said.

Dania frowned. 'Never believed in it.'

AxMan checked himself for damage in turn. 'You were lucky not to have been hurt yourself.'

'Luck? I've got a few cuts,' she said, pulling fragments of glass from her arm. 'It's nothing. Women have to put up with more than this once a month. Then childbirth. Men have no idea.'

* * *

They pushed Jamie's Limos's limo into the heavy undergrowth, then Dania got them all to cover it with branches and leaves. To AxMan's surprise, she had a good eye for camouflage, and before long the Mercedes was invisible from the track.

'How many bullets you got left?' Freddie asked Dania, but she shook her head.

'Phone?'

Dania held up her mobile with a grimace. It had been hit by a bullet, was smashed and bent. AxMan reported from the dashboard clock: they'd been here fifteen minutes already.

Freddie told everyone to search the limo quickly for anything that might be of use. This produced the grand total of an open packet of plantain chips and a bottle of distilled water. With a quiet shout of triumph, AxMan discovered a first aid box in the glove compartment. But the box turned out to contain only a note:

*We care about your health. The contents of the box have been temporarily removed to help with ongoing cash-flow initiatives. Feel free to leave financial donations to help future users.*

*Jamie J Jameson, CEO Jamie's Limos.*

Dania found two books on the back seat. One by Donald Trump on how to make a deal and the other by Ayn Rand on how selfishness makes you strong. Meredith Heel had inscribed her own name on them and filled the pages with neat notes and underlinings.

'These might be useful,' Dania said. 'For wiping ourselves when we have a shit.'

Just then, they heard a car whining up the track towards them. Freddie turned off the lights and darkness returned, dimly broken by moonlight filtering low through the trees. They watched as Dania's car rattled past, a yellow Honda Civic rammed with mercenaries waving guns.

Once the car had disappeared, Freddie led the others out onto the narrow dirt road, away from the kidnappers' village.

Lucky Strike must have got busy on his phone because they hadn't been walking ten minutes before army helicopters clattered overhead, searchlights flickering across the tree canopy. The four dived to hide in ferns beside the road.

By the time the helicopters had chucked it in, the moon had set. Total black. Freddie wanted to press on, but AxMan asked to stop so Micky could rest.

'We're not on tour,' Freddie said in the darkness. 'There's no green room.'

But to AxMan's surprise, Dania supported him.

'No point in going round in circles,' she said. 'We'll either step on a running snake or end up back at that village again.'

'You have snakes?' AxMan asked.

'Nothing to worry about, musician. Just be careful where you lie down.'

As she spoke, they heard the Honda returning. Freddie hissed them to get into the undergrowth. The car passed more slowly this time – the kidnappers waving their guns with less gusto.

Once their rear lights had disappeared, AxMan groped his way to a tree and settled against it. He felt Dania join him and push his share of the plantain chips into his hands, along with the bottle of distilled water, which tasted like it had come straight out of the Mercedes's engine.

'So, what were you doing there, sis?' Freddie said, his voice from the other side.

'Saving your life, bruv. Good thing I left straight away yesterday when you said we were safe. I was driving off when I passed the cops down the road, heading in.'

'Women's intuition?'

'For sure. I watched from the other end of the street. I saw you all shoved into that van, so I followed you.'

'I call that women's luck.'

AxMan said, 'Luckily for us, you thought positively.'

'Your friend thinks positively. Myself, I find it's better to expect the worst.'

'But surely that way you suffer more. Take today. If we'd expected to escape, then got killed, we'd have had a whole day of happiness and a few minutes of pain. But if we'd spent today thinking we had no hope, then we'd have had a whole day of pain for nothing. Because in the end you turned up.'

'Because I was thinking negatively,' Dania said. 'Anyway, this morning I called out to you, but you never answered.'

'I told you it was a sign,' Micky said from closer to the ground. 'Not a bird.'

'She's a woman,' Freddie said. 'She don't know how to signal properly.'

'Well, you owe this woman,' she said. 'I burned a good Saint Laurent scarf setting light to that bloody presidential SUV. And I can remember how to shoot, Mr Forrester. Even though,' she added with emphasis, 'violence still disgusts me.'

Freddie grunted and Micky didn't say anything. Indeed, judging by Micky's snores, he'd fallen asleep.

AxMan tried to get comfortable lying on unguessable roots and tendrils. There was a deal of rustling. Smells assaulted his nostrils, animal smells of hot fur, flesh, slime and decay. Non-human things could be heard moving around, snuffling, buzzing, fluttering and slithering. Things that only valued him as a source of food.

He didn't belong here. He belonged in cities, where you could see at night, watch TV, share a spliff with friends. Eat. Not get eaten.

He tried his best to think positive and ran through as many of Micky's self-help quotes as he could remember. He was still alive. He had somewhere to sleep. He didn't have to face that jail food any more. But the positive thoughts kept slipping out of reach and the doubts returned, like the insects circling, each taking its bite.

# 32 Three Mountains

Whether thanks to positive or negative thinking, AxMan woke at dawn to find he'd slept after all. A grey mist filled the forest on all sides, turning trees into ghosts. The others were already rousing. They all had a shit and wiped themselves on the book on deal-making or the one on how it's good to be selfish.

By this time, the mist was starting to lift and AxMan could glimpse wooded mountainside, glimmering in veiled sunshine.

'Wow!' he said. 'That's some view. Spiritual! You're so lucky, on this island, like this is your like ancestral inheritance.'

'I'm not some fucking native tracker,' Freddie said. 'I live in the city.'

'So, where are we, City-boy?' Dania squinted into the pines.

Freddie scratched his ear. 'Either halfway up the mountain or halfway down.'

'Which way do we go then?'

Freddie pointed down the slope, then pointed up, then changed his mind again and pointed down.

'You certain?' AxMan felt unconvinced.

'Man's intuition,' Freddie said emphatically and set off down a narrow path.

AxMan followed, admiring the view like it had been created for him as some kind of massive VIP lounge. Dania was behind him, sighing and kicking the stones out of her way, and at the back he could hear Micky, who refused to be negative about his wounds, despite Dania's encouragement.

'Expect the worst,' she said, and was happily outlining the many potential bad outcomes, from gangrene and tetanus to sepsis and death, when AxMan suggested that they concentrate on the path ahead.

Dania gave him a brief smile. It was the first from her that he'd seen.

\* \* \*

The morning heat pressed down on Dania as she walked. Miles of forest varied only in their shades of brown and green. The gun in her belt hurt her side and her boots had been bought with clubbing in mind, but Dania refused to let AxMan see any sign of her discomfort. She'd had enough dealings with celebrities. Other people's problems made as much impact on them as a custard pie on a tank.

She didn't doubt AxMan would not be short of women. But despite his impressive height and beard and strong brow and blue eyes, despite these things, his charm didn't affect her. Nevertheless, she felt she ought to engage him in conversation, if only out of a sense of responsibility. After all, she and Freddie had invited him to the island.

Trouble was, notwithstanding her years of producing rock and pop CDs, her knowledge of what to say to rock stars was still as thin as a low-calorie crispbread. So, a week before AxMan was due, she'd made a point of dropping into the Forrester Music studio, where her engineers, George and BJ, were supposed to be adding the final polish to a Dylan album they were pirating.

Sitting, boots up on the mixing desk, she guided the conversation to what a rock star might be interested in talking about.

'Groupies and wah-wah pedals,' George told her with authority, having had a brief fling with the lead guitarist of an all-female Led Zeppelin tribute band.

'What are wah-wah pedals?'

'Something they make music with. Like you stand on them and they do something or other.'

'You think I should get him one? As a welcome present.'

George adjusted his fly. 'I don't think a wah-wah pedal would be considered an appropriate gift.'

'What else do they talk about?'

'Amplifiers, Eric Clapton, groupies, laser beams… and they go on a lot about riders. They always seem to have problems with them.'

'Riders?' Dania tried to imagine AxMan on horseback.

'Apparently. Very important, they seem.'

Now, as they walked on down the narrow path between the trees, Dania turned to AxMan with trepidation. 'How are your wah-wah pedals?'

AxMan looked taken aback. 'You want to know about my wah-wah pedals?'

Dania grew wary. 'If you want.'

'Do *you* want?'

'Perhaps.'

'What's this wah-wah?' Freddie called from in front.

'Music talk,' Dania explained.

AxMan scratched his beard. 'Do you have a problem with my sound?'

'No, not at all,' Dania said. This wah-wah topic wasn't turning out as well as she'd hoped. She regrouped. 'You've got issues with your riding friends?'

'Now riding!' Freddie said. 'We going on horses?'

'No riding issues,' AxMan answered, looking confused. 'Have you?'

'Not at all. You've got a stable?'

'Not me.'

'Oh.' Dania withdrew her forces in order to try a flank attack. 'How are the groupies?'

'Shit, man, I don't know what Cla-Rice said on YouTube, but she was just upset.'

'Ah.' Dania fell silent.

* * *

AxMan began to feel sorry for the woman, for all her bolshiness. Music execs were strange. She'd obviously been trying to broach some difficult issue but she couldn't bring herself to get the words out. Maybe it was his last record. AxMan decided to help.

'You want to talk about *Wankers*?'

'Wankers?' It was Dania's turn to look confused. 'You have a problem?'

'No, man. Not me. I thought you might.'

'Not particularly.'

'That's OK then.'

'Fine.' She stalked off and joined Freddie in front.

AxMan watched her from behind, thinking how different she was from his beloved ex-girlfriend. Taller than Cla-Rice. And a very different approach to life. Cla-Rice was still his muse, he supposed. He wasn't sure how these things worked. Could someone resign from being a muse or did she have to change her status on Facebook?

They were heading over a small rise when the dirt path widened for no obvious reason into a fully tarmacked four-lane motorway, still free of traffic.

'I don't like this,' Dania said. 'This isn't the way I drove when I followed you, and now there's this wide road with nothing on it.'

'More woman's intuition?' Freddie asked.

A short time later, they passed a sign for Three Mountains. The name rang a bell with AxMan, but he couldn't think why. A song? Or a festival he'd played once?

'It's the name of the region,' Dania said acidly. 'We're in the north-west of the island, near the coast. There are three mountains.'

'Yes, but why would I have heard someone say it?' AxMan walked on. It was recent. On the plane? The airport? The jail? None felt right.

Ahead of him, Freddie crested a second rise. Then, without warning, he halted in the middle of the road. 'Hell!'

AxMan ran to join him, out of breath. Below, the road curved sharply down to an enormous clearing. A large building stood in the centre, by a stagnant lake, the water a startling emerald green. Around it ran a grid of roads and smaller buildings. From where they stood, it looked like a toy village.

They descended. Hoardings announced that this was "Three Mountains A" and warned pointedly that entry without permission would result in permanent injury, dismemberment and death by the security guards of Gropius-Plante. To add force, a fifteen-foot fence ran round the entire area, topped with razor wire and yellow and black nuclear signs.

'Gropius-Plante,' said AxMan. 'I know that name too, I'm sure.'

Dania peered through the wire fence. 'There's no-one here.'

Close up, they could see that few of the buildings were complete. Wooden signs pointed to every amenity a small community would need – shops, hotels, bars, doctor, dentist, a gym – but none of them were more than concrete shells, like the builders had lost interest and wandered off to do something more fun.

The large centre building was square and windowless. Around it stood other sheds, connected to power lines that ran on steel pylons, disappearing into the forest. A large bird of some kind flapped up from a roof and circled above them, before wheeling away.

'I don't like it even more,' Dania said.

'I was hoping there might be some drink here,' said Micky. 'I'm parched. And eating something might be nice too.'

'And no squatters,' AxMan added, 'which is weird. I don't care how far from the rest of the world, squatters always get there.'

And so, they returned to the road. What they didn't notice, hidden in the foliage, was a security camera which silently came to life and patiently panned with them as they passed along the brand-new highway, before turning off again.

# 33 Lunch

Four hours later, the forest finished, cut in a line like by a guillotine. Weary of foot and empty of stomach, they'd reached the foot of the mountains. In front, a flat prairie of fields with low plants, little higher than AxMan's knee. That strange dual carriageway went on through the fields, a sword straight to the horizon. All that time, they hadn't seen a single car.

AxMan looked right. 'Pineapples.'

Micky looked left. 'Peppers.'

'Lunch,' AxMan said.

'I wouldn't,' said Freddie.

'Are you sure?'

'Unripe and indigestible.'

'Don't listen to him,' Micky advised, picking a small pepper. 'If the universe has seen fit to provide this for us, we should be grateful.'

Negativity fought hunger and hunger won; AxMan joined Micky and fell to eating a meal of unripe pineapples and acid green peppers. Freddie hesitated, then chose to sample a little, while Dania looked on with disdain.

'Women,' she said, 'know how to go hungry.'

They'd finished all their water some time before, so AxMan tried scooping one of the puddles that lay around the plants, sipping from his hands. 'Do you think this water has a strange acrid tang?'

'Fine by me.' Micky drank deeply. 'Reminds me of some pills I once got off the sound crew at Download.'

Dania snorted. She seemed to have cooled towards AxMan since their last rather odd conversation about wah-wah pedals, but he didn't understand why.

'What do we do now?' he asked.

'OK,' Freddie said, 'here's the reality. Go back into the forest, and wander in circles. There's no food and we die of hunger. Go forwards into the fields, there's nowhere to hide and we die of being shot. Stay here and we die of eating nothing but unripe pineapples and peppers.'

AxMan threw down a pineapple core. 'Shit. I'd have been better off shot, stabbed and run over by Lucky Strike. Then at least it would all be done with.'

'You got suggestions?' Freddie asked.

'Yeah, I'd like to go home. I'm about to lose my house and all I own to the lawyers, but I think I've seen enough of this island to last me a lifetime. Which won't be very long at this rate.'

Freddie pointed across the fields. 'The sea's that way.'

AxMan stood up. 'I'm decided then.' And he started walking down the empty freeway.

'Ax!' Micky called. 'Are you sure?' He looked fondly back at the trees with their many hiding places. 'Shouldn't we take a vote on it?'

'Fuck, no.' Freddie stood to follow. 'This isn't a rock band.'

Dania stood up too and brushed herself down. 'I'm getting fed up with this island myself.'

\* \* \*

For an hour, the four of them walked along this deserted four-lane motorway. No living creature seen, only peppers, pineapples, not counting a single turkey vulture which cruised above them, a patient undertaker waiting for new business.

AxMan dropped back to accompany Micky, whose limp had worsened and who was holding his hand to his stomach. About two miles further, Dania stopped, pointed. There was a dark shape in the distance and it was moving towards them.

'Shit!' Freddie said.

AxMan looked around. The plants were too low to hide in and the forest lay far behind them. The shape travelled slowly and resolved into a tractor, spraying crops from a boom.

'Just pesticides,' Freddie explained.

'Pesticides?' Micky repeated in a low voice. He massaged his stomach with an air of it not being much of an issue, but his skin had the pallor of an unhappy frog.

Dania nodded. 'We're very lucky on this island. This is where the major companies come to experiment with their new chemicals.'

'Experiment?' Micky said meditatively.

They walked on, but Micky dropped further behind, wheezing. 'I'm thinking positively,' he said, between gasps. 'But at the same time, I'm concluding I don't feel at all well.'

AxMan felt Mickey's forehead. 'Folks, we need to get help.'

'Help from who?' Freddie said. 'The emergency services maybe? They'd love to sort out his indigestion. With a bullet.'

AxMan grabbed Freddie by the arm. 'Hey, I'm saying he's in need.'

Freddie glared at him and AxMan let go sheepishly. 'I mean–'

But just then Micky gave a low sigh, slid slowly down onto the hot tarmac and lay groaning to himself.

'That's an impressive bout of indigestion,' Dania said.

AxMan looked across the vast fields. There was no-one except the crop-sprayer. AxMan went to wave, but Freddie pulled his hand down.

'No.'

AxMan jerked his hand away. 'Fuck you, that's my friend on the ground there.'

'I hate to rush you,' Micky said. 'But I'm losing sensation in my fingers and toes.'

Before Freddie could stop him, AxMan ran towards the crop-sprayer, shouting. He pulled off his gilet and waved it. Freddie called him back, but it was too late. The crop-sprayer came to a halt. The operator could be seen climbing down, a small figure in the heat haze. He took out his phone.

'Great,' Freddie said. 'Now you've got us all killed.'

# 34 Poisoned by The Man

Ten minutes and AxMan watched an expensive Land Rover weave its way across the fields towards them. The driver stopped and jumped out, introduced himself as Trevon Poynter, farm manager for Fruitcancorp International. Late twenties/early thirties, dark-skinned, lean and shaven-headed, he moved with ease, like he was used to being in charge. Reminded AxMan of Pissoff's record execs. Next thing, he bent over Micky and prodded him sharply in the ribs. to AxMan's surprise, Micky pushed him away.

'He works for The Man,' he said hoarsely. 'The Man poisoned me.'

'I no poison no-one.' Trevon straightened up. He had a Jamaican lilt. 'However, I must say he don' look good.'

'I'm not getting saved by The Man!' Micky croaked.

AxMan kicked the road in exasperation. 'Hey, dude, I understand you, but you should let The Man save you this time.'

'Listen, The Man–' Micky didn't finish his sentence.

Freddie grabbed him by the Muse T-shirt and threw him onto the back seat of the Land Rover. 'Sorry, my hearing seems to be going,' he said.

'Must be The Man's doing,' Dania said.

As they lurched and juddered over the rutted access track away from the main road, Trevon turned to them, one hand on the wheel, and argued whatever the problem was, it couldn't be pesticides. 'Not possible, sir. Fruitcancorp take the health of its employees and customers very serious.'

Micky started to froth at the mouth. 'Thinking positively–' he began. And slipped into unconsciousness.

Trevon glanced over his shoulder. 'Shi-i-it,' he said and accelerated hard.

Soon they skidded to a stop at a rectangular steel hut, as impressive as a large Portaloo. This, Trevon explained, was the Fruitcancorp Benkuda North Province Farm Management Centre. A grand name for three rooms. Trevon worked and slept in the first, cooked in the second and bathed in the third. He carried Micky into the bathroom, where the little man lay between the steel shower and toilet basin, pale and unmoving.

AxMan flapped his arms. 'He's dying, dude.'

'We all die,' Dania said.

'Thank you, that really helps.'

Freddie turned to the farm manager. 'You got some kind of antidote?'

'I telling you it's all safe,' Trevon said irascibly. 'You were stealing our fruit then?'

They didn't answer. Trevon shrugged. 'Is no skin off my nose, blood. However, you three seem OK.'

'He had more,' Dania said emphatically, 'of everything.'

Trevon still seemed unconvinced, but went to his computer and googled the name of one of the pesticides they used.

'May cause oral or nasal discomfort,' AxMan read over his shoulder, 'tingling and irritation, nausea, vomiting, diarrhoea, loss of limbs, blindness, infertility and death.'

'Don't trust those environmentalist do-gooder websites,' Trevon said. 'They making me angry. Always exaggerating. Without those chemicals, the birds and insects eating everyting. You townies think this some kind of beautiful countryside, but to us farmers it's a war zone. But with this stuff, we winning. No weeds. No insects. No birds. I'd feed these chemicals to my children if I was able to have any.'

Micky gave a strange gurgle from the bathroom. AxMan called to him, 'Hold on there, Micky-boy. Think of what Tom Toggler would say!'

Dania took over the mouse and scrolled down. 'Do you have a stomach pump?'

Trevon didn't, but digging reluctantly through his first aid box, he astounded himself by finding phials of antidote. 'Odd,' he said, shaking his head. 'I don't understand why we have all these unnecessary medicines.'

AxMan grabbed them. 'You see, the power of the universe. As Micky would say, if he wasn't in a semi-coma.'

'The power of the first aid kit,' Dania replied.

She followed AxMan into the bathroom, prepped a syringe and located a vein in Micky's arm. 'This is one advantage,' she said, 'of living among drug dealers.'

At the first injection, Micky jerked half-awake and stared around, looking sorry for himself. He insisted woozily that every experience was good experience – then passed out again.

# Track 4

# 35 Tell Me They're Dead

'Tell me they're dead and everything's under control.'

Meredith stared at her laptop screen, her lunchtime cappuccino getting cold. Martin Plante could be seen on Teams, sitting in dappled sunshine in his large conservatory in Newbury, sipping a mid-afternoon tea.

'Everything's totally under control, sir,' she said. She'd set up in a side office in the presidential palace. Lucky Strike had stomped off to shout at people. Especially if they forgot to call him Mr President. He'd spent most of the helicopter flight from Three Mountains insisting she repeat "Mr President" over their in-flight intercom at frequent intervals. He said it sounded sexy.

Meredith hated being objectified, but let that pass and said 'Mr President' in as business-like tone as possible. Despite that, he'd grinned like she'd just fellated him. No matter. Let him enjoy his moment. Time to cut off his balls later.

'And they're dead?' Martin Plante insisted. 'Deceased. In the morgue?'

She had hoped to string her boss along until they actually were. She hated AxMan even more than she had before. Fucking artists. Always buggered things up. 'It's all in hand, sir.'

Plante's dewlaps flapped as he took a vicious bite out of a bun. Meredith caught the distinct feeling he wished it was her head he was biting off.

'So they aren't? Dead? Those two shits?'

'Not exactly.' She hesitated, searching for the right words, hoping he'd think it was a frozen connection. Unfortunately, she could see from his face that he was buying this as readily as he would a supermarket Rioja. She cleared her throat. 'And it's four shits now.'

Plante glared through the screen. 'Four? They're breeding?'

'We–'

'Don't insult me with excuses, Heel. Just sort it out, whatever mess you've made. Our share price is taking a hit. And get on with the rest of the agenda. Has your president picked his cabinet yet? Did you give him the list of choices?'

Again, Meredith hesitated. It hadn't been a calm discussion. 'President Lucky Strike Morton has some ideas of his own. Family and–'

'It's not his job to have ideas,' Plante said, stabbing the remains of the bun with a knife. 'But, no. I'm not a hard man. Let him appoint a few friends and family. It's good to make him feel he has a say in these matters.' He speared a knob of butter. 'Talking of which, I'm told you have your own ideas. That you support abortion rights and freedom for gays. Your leftie parents, I assume.'

Meredith froze. How did he know what her views on gays and abortion were? Then again, Martin Plante seemed to have access to any information he wanted.

'I do think,' she began, stumbling, 'that there are certain moral ways of living–'

'I don't give a damn,' Plante said. 'Do what you want with gays and foetuses. Just get the other stuff done. And moving on with the next two nuclear power stations would be a good idea. Maybe add a third? It's time you upped their debt again. We need the money. Serve them right for thinking they can vote for idiots like Isobel Bachman.'

'Yes, sir.' Meredith could hear shouting from the direction of the presidential main office. Lucky Strike's wife was complaining to him about the quality of the First Lady's apartment. Only six bedrooms, north-facing, five bathrooms, none with rain shower. Her voice echoed down the corridor. 'What paesano doesn't have a rain shower nowadays!'

Meredith made an effort to refocus on her boss, who was reaching forward to end the call.

'And kill those four shits.'

# 36 It's a Cut-throat Industry in Fruit and Veg

AxMan waited in Trevon's office for Micky's condition to improve or worsen. An army chopper flew over the farm, hovered, then slouched away. AxMan ducked from the window. Then realised Trevon was watching him from the door.

AxMan tried to sound nonchalant. 'They come often?'

'Now and then.' Trevon sat at his desk. 'Searching for rebel gangs.'

AxMan watched the helicopter disappear beyond fields that stretched out of sight.

Trevon swivelled in his chair. 'Impressive view, nah? One of the largest farms on the island. Believe it, blood. Pineapples, peppers, sugar cane, cocoa beans, coffee beans, coconuts, spices, herbs, bananas – large and small – tomatoes, cucumbers, cantaloupes and mangos.'

AxMan said he was surprised, given this abundance all around them, that there was so much hunger in Benkuda.

'Oh,' Trevon said. 'None of this to be eaten here, blood.'

AxMan was now doubly surprised, as he had found that people generally needed to eat.

'Yeah, but can you make money out of it? You have to add value. That how business works. I don't know who you are…' He paused and inspected AxMan with curiosity, but AxMan felt it best not to answer.

Trevon continued regardless. 'Take the pineapples. Pick one off the ground here, it's worth ten Benkudan cents. But you cut it in slices or chunks, add sugar syrup so no-one notice it going stale, you squeeze it for juice, can it, freeze it, design an ad campaign. Now you sell that one pineapple total ten Benkudan dollars.' He tapped his computer screen with pride. 'But of course that's a price that the local people can't afford.'

'That seems a bit unfair,' AxMan said.

'No way.' Trevon waved a hand at the bundles of papers piled up in his in-tray. 'We sell to the rich people in Europe and America. Then all the cash that come back can be spent on ting like schools, power stations, hospitals, computers, airports and roads.'

'That makes more sense,' Freddie said, who'd come in and caught the last sentences. He flung himself lengthways on the office sofa. 'Except the fucking schools and hospitals are falling down, there are always power cuts, and the roads are full of potholes.'

'They certainly are,' Trevon said heatedly. 'But that not my fault. All that adding value come at a cost – refineries, canning factories, distributors, lorries, container ships, advertising, overheads and shareholder dividends. At the end of it, there no money left for those other ting.' He spread his arms wide.

'Let me get this straight,' AxMan said. 'You grow things nobody can afford, so it has to be sold abroad to make money for the local people, but the costs mean that they get nothing after all.'

'Put like that,' Trevon said irritably, 'just show how little you understand modern farming.'

\* \* \*

Freddie waited for Dania, who'd stayed monitoring Micky's health status in the bathroom. She called out at regular intervals there was no change. At each update, AxMan muttered a lament.

'He's not dead yet,' Freddie said, after the fifth time. He was thinking about their parents, who were God knows where. Being forced to do God knows what. Who'd be looking after *their* health? Who'd be muttering a lament for *them*?

Trevon looked up from his phone and examined them more carefully. 'I meet you two somewhere before?'

'No.' Freddie was picking dirt out of his fingernails. 'I doubt it.'

The farm director rubbed his hand over his head in thought. 'Where you coming from?'

'Up in the mountains, back there,' AxMan said from by the window.

Freddie gave a sigh. 'You want to tell him everything?'

'You came from Three Mountain A?'

'We came past there,' AxMan said.

'Three Mountain? Blood, you're lying. Nobody go to or come from Three Mountain A. One day, they start the power station up there… Fish dying. People getting ill. One day, they stop. Everyone left. You lucky you didn't eat anything up *there*. Ha!'

'So that was a power station we saw,' AxMan said.

Trevon leapt up. 'Hey, I got it. You that gangster and terrorist pop star–'

'*Rock* star–' AxMan blurted.

Freddie glared at him. 'Well done.'

'You *are* them,' Trevon said, with a widening smile. 'You all over the news for that concert you coming to do. Everyone very excited. Big crowd expected.'

'Well–' AxMan began, looking modest.

'You in the news again, today.'

Freddie said, 'Don't believe everything they tell you.'

'I never believe one single ting they say.' Trevon went to the window and pulled down the blinds. 'Yet if I'd known I wouldn't have brought you back here.'

Freddie got ready to stand up. 'You going to shop us?'

'Man, I got nothing against you.'

'We're not murderers,' AxMan said. 'Well, *I* didn't kill anyone.'

'Yeah, I believe you. But the police, they offering big, big rewards.'

'There you go.' Freddie kept eyes on the farm manager. He reckoned he could take him if he had to. He sat forwards. 'How big a reward do you get for shopping us?'

'I don't shop you. No, no, no. But my workers. If they don't spy for Goodnessfoods, Real Greens or Vitafreeze, they spy for the government. It's a cut-throat industry in fruit and veg.'

Like that, AxMan slapped the wall. 'I've remembered!'

Freddie jumped in his seat. 'Don't fucking do that.'

'Remembered where I heard about Three Mountains,' AxMan said triumphantly. 'It was when… they…. he…' He glanced uneasily towards Freddie and mimed holding a gun. He mouthed 'Assassination.'

'When you saw Lucky Strike shoot the president?' Freddie said. 'Just say so. He knows who we are now.'

Trevon was watching them, open-mouthed. 'You saw the president shoot the president. I mean, the new president shoot the… You saw that?'

AxMan nodded anxiously. 'And that's what the economist said before they… did it.'

Freddie scrutinised him. 'She said "Three Mountains"? I don't believe you.'

'She told Bachman the riots were all planned long in advance. "After Three Mountains."' AxMan reached into the back pocket of his jeans and pulled out the business card that Meredith had given him.

'*Meredith Heel, Economic Adviser, Gropius-Plante,*' he said. 'Like at the power station – and GP on the kidnappers' uniforms.

# 37 The Logo

Before Freddie could reply, Dania rejoined them.

'The invalid is mending,' she said. 'Slowly and grumpily. And telling me how positive he feels about escaping... ah...' She glanced at Trevon.

'He knows,' Freddie said.

'Man, I feel we can trust him,' AxMan said fervently. 'And he can't call anyone without us seeing him.'

Freddie grunted. 'I trust my crew. I'm not so sure about trusting anyone else. It's running across a road with your eyes closed. It never ends well.'

'I'm pleased your guy is better.' Trevon sank back into his chair and rubbed a hand over his scalp. 'I suppose you'll be going north to the sea.'

'What's it to you?' Freddie said.

Trevon blew his nose nervously. 'There's a fishing village ten miles up the road. You could get a boat off the island, but...' He trailed away.

'But what?'

'You make me 'fraid to open my mouth.'

'Go on!'

Trevon folded up his handkerchief with care. 'They say that village run by this... family. You probably know all about such.'

Freddie gazed at him. 'You mean gangsters? Go on, say it.'

'Kind of, yeah, blood... I mean, not to insult present company. But I don' go there.' Trevon trailed off again and looked as if he'd swallowed one of his own fruit cans whole, tin included.

AxMan gave him a reassuring smile. 'No insult. We'll take our chances.'

Micky, meanwhile, had grown strong enough to limp back to Trevon's office before sagging onto the couch next to Freddie.

Trevon eyed Micky with what could have been a guilty conscience. 'Though, hey, listen,' the farm manager said. 'I can drive you part way.'

'I knew it,' Micky said. 'Positive thinking. You never know how things are going to turn out. If I hadn't drunk the pesticide, we wouldn't have found this man. Positive thinking.'

'Or negative thinking,' Freddie said. 'Because, if we'd been as stupid as you, we'd all be lying spark-out on the road back there, and none of us would have been able to find anyone.'

'Hey.' Trevon got out his keys and opened a cabinet. 'Enough of the pesticide.'

'You know, man,' AxMan said to Freddie, 'you have a lot of inner anger yourself.'

'Perhaps my fucking anger is what's kept me alive these years.'

AxMan shrugged. 'And you want to watch out. All that blood pressure. It's not good for you.'

Micky stretched his short arms and legs to see if they still worked. 'Anyway, what are we waiting for? I'm ready.'

'Assuming I'm still trusted, blood.' Trevon took out four T-shirts, bright red, with *Fruitcancorp* in letters shaped like overjoyed cartoon fruit. 'Wear these in case anyone sees you. People will think you're seasonal pickers.'

Micky looked at his and puffed his cheeks.

'Too small?' Trevon asked. 'I got larger.'

'No, it's nothing.'

'What?' Freddie asked.

'It's the logo.'

He peered tetchily at the front. 'What wrong with this logo?'

Micky tossed it back. 'It's The Man's logo.'

AxMan turned to Trevon. 'Ignore him. He doesn't know what he's saying.'

'I know exactly what I'm saying,' Micky said. 'It's bad enough taking all this medicine from The Man without having to advertise him.'

Trevon jammed the T-shirts onto the shelf again. 'That's it then!'

Freddie threw up his arms. 'I don't believe it!'

'I don' have to help.'

'Apologise,' AxMan said to Micky. 'Or we don't get our ride.'

'You've changed. What about sticking it to The Man?'

'That was when I was eighteen. Right now, I just want to stick myself in a boat and not in another jail.'

Micky shrugged. 'OK, I give in.'

'Thank fuck for that,' Freddie said.

'As in your song, Ax. *Kapitalist Krap. It's not the picture on my chest, but the picture in my heart.* I'll wear that Fruitcancorp T-shirt, but in my heart I'll be remembering when you had principles.'

'That's not fair—'

'And about saving the planet from processed foods.'

Trevon jangled his keys in his hand. 'Save the planet from me, blood?'

'He doesn't mean that.' Freddie eyeballed Micky. 'Does he?'

'He does have a point,' AxMan said.

'I get it. Your friend don't want be driven by The Man, in The Man's air-conditioned Land Rover, fuelled by The Man's petrol. Well, he don't have to!' Trevon slammed shut the cupboard door.

'It was the poison talking.'

'Not again the poison!'

'Forget the poison. He is definitely going to apologise.'

Freddie hissed at Micky, 'Apologise and just wear the egg-sucking thing!'

Micky struggled with the words. Finally, he managed a quiet, 'Man, I'm sorry.'

Trevon put his hand to his ear. 'What? I nah hear that.'

'I'm sorry,' Micky said louder.

'Still can't hear.' Trevon shook his head slowly. 'Maybe this is one of those non-apologies that politicians talk about.'

'I fucking apologise, OK!' Micky yelled.

Trevon drew breath. 'OK, blood. I accept that—'

'I apologise for saying what I think,' Micky continued, warming to his theme. 'I apologise for this thug trying to strong-arm me into abandoning my beliefs – I apologise for AxMan, who's forgotten his balls – I apologise for you, Trevon – working for The Man who is screwing up the world. I apologise for you – taking money from The Man. I apologise for you being The Man's man... man...'

# 38 A Man's Needs

Nobody spoke for the first half mile. The freeway had finished and a dirt road rose up towards the northern hills, smelling of burnt earth. The fields either side filled with low-sprouting sugar cane. AxMan could feel blisters the size of coconuts forming on his feet and from time to time he cast a nostalgic eye at the farm office far behind them and thought about Trevon's air-conditioned Land Rover.

'So what was all that about?' Freddie asked finally.

'Talking truth to power,' Micky said.

Freddie kicked a large stone with venom. 'That farm guy helped us and was going to help us some more and you pissed him off till he threw us out. How bloody good was your truth then?'

'I thought you survived because you believed everyone was out to scam you,' AxMan said.

'I thought you believed people can change.' Freddie struck out at the sugar cane. 'Great, well done, egg-suckers. That was a good job done. Who wanted to ride in comfort? Who wanted to show gratitude for that man saving Micky's life? Much better to have sodding truth, yes?

'I'm really glad we're not sitting in his nice air-conditioned jeep. Because that would have been The Man's jeep, made by The Man and paid for by The Man's money. And anyway, what's all this shit about The Man anyway? I thought pop singers, sorry, *red-metal rock* singers just wanted to make money and snort yayo up the nose.'

'Some of us are politically aware,' AxMan said. 'I'm sorry if you're happy to stay in a fog of complacency.'

Freddie strode on. 'I should never have got involved with musicians.'

'I told you,' Dania began. 'Musicians are always trouble.'

'Thank you for being so fucking right!'

At that moment, three helicopters roared up from behind the hill, firing rockets. Axman dived for cover into the sugar cane followed by the others. Micky shouted in pain. Dania grunted and her lower half landed on AxMan's head.

But the rockets weren't aimed at them. As the helicopters passed overhead, AxMan could see between Dania's legs. The first chopper slanted down towards the valley below and strafed the farm before they all landed in the fields next to the office. Soldiers leapt down, taking up positions around the outbuildings, some of which were on fire.

For a second he thought Trevon had ratted on them, but then a group of soldiers stormed the main office and dragged the farm manager out at gunpoint. One hit him with the butt of a rifle. The other soldiers deployed in all directions, searching.

'Looks like he was right,' Freddie said, keeping his head low. 'He couldn't trust his own workers.'

AxMan felt Dania shift above him.

'Stay down,' Freddie said. 'They're still too far away to see us if we don't move.'

Dania took a look at AxMan under her crotch and neither of them moved.

After fifteen minutes, AxMan noticed the soldiers seemed fully occupied torturing Trevon. Freddie said it was probably safe to get going again while they were distracted. 'Just keep below the level of the canes.'

Micky clutched his upper arm. 'I think I've broken my shoulder.'

Dania looked down at AxMan. 'You got any damage?' she said softly and sounded almost concerned.

He felt his guitar hand gingerly. 'No, it's fine.'

'For shit's sake,' she said, jumping up. 'Not everything is about your music.'

AxMan stretched carefully. 'It was strange. While I was down there, I found myself remembering when I first met Cla-Rice. She came backstage when I was playing at—'

'We should move off as soon as possible,' Dania interrupted. 'You never know what will happen next.'

From the ground, Micky suggested that it was a good thing that farm guy wasn't driving them. Indeed, it could be said that they, Micky and AxMan, had saved them. 'No need to thank us though.'

Freddie walked over to inspect Micky's shoulder and announced it was merely dislocated. He gave a sudden sharp wrench. There was a loud crunch and Micky would have screamed if Freddie hadn't clamped a hand over his mouth.

'There you go,' he said with a smile. 'No need to thank me though.'

\* \* \*

Soon dusk fell and they lay down by the path. AxMan felt hot, dirty, hungry and thirsty. It reminded him of Glastonbury, except for the lack of drugs and vegan catering. He gnawed at some cane stumps for energy, but there was nothing to drink except for the pools left around recently sprayed plants. These he avoided, as did Micky, who glared at each puddle like it was a personal enemy.

'Dude,' AxMan said, 'Trevon knows where we're going. You think he'll tell?'

'Possibly,' said Dania.

AxMan thought she looked more nervous than he'd seen her before.

'He could,' said her brother. 'There's only one problem.'

'What's that?' AxMan asked.

'There's no other way for us to go.'

\* \* \*

Next day, they set off again at dawn, scanning the horizon for more choppers or army trucks. To take their minds off their empty stomachs and nagging thirst, AxMan sang snatches of his more recent songs. Oddly, the others appreciated them less than he'd hoped.

Micky limped, clutched his ribs and stomach and groaned frequently, while insisting it was all for the best. He'd begun quoting Tom Toggler on things being all for the best in the best of all possible worlds, when Freddie said, 'Voltaire.'

'Toggler.'

'Fucking Voltaire.'

'Tom–'

AxMan surprised himself by telling his friend to shut up.

An hour took them to the crest of a new hill. Freddie reached it first and stopped.

'Another nuclear power station?' AxMan asked, hurrying to join him, but it wasn't another Three Mountains. The land dropped sharply away and below, glittering blue and silver in the sunshine, lay the Caribbean.

'Over there,' Freddie said, squinting at the horizon, 'is the way to Sainte-Âne and safety.' He looked down. 'And there are boats.'

Beneath them, a small fishing village seemed glued to the cliffs: around three dozen little corrugated iron cubes, scattered like dice, and a cluster of fishing boats pulled up onto the beach for protection. Other boats could be seen further out to sea, moving slowly.

AxMan's spirits lifted. He never travelled well by ship, but the romantic side of him couldn't deny the beauty of the scene. He'd been letting Micky lean against him, but seeing the village gave Micky a burst of energy and the little man hobbled forwards on his own.

'You think the natives are friendly?' AxMan asked.

'These places don't survive by being friendly. They survive by cutting throats of people who have a different surname from them.'

Dania sniffed. 'Always the violence with you.'

Freddie slapped his hand on his forehead. 'My violence paid for your clubs and your Ralph Lauren scarves. And kept our parents from having to eat fried rat.'

AxMan eyed the steep path down. 'Might the police be waiting for us?'

'You're getting the hang of this,' Freddie said with a thin smile. 'There's only one way to find out.'

They picked their way along the winding path towards sea level. AxMan moved up alongside Dania. She was striding forward with energy yet also a very feminine elegance. Once more he was struck by how different she was from Cla-Rice. Maybe it was the possibility of escape growing closer, maybe it was the possibility of danger, but something made him think about—

He scratched his beard. 'Can I ask you something? Something personal?'

Dania turned to him. 'Ask me?'

'You're a woman.'

'It has been said.'

'And, hey, an attractive one.'

Dania demurred, but moved closer.

'It's not easy for me to share this.' He could feel the warmth of her body pressing against his side as they walked.

'Go on.'

'You understand that women and men have needs.'

Dania flushed slightly and shot him a glance. Having started, AxMan wasn't sure how to continue. 'Look, I don't even know if you've got a boy-friend, a partner, anyone…'

'I have had. Not so many as you, I assume. Though don't take it for granted just because we're thrown together here—'

AxMan broke in. 'You see, I've been worrying about Cla-Rice and would, like, appreciate some advice. From a woman.'

They walked on for a few more steps before Dania spoke again. 'Your woman… Clarinda…?'

'Cla-Rice. It's the name she chose for herself. She says it's French or something—'

'OK, enough about French!' Dania was scrutinising the stony track ahead, shimmering in the mid-morning heat. 'What advice do you want then?'

AxMan ran through a few memories. 'You know how women try to play hard to get – I mean, all right, she was amazing in bed, she'd trained as a dancer and there were things she knew how to do—'

Dania interrupted. 'Fine! There's bed and there's feelings.' She sounded surprisingly irritable.

'Of course. But I'm thinking, maybe despite everything she's said, she really cares. I mean, three years don't disappear like that. She might be making an album with The Font, but she's writing a song about me.'

'The Font? What's The Font? Something on a computer?'

'Exactly. That's what I told her.'

Dania frowned. AxMan tried again. 'It was *me* she's writing about. So surely it's me she cares about. Even if she trashes me. Surely?'

Dania scuffed her shoes against stones and weeds as she walked. 'It doesn't sound—'

'You're right.' Suddenly AxMan saw the truth. 'I mean, The Font. All *he* did was play for Oxfam. Look at me, I'm here risking my life. I think she knows that, deep inside.' AxMan walked easier. It was as if his shoes had more spring. He stretched, breathing in the slight breeze, fragrant with distant salt water and seaweed.

'Has anyone told you, you think too much?'

'Yeah, Cla-Rice did all the time. You must meet her. She's a beautiful person. Inside. As well as having great tits and legs. But that's not really important—'

'Indeed. Not important at all.' Dania sped up without another word and joined Freddie in front, putting her arm in her brother's. She seemed upset about something. However, before AxMan could ask what, Micky gave a yell.

# 39 White Crab

All AxMan could make out was a waving of leaves as Micky tottered into the bushes and disappeared. Then came a more anguished cry. AxMan dived into the forest, following the voice, until he found Micky wrestling a vicious barbed wire fence, as if caught by a razor-sharp octopus.

'Coconuts!' Micky shouted. Beyond the fence stood a grove of coconut palms. The others joined AxMan and helped disentangle Micky, who wiped away the blood, insisting the cuts didn't hurt nearly as much as his other wounds. Then, taking two fallen branches, Freddie pushed the strands of wire far enough apart for them all to slide through. Once on the other side, Micky limped to the nearest palm.

'This only shows the power of the mind,' he said, shaking the trunk. 'Like in *The Unseen*, book and video. Focus on what you want. For the past evening and morning, not counting when I was asleep, I've been focusing on a six-pack of ice-cold lager and a burger and chips, and here we are! A forest full of coconuts.'

AxMan was impressed.

'Coconuts aren't beers or Burger King.' Dania squinted upwards at the swaying tree.

'A can of lager is a container of drink,' Micky said firmly. 'And so is a coconut. It also contains food, like a burger does. QED: the power of the mind.' And to prove his point, a coconut detached itself and bounced off his head.

Micky was brought back to consciousness by AxMan slapping him a number of times. The little man insisted that it was just a light bump and that the pain was useful in taking his mind off the infected dog bite, the gunshot wounds, the bruised ribs, arms and ankles, the stomach ache, the dislocated shoulder and the cuts from the barbed wire. If he'd missed some injuries, he promised to add them later.

'That's good,' Freddie said. 'We'd hate you to forget them.'

Dania smashed open the coconut with a sharp stone and shared out the water and meat inside. 'This may be all we get for some time.'

'Nah,' Micky said, chewing enthusiastically. 'I'm going to visualise that the fishing village down below us is jammed with friendly generous people, who love AxMan's music and are excellent cooks. "Trust the universe and it will repay you," as Bruno Benderbander says in *Believe and Succeed*.'

'Personally,' Freddie said, 'I've usually found it safer to visualise a village filled with thugs who will betray me for the price of an ounce of coke.'

'I find it better,' Dania said, 'just to get on with things.'

At which point, AxMan went behind a bush to get on with personal things. He was only there a minute, but when he came back the others were standing motionless in the clearing. 'Hey, guys?'

They didn't speak.

'Is it something I said?'

A voice spoke behind him. 'Stay still, motherfucker.'

He stayed still.

'Turn round slowly.'

'Sorry, mate, you want me to stay still or turn round?'

The answer came as a whack to his head. 'You fucking stealing our coconuts?'

AxMan turned.

A man stepped forward, holding a shotgun. He was short, pale and thin as a stoat, with a straggly beard, a few strands on his chin that looked like they'd have preferred to be somewhere else. He shouted, 'Boss!' Then patted them down, finding Freddie's pistol. 'Coconut thieves who are packing?' He jiggled on the spot with amusement.

'No bullets,' Freddie said, raising his hands.

'No shit.' The man held the pistol to AxMan's head. 'You definite? Not one hidden in the chamber.'

'Better check,' AxMan said quietly. 'People can make mistakes.'

'I'll check, yeah.' He pulled the trigger. Dania screamed. There was just a click. The man giggled again. 'All clear.'

'For fuck's sake.' AxMan took a step forward, but the other man raised his shotgun.

'You wanna speak to the complaints department?'

There was a sound from the jungle and a large man emerged, with a small moustache and an evil glint in his eye.

He stopped. 'Shit!'

'Pontiac!' Freddie said.

'The fucking Forresters. Who'd believe it!' Pontiac went to Freddie and hugged him warmly, then hugged Dania, who seemed less impressed.

Freddie slapped him on the back, then introduced him to AxMan and Micky. 'This is Pontiac. My lieutenant. My number two!' Freddie slapped him a little harder. 'Pontiac, your man almost iced us.'

Pontiac smacked his man across the face. 'Edsel's an idiot and a fool–'

Edsel didn't seem too pleased at this and jiggled his shotgun up and down in his hands. Pontiac apologised again, punched Edsel on the head, hugged Dania once more, shook hands with AxMan and apologised a third time. 'Edsel! Give my chief his gun back.'

Edsel tugged on his few strands of chin-hair, but didn't hand it over. 'You trust them, boss? They were stealing.'

'We didn't know–' AxMan began.

'Don't worry about it.' Pontiac thumped Edsel on the ear that was nearest him. 'Trust? This is *my* boss, my boss's sister, my boss's pop singer–'

'Rock singer,' Freddie said, before he could stop himself.

'Thank you,' AxMan said.

Freddie shrugged. Pontiac spread his arms warmly. 'But what are you all doing alive? Everyone's saying you're toasted brioches, not that I believed them for a minute.'

AxMan said they were, so far, ungrilled, but aiming to leave the island.

'Well,' Pontiac exclaimed, 'we can talk about leaving later. You're safe in this village. I run the place. Don't look startled. And leave those sodding coconuts. We got better food for you at home.'

He led them along an overgrown path to a gleaming new Cherokee SUV. Edsel drove them down a winding cliff road towards the village. He and Pontiac made an odd couple, AxMan thought: Edsel shorter and thinner, with his threadlike beard, and Pontiac, larger in all directions. Edsel jiggled with excitement as he drove, making the Cherokee veer worryingly close to the cliff edge.

'I apologise again for Edsel,' Pontiac said. 'He used to work in one of the smaller gangs near the docks. In that place, they shoot first and use their brains later.'

Edsel grinned stupidly as the offside tyres skidded along the edge.

The SUV entered the single street that made up the fishing village. AxMan was surprised there were only a few people around. Those he could see appeared to be either very old or very young or on crutches. Fishing boats lined the beach, but as they drove closer he noticed they had large holes in their hulls. The people watched them with apparent suspicion. AxMan wondered if Freddie might be right about how many locals would be happy to betray them.

Pontiac said sharply, 'Get down!'

Axman, Freddie, Micky and Dania dropped in their seats. Squinting up through the tinted windows, Axman saw they were approaching a dilapidated concrete police post above the road. Outside, sat a policeman with a machine gun. He shielded his eyes broodingly as he observed them pass.

The car sped away and up a hill.

'OK,' said Pontiac. 'You can sit up again.'

Edsel skidded into a driveway to park by a large house dug dramatically into the side of a crag.

Pontiac climbed out heavily, led them to a courtyard, yelled for his wife. A short intense woman emerged, greeted them with a smile and insisted she'd go have the maid bring breakfast.

AxMan looked around at the low building, which extended an impressively long way in all directions, painted bright blue and yellow. Pontiac caught his eye proudly.

'This was my father's.' He snapped his fingers at Edsel to shift bamboo seats into the shade for them all. He did it with ill grace.

The maid brought fried cheese, cassava bread, avocado and fresh ground coffee. Edsel joined them, still squinting towards AxMan and the others, like he could trust them no more than a scorpion in his underpants.

Pontiac handed round the plates. 'Take what you want. My father was poor fisherman. But the poor always share. Poor like the Forrester family were poor farmers.'

Freddie sucked in his lips without smiling.

'Sorry, boss.' Pontiac patted him on the shoulder. 'Just telling the truth, yes? You and me, if we wanted shoes, we didn't eat two days. This is the truth.'

Dania looked towards Freddie. 'It's a fact.'

Freddie stabbed at a slice of avocado. 'I've never pretended different.'

'This doesn't look like the house of a poor fisherman,' AxMan said.

Pontiac leant forward and winked heavily. 'White crab.'

'Ah.' Freddie nodded.

But AxMan was confused. 'White crab?'

'Here's some more real life to learn about, not like your songs.' Freddie reached for the coffee pot. 'Here in the north, there are boats that cross to Florida with certain… goods–'

'Sometimes they see customs patrols,' Pontiac interrupted. Freddie didn't look too pleased to be talked over.

'So they get rid of said goods–' Freddie continued.

'Overboard,' Pontiac explained. 'Intending to come back to collect, but sometimes, a local fisherman catches it in his nets first. A nice haul of white crab. Then the fisherman has a happy holiday selling his white crab. Perhaps enough to live off for the rest of his life. Long as the owner doesn't find out where it's gone.'

Pontiac happily tapped his hands on his pudgy thighs. Freddie sipped his coffee in silence.

'Your father caught white crab?' AxMan asked.

'It made him the big man of the village. Enough to start his own drugs operation. But did it make him happy?'

'Not happy?' Freddie said thoughtfully.

'More money than he could ever spend. But started to hate it. Always looking behind him. Hired bodyguards, but was afraid to go out.'

'I want to meet this man.'

'You're two days too late.' Pontiac inspected his fingers. 'Floating face-down in the bay. With my mother and brothers. Orders of President Sodding Lucky Strike.'

AxMan expressed his shock and commiserations. Pontiac waved them aside with a large warm hand, like death was something that would have come soon anyway.

'But you're alive,' Dania said.

'I'm a lucky bastard, aren't I? After the prison break, I walked and hitched my way back. By the time I got here, the cops had been and gone.'

AxMan scratched his beard. 'Micky, what would Tom Toggler and Bruno Benderbander make of all this? Poor fisherman becoming rich, but not happy, and then, like, getting bumped off. I'm finding it difficult to see the positive side of it all, dude.'

Micky enthusiastically ladled more food onto his plate. 'Pontiac's story might seem negative–'

'Too true.' Freddie poured himself more coffee. 'I'm looking forward to seeing how you're going to get anything life-affirming out of this one.'

'But examine things in the round,' Micky continued. 'If his father hadn't found the white crab, he'd have stayed poor. Then some other, worse, gangster might have taken over the village. Then we might have been accused of stealing coconuts by the other worse gangster who could have shot us all. Then where would we be?' He sniffed a portion of fried cheese for chemicals, just in case.

AxMan frowned. 'You must be on the mend, because you're making my head hurt again.'

Freddie raised his glass. 'For once, you and I agree.'

# 40 Head Honcho

They finished their breakfast, which was considerably tastier and less laden with chemicals than Freddie had eaten for some time. Pontiac offered him a cigar, but Freddie couldn't stand the things. Pontiac lit one for himself and wandered to the edge of the terrace. Freddie joined him. There was a partial view through trees to the ramshackle rusted houses of the fishing village below.

He turned to Pontiac. 'So you're the head honcho of all this.'

'Not now. Shit!' Pontiac dipped his head and spread his hands wide to emphasise his lowly status. 'This is yours. You my boss. Always my boss.'

Freddie shook his head. 'I believe in the old rules. This was your father's. In this village, you're the boss.'

Pontiac clapped his hands warmly. 'Thank you. If you say I'm the capo here, then I'm the capo. But you'll have anything you want.'

Freddie contemplated him with care. 'Well, for a start, you got lead for my pistol?'

Pontiac said he could think of nothing more important. He flicked his fingers urgently at Edsel, who made a face and went off, coming back with Freddie's gun and a box of cartridges. Pontiac thrust them at Freddie. 'You must feel naked without them.'

'True,' Freddie said, loading his gun. 'I'd kind of been getting used to it though.'

Pontiac shook his head. 'You don't want to get too used to that kind of thing. Next, you'll be getting used to a bullet in the head… At least we knew where we were under Bachman. You either bribed the cops or got a beating. Life was simple and we didn't know it. Lucky's been making speeches, saying he's protecting the ordinary people from rebels.'

Pontiac waved at the trees beyond the compound. 'You see rebels? He's making us afraid, so he can pick our pockets while we've got our hands over our eyes. We should have shot him years ago.'

'It's on the bucket list.' Freddie slid his gun into his belt. 'He took my folks. And aunts, uncles, cousins. Took them God knows where.'

Pontiac dragged deeply on his cigar. 'Just more of the Disappeareds. Once they've gone… sorry, boss.'

'I hate the thought of leaving them to rot.'

'But, boss, you're not safe in this godforsaken crotch of a place. The cops come round all the time. They could decide to turn the place over just for laughs. I pay them off for me, but no green would be enough to cover you and the pop singer.'

'Yeah, I know.' Freddie gazed out for a minute at the village below. The jumble of corrugated iron roofs looked deceptively peaceful in the morning sun. A cock crowed and a dog answered it. 'So we'd been thinking of hitching a lift to Sainte-Âne.'

'You and a thousand others.' Pontiac knocked his ash into the neighbouring garden below. 'The government isn't that dumb. Yesterday they came and knocked holes in half the local fishing boats and nicked the rest for Lucky Strike to run his own drugs. The men who were here when they came got taken to work for him. The ones out fishing have tried to stay there since and only dock when they think the pigs aren't here. Their families never had much and they're starving already.'

Freddie took in this news. Once more, Lucky Strike was ahead of them, or more likely the economist, Meredith Heel. Pontiac buffed him on the shoulder. 'Don't worry, boss. We've been deeper in the shit before.'

Freddie was not reassured.

* * *

AxMan spent the rest of the morning in a strange mood. Pontiac set off, saying he was going to talk to a friend of a friend of a friend and instructed them all to treat his place as home. AxMan didn't want to treat it like home. He wanted to treat his home as home. And home seemed further away than ever.

He mooched around, trying to find something to take his mind off matters. It wasn't easy. Thing was, other people's homes annoyed him. They were always arranged wrong. Rooms were not laid out the way he liked. Food and drink were never quite what he wanted. You could never relax. There wasn't even a guitar to play.

Every room he went in, he found Pontiac's wife washing linen; or the maid cutting vegetables, or Dania bickering with Micky about whether things were positive or negative. Was a headache positive, because it warned you of potential disease? Or negative, because of the disease it warned you about? Or positive because you ended up being treated? Or negative because a person could be doing something more useful instead?

How was it other people could just let time pass doing nothing? AxMan would rather eat his own foot.

Pontiac came back shortly after one, looking pleased with himself, and over lunch in the courtyard he announced he'd found a boat. 'You'll like it. Not too showy, but comfortable. We wait till dusk. If anyone stops us, we're night-fishing for snappers and stingray.'

'Whose boat?' Freddie asked. 'They can be trusted not to talk?'

'No sweat.' Pontiac patted Freddie on the arm with a thick hand. 'To-night, we'll get you safely across the straits to the Donkeys.'

'The Donkeys?' AxMan asked.

'You don't want to know,' said Dania.

'If this is where we're going, I do.'

Freddie sniffed. 'The nearest island is called Sainte-Âne. And because we're neighbours we hate each other. We speak the same language, but they speak it funny. We eat the same food, but they cook it in a weird way. Worst of all, thirty years ago their football team beat us by scoring in the last minute with a handball the referee didn't see. We've never forgiven them.

'They call us Turnips, because of the shape of our island. It's a joke that always has the Sainte-Ânians rolling in the aisles. What they forget is that their country was named by an idiot nephew of Napoleon, who meant to call it after Saint Anne, but misspelled it Sainte-Âne with a circumflex. Which means Saint Donkey. If you want to get them going, ask them how they like their hay cooked. Now, however, it seems we're going to be eating hay with them and swallowing their jokes too.'

'Doesn't sound like we've got a choice.'

'I hate running away. I hate leaving my family to be pissed over by Lucky Strike.'

'The world's upside down.' Pontiac refilled their glasses of rum. 'Lucky has turned into a politician and is fertilising his own business, while he sprays weedkiller over ours. It's not fair. It's difficult enough running a crew at the best of times. News in the village is he's going to make us all great again by building more power stations.'

AxMan nodded thoughtfully. 'I don't know so much about upside down, but aren't power stations good things. I mean, if they work properly. I keep thinking about this strange empty place we saw in the mountains.'

'Three Mountains?'

'You know it?'

'Everyone here knows it. How it goes: the Brits and Americans lend Bachman a ton of green to build a power station and highway nobody wants, but the money goes straight back to them to build it. Our people go rushing up there to work for miserable pay, but more than they can get selling fish. Then the fish and people start to die. Those who don't die are crippled. So they lend Bachman a new wedge, which they take back to pay for closing it down. Now, everything sits there doing nada in the middle of nowhere, while we still pay them interest on the loans. Nice work if you can finagle it.'

'So why would Meredith Heel, like, say "Three Mountains" to Bachman before Lucky Strike shot her?'

Pontiac raised his eyebrows. 'That's what she said?'

'While I looked through the crack in the door.'

'My guess?' Pontiac said. 'It's like us. We lend little amounts to little people and if they don't pay, we cut off their fingers. These big boys, they lend big amounts and if you don't pay up, they whack the president. Bachman was in to them for two more power stations and they heard she was about the cancel the deal.'

'We're in the wrong business, Ponty.' Freddie swirled the ice around in his rum. 'Lending money to build a power station nobody wants and getting paid to do it out of the cash you lent in the first place. That's ingenious. I've been wasting my time on small change, working with small-time thugs, when I could be building power stations – or growing peppers and pineapples and charging people through the nose for turning it into chunks and smoothies. All legal. I could be listed on the stock exchange and dining with the big movers and shakers.'

Pontiac grunted. 'Well, after tonight, you'll be the other side of the straits with the hay-eaters and you can move and shake all you want.'

# 41 An Old Friend

As sunset approached, the six of them set off in the Cherokee, taking the short drive down to the village harbour. Children played in the sea, diving and splashing off the rocks, which sparkled in the dipping sun, like a jewellery store display. Pigs snuffled around a concrete pen, while two teenagers occupied themselves gutting fish. The police post seemed closed and dark, but it was difficult to see inside.

The scene reminded AxMan nostalgically of his childhood home, playing under the sprinkler on the lawn, pretending to be an explorer fighting his way through a mountain waterfall. Was it that life really was simpler? Or perhaps it was him who'd been simpler then.

Edsel stopped the SUV next to a short wooden jetty and brought out a serious-looking rifle.

'Dangerous waters,' Edsel said with a giggle, when he caught AxMan glancing at it. 'Pirates, mobsters…' He giggled again.

'Well, keep it away from this mobster,' Freddie said, climbing out of the car. An ancient sports fishing yacht nodded lazily in the water alongside the jetty, with a scratched dark blue hull and cracked windows.

'Get moving, before the cops turn up.' Pontiac jumped onto the rotting quay.

'Are you sure that will get us to Sainte-Âne?' Micky mumbled. 'I'd feel safer on a plank of wood.'

'This could get us to Australia.' Pontiac slapped a hand on the side of the boat, which creaked worryingly. At this, a slim figure appeared from out of the galley.

'Jamie J Johnson!' AxMan exclaimed.

Jamie gave a wide smile. 'AxMan! Micky! Mr Forrester! My old mates! I'm sorry I couldn't help you with your kidnappers before. Still, all's well that ends.'

'All's well that ends *well*,' AxMan corrected.

'Isn't that what I said?'

'You know him?' Pontiac asked.

'We know him,' AxMan said. 'But what's with the boat, Jamie? When we last saw you, you had just one car, which belonged to your uncle.'

'Jamie's Limo, which you left in the jungle without the key,' said Jamie.

'It had to be done.' Freddie stepped onboard. 'All's well that ends.'

'No sweat.' Jamie's smile widened even further. 'You did what you had to do. That's business. So now I'm Jamie's Cruises.'

Yes, AxMan could see now 'Jamie's Cruises' hand-painted on the flybridge in red.

AxMan introduced Jamie to Dania and she joined them on the rear deck, followed by Edsel and Pontiac. Micky stayed on the quayside. AxMan beckoned to him. 'What are you waiting for, dude? The rust's moving faster than you are.'

'Me and boats,' Micky said.

'This is the safest boat on the planet,' Jamie declared. 'It belongs to a cousin who's gone shares with me.'

Micky shook his head. 'I just have this bad intuition about all this.'

'Get on here,' Freddie said, 'before the pigs get back for the night shift, or you'll have PTSD to add to it.'

'Tom Toggler said, listen to your intuition or–'

AxMan jumped off the boat, grabbed Micky by the arm and dragged him protesting up the gangplank. 'This man's intuition tells me if you don't get on this rust-bucket, there'll be another head floating in the water to go with those fish-heads over there.'

'OK, OK,' said Micky, half-falling onto the deck and catching the rail just in time. 'You know, man, these gangsters are a bad influence on you.'

A small crowd of villagers had been gathering at the sight of these strangers. One of them started getting out his phone, but Edsel waved his gun at him and he decided he had better places to be.

Then Jamie started Jamie's Cruises' engine and they set off. The fishing village soon lay behind them, glowing blood-red in the last of the setting sun. Edsel sat sullenly up on the flybridge, toying with his rifle. Dania leant against the rail with her eyes closed and a faint smile, like she was on holiday. AxMan watched with a mixture of relief and sadness as Benkuda grew more distant. He'd arrived with such hopes. He'd wanted to help make peace and was leaving the island with even less of it.

'If we see any coastguards,' Pontiac said suddenly, 'I do the talking. You hide below deck.'

'Coastguards?' AxMan scanned in all directions.

'And Edsel's gun?' Freddie said. 'If they see it?'

'He has a licence to shoot crocodiles and pirates.'

Edsel grinned at the thought.

'I don't see many crocodiles,' Dania said. 'Or pirates.'

After fifteen minutes, Pontiac said, 'Over there in a short time you will see the island of Sainte-Âne. Near where the sun just disappeared.'

'Romantic.' Dania shivered as an evening breeze started up and without thinking, AxMan put his arm around her shoulders. To his surprise, she didn't tell him to piss off.

'You know,' he said, gazing at the water rushing past the hull, 'I realised I haven't thought about Cla-Rice since this morning.'

Dania crossed her arms. 'Wonderful.'

'I mean–' AxMan said.

'Sometimes it's better to mean nothing.' Dania turned to face the sea, but she didn't remove AxMan's arm.

Pontiac, meanwhile, wasn't looking in the direction they were going but at the coast behind them. AxMan followed his gaze, but there was nothing to see except a darkening line of mangroves. Then Pontiac turned to Jamie and gave a brisk nod.

Jamie turned off the engine. The sound died away, leaving only the slap-slapping of waves against the side. Pontiac beckoned to Edsel, who jumped down from the flybridge.

'Is there a problem?' AxMan asked.

Pontiac gave a sheepish grin. 'I'm sorry. Money is money. You'd have done the same.'

Freddie pulled out his gun and aimed it at Pontiac's head, but the other man seemed unconcerned.

'Shit,' Dania said.

AxMan looked from one to another in confusion. 'What's he talking about? What's going on?'

Pontiac didn't move. Freddie held his gun to Pontiac's head and pulled the trigger.

# 42 Dead or Alive

The gun made a dull click. Three or four gulls circled them hopefully with a cry then were gone. Nobody spoke.

To AxMan, Freddie seemed surprisingly unsurprised. He said to Pontiac, 'The cartridges you gave us…'

'Sorry, boss. Blanks.' Pontiac gave a crooked smile and tapped a number on his iPhone. 'Luckily, I have a signal.'

'Signal?' AxMan asked.

'He's done a deal,' Freddie said heavily. 'And he must show proof.'

AxMan still didn't get it.

'Our wonderful law-and-order-loving president offered a reward for us,' Dania explained. 'Dead or alive. And Lucky Strike wants a ringside seat. Live. Or in our case dead.'

AxMan took a step back. 'They're selling us out?'

'Now you get it.'

Pontiac spread his arms. 'It's not just the money… well, it is the money, but he also threatened to send my family to the National Football Stadium.'

'The National Stadium?' Freddie picked up on the words and moved slowly towards him. 'Is that where he took my folks?'

Pontiac ran a finger over his moustache. 'I'm not supposed to say.'

Freddie moved slightly closer. 'What's it matter? You're going to kill us anyway.'

Pontiac nodded. 'Maybe.'

AxMan swallowed. He was getting pissed off after everything they'd gone through. All they needed was a few more miles across the sea. 'Let's talk about this.'

'He's right.' Freddie closed the gap a little more. 'Let's talk. Tell Edsel to put his widowmaker away. We forget this ever happened.'

'Nothing to talk about.' Pontiac drew his revolver, pushed it into

Freddie's face. 'I tie you up. Throw you in the sea for the sharks' tea. We watch them eat. The president sees on screen, like a movie. Edsel directs. He got an eye for a good composition... Mr President?' (This to the phone). 'Are you getting a picture?'

He panned the iPhone round. AxMan could see a tiny Lucky Strike watching in the presidential office at the presidential desk.

'This is your president speaking–' He leant forward seriously.

'Get on with it,' Meredith Heel could be heard off-screen.

'Forrester!' Lucky Strike spotted Freddie. 'No extra sisters around to save you this time?'

'If I'd have known,' Freddie said evenly, 'I'd have asked my parents to have more.'

'And by the way my name is Dania,' Dania broke in. 'I don't want to sound ungrateful but it's nice to have your name remembered by the man who's having you killed, even if he is a self-opinionated thug.'

Meredith leant into view on the iPhone. 'Just get the hell on with it.'

'Listen, dude,' AxMan said. 'I'm getting fed up with this–'

'No time to argue. The president has a shed-load of decrees that I've drawn up for him to sign.'

'About the Three Mountains power station?'

'What do you know about the power station?' Meredith could be seen screwing up her eyes as she strained to watch the screen at her end.

'More than you think. Any more fish died recently? Or people?'

Meredith hesitated, then shook her head. 'Sorry, not taking that bait. Ha! Pun intended. You're just trying to delay. Get on with it! We announced your deaths ages ago, now we need to get rid of you, otherwise everyone's going to be severely disappointed.'

'What about the press release?' AxMan said. 'Shot, stabbed and run over.'

'Fuck the press release. The most anyone will find is some chewed-up bones that might wash ashore in a few years. By which time, everyone will have forgotten all about it.'

Pontiac tossed the iPhone to Edsel, who tucked his rifle under his arm and walked around to look for a good angle, like on a Hollywood set.

'You don't need to kill Dania,' AxMan said warmly. 'Nobody has announced her death.'

'Thank you.' Dania smiled. 'I appreciate that.'

'All of them!' said Meredith Heel on the iPhone in Edsel's hand, as if her favourite toys were about to be snatched away from her.

Dania sniffed. 'You're probably right. If you don't kill me too, I'll come find you and cut your tits off.'

'I'm told Dania's the non-violent one of the family,' AxMan said.

'Remember to include the frightened one with his eyes closed,' added Lucky Strike, but Micky, leaning against a lifebelt, opened his eyes and insisted he wasn't frightened. Just thinking positive, something he advised the others to try.

Edsel lined up the phone. Pontiac picked up a coil of rope. Freddie stiffened. AxMan tried his hardest to think of something to do.

'Hold on.' Edsel laid the gun down and squared off his hands, looking through them like he was directing *Fast and Furious*. 'You know, against the darkness of the coastline. With those violet clouds. They call it the Magic Hour—'

Meredith said she didn't care a Venezuelan bolívar about violet clouds, as long as she could see clearly they'd been tied up and thrown overboard.

Edsel spat over the side of the boat at the lack of appreciation of his work. 'Camera ready,' he announced grumpily.

Pontiac approached Freddie first. 'Turn round.'

AxMan tried to go over his songs. They were full of fights being won. What had he said to do? Looking back, they all seemed stupidly vague about specific action. And none of them dealt with being shark-food. The Man seemed so much easier to beat with a guitar backing. 'However much he's giving you for this, Pontiac, I'll pay double. Out of the reward the British government will give to get us back. Plus the royalties from my next album.'

'No!' squeaked Meredith's image, in Edsel's hands.

'Then of course there's the money from the peace concert. Which will be all the more necessary, thanks to Lucky Strike screwing the country dry.'

Pontiac scratched his double-chin. 'You have a point—'

'No, he doesn't!'

'However,' Pontiac continued, 'according to Wikipedia your last album earned less this year than my pool cleaner. The British government thinks you're a terrorist, and anyway is about as generous as a cat's arse. And as for your scam concert—'

'Scam?' AxMan broke in.

On the iPhone, Lucky Strike laughed. 'He didn't know, your pop singer?'

'What's he mean, our scam concert?'

Freddie turned to him. 'Do we have to talk about it now?'

'I don't see another time to talk about it, man.'

'Pop singer…!' Lucky Strike could be seen slapping his desk in amusement. 'Fucking Forester was working with Bachman to soak the charities, charge them special rates for cars, Portaloos, medicines, tents, you name it. It was an earner.'

'You're lying.' AxMan was so shocked that he hadn't even challenged twice being called a pop singer. 'He's lying, isn't he? You're cynical, but you're not that cynical, are you? I mean, there are actual poor people out there, man, with actual needs. And actual charities doing actual work.'

Freddie didn't speak and Dania scrutinised the deck.

'Fucking hell.' AxMan felt like a kid who'd been told the tooth fairy kidnapped lonely orphans in her spare time.

To Freddie's credit he did redden. 'We didn't have a choice. Bachman was going to kill us.'

'And the concert was going to be real,' Dania said. 'We hoped. Some of it.'

'Got it, now!' Edsel jiggled with amusement. 'This is the rock-singer cunt who was supposed to be making the gig happen?'

'Too right.' AxMan punched the side of the flybridge. 'I'm the rock-singer cunt. I believed it. More fucking cunting fool me!'

'Stop it!' Pontiac stamped a large foot on the deck, sending clods of rust flying. 'I'm in charge of this killing.' He twisted the rope in his hands. 'Do you think I'm enjoying this? Drowning my own chief for money, even a very large amount of money. Can't the four of you let me just get on with it?'

He approached Freddie again. Blow flies circled in and out of the cockpit. Freddie seemed to be eying the distance to see he'd have any chance of jumping him without getting shot by Edsel. With a pang of nerves, AxMan realised that if he did, someone would have to jump Edsel at the same time. But he'd never fought anyone in real life. All his fighting had been in his songs.

Dania said, 'Stop. Look over there.'

'Oh, Mother of Christ!' Pontiac grew even angrier. 'You think I'm an idiot?'

Micky pointed out to sea. 'Boats.'

'Good try, guys,' Meredith said on the phone.

'I admire your desire to survive,' Lucky Strike added, nodding into shot and out again. 'Forrester first, then the singer.'

A bullet whined off the top of the bridge. AxMan flung himself to the floor.

'What the fuck are you doing, Edsel?' Pontiac shouted.

'It wasn't me,' Edsel yelled.

More rounds tore past the outriders and ricocheted off the hull. Someone was firing from out at sea. The iPhone skidded out of Edsel's hands and across the deck.

'No, no, no!' Meredith squawked from next to a bilge bucket. 'Not fucking again! I don't believe it. Just kill them.'

'I told you to think positive, didn't I?' Micky shouted from the ground by the guard rail. 'We're being rescued.'

'I don't think so.' Freddie was keeping as flat as possible. 'Pirates.'

'Pirates?' AxMan frowned. 'With eye-patches and parrots?'

'Not such fun. With machetes and motorboats.'

'Jamie, start the engine!' Pontiac shouted to the flybridge. 'Get us the fuck out of here!'

'Good idea. Jamie J is getting the fuck out of here,' Jamie said and he dived over the side.

'Come back!' Pontiac yelled.

AxMan raised his head to look over the rail. Two speedboats headed towards them. He'd read about these guys, but tried not to think about them. More interested in slave trading than buried treasure. The speedboats circled them. A grappling hook clattered.

'Give me some proper bullets!' Freddie shouted to Pontiac, but it was too late. Men were already clambering on board, slashing with machetes. They did not look at all like AxMan's childhood memories of Long John Silver.

AxMan forgot about not being violent, grabbed a nearby bilge bucket, swung it at the nearest pirate. The smell of rotten fish made the pirate pause. Across the deck, Dania had found an iron spike and was stabbing at three who'd surrounded her.

But there were too many of them. Two got behind her and pushed her, swearing loudly, over the rail and into the nearest speedboat.

AxMan forgot even more about non-violence. Shouted, 'No!' and tried to follow. A pirate blocked his way. But to his amazement Micky jumped into the boat after her.

Before AxMan could do anything, the speedboat revved its motor and swung away. He watched, aghast. He could just about make out Dania and Micky in the dwindling light, standing up in the back of the boat, punching, kicking.

'I may have been bitten by a customs dog,' Micky was shouting, 'banged about by police, kidnapped, shot, poisoned and knocked out by a coconut, but I once took a class in Aikido and I'm going to use the energy of ki to–'

Right then, two pirates attacked him with machetes. To AxMan's horror, he saw the little head slice off, bounce over the side and drop with a splash into the heaving black sea.

'No!' he yelled again.

He put one leg over the rail to dive after his friend, but Freddie grabbed his arm. AxMan fought him, struggling to swim out to the boat. 'Let go of me!'

'It's too fucking late!' Freddie shouted.

'Fuck you!' AxMan shouted back, but Freddie was right. The speedboat was already two hundred yards away.

There were still pirates on board the fishing yacht. One scythed at AxMan with a knife. AxMan stabbed furiously with the bilge bucket. The man leapt back, spattered with green water. If this was using his inner anger, AxMan thought, then maybe it wasn't so bad.

But the pirate was not so easily deterred, came again, swinging. AxMan yelled a battle-cry and promptly tripped over the rope Pontiac had dropped. The pirate stood over him, knife raised.

However, the knife never came down. Instead, shooting came from a different direction. The pirate paused and turned to his colleagues in consternation.

Squinting under the guard rail, AxMan could make out three dinghies racing toward them out of the gloom. All but one of the remaining pirates jumped down into the second speedboat and raced off.

In the confusion, AxMan fought back against the man standing over him, kicked him in the leg. He, in turn, realised he was being abandoned and – deciding survival came before business – dived into the sea with the rest. The speedboat paused only to curve round and pick up the leftover pirates before accelerating after the first in a blue cloud of carbon monoxide.

Silence fell, broken only by the waves surging and the engines of the three approaching dinghies. AxMan took a deep breath where he lay. Exhaust fumes never smelt so good.

'Guys!' Meredith screeched from the phone, which had been kicked under a seat. 'Finish the job! Please! For me!'

'Get on with drowning the bastards–' Lucky Strike added, for clarification.

Pontiac picked up the rope. But voices called out from the dinghies for them to put their hands up. Pontiac and Edsel raised their hands.

Then they took another look at the approaching dinghies and lowered them again.

'Looks like the execution goes ahead as planned.' Pontiac ran his hand over his moustache and beamed with pleasure.

The dinghies were filled with army soldiers.

# 43 You Had Me at Crocodile

As the soldiers climbed on board, AxMan's spirits sank. So near yet so far. He resigned himself angrily to his fate. Life was cruel. It offered him hope, then snatched it away again.

A young female officer looked him up and down. 'It's the rock singer!'

'No, not at all.' AxMan didn't even care that she'd got the genre right. 'I'm not AxMan. I'm not a rock singer. AxMan is dead, haven't you heard?' he added quickly.

'Don't believe him,' Lucky Strike called from under deck seat. 'He's AxMan. And that's the criminal Forrester. Execute them for treason. That's an order from your Commander in Chief.'

'You're AxMan, for certain.' The young officer held out her hand. '*Kick de Man when he's down, Fight 'em in de Tescos and de Aldis*. I'm a fan.'

'Shake her bloody hand,' Freddie said. 'She's on our side.'

AxMan peered at her. On closer inspection, none of her uniform matched. The vest, jacket and trousers were all in different shades of green.

'My name is PanAm. Lieutenant of the Pro-Democracy Rebel Army.'

AxMan hesitantly shook PanAm's hand. 'Always happy to meet a fan.' He made a wobbly devil's horns. The rebel soldiers lowered their rifles and started shaking hands all round.

'Not those two.' Freddie pointed to Pontiac and Edsel. 'You can execute them.'

Pontiac and Edsel raised their hands again. 'I am on your side too,' Pontiac said, holding his arms as high as possible. 'I was being forced to do something that was not my choice.'

'Bullshit,' said Freddie. 'You were selling us out. Throw them overboard for the squid to eat.'

PanAm looked at AxMan. 'Is this true?'

'I don't know. I mean, they *were* about to kill us, but–'

The young rebel officer went over to inspect Pontiac and Edsel, whose scraggy goatee shook with fear.

'Our leader will decide,' she announced. 'Meanwhile, I am taking ownership of this flagship of the Rebel Navy.'

'You have a rebel navy?' AxMan was impressed.

'We do now. We need to go back to Benkuda. Does anyone know how to drive this?'

A voice came from the sea. 'I do.' Jamie scrambled back over the guard rail, dripping wet. 'Jamie J Johnson, reporting for duty for the Rebel Navy. No need to be getting-the-fuck-out-of-here after all, it seems.'

A squawk came from the iPhone under the deck seat. 'You'll regret this. This is not the will of the people–'

'Excuse me,' AxMan said to PanAm. He swept the phone out with his foot, stamped on it, picked up the remains and tossed it over the side.

'I never thought I'd be so happy to oppose the will of the people.'

\* \* \*

The newly appointed Rebel Navy flagship – RN Jamie's Cruises – turned back to Benkuda, escorted by the three dinghies. It entered a narrow channel into a mangrove swamp. By now it was almost night and the boat's headlamps only lit a distance of about ten yards ahead.

AxMan stood in the prow, trying numbly to make sense of what had happened in the last hour… last day… last four days. Mangrove root cables rose on either side like a battle between giant spiders.

'Where are you taking us?' he asked PanAm standing next to him, but she didn't answer. From time to time, pairs of eyes glittered in the darkness.

'Nile crocodile,' PanAm said as they passed a pair. 'A big one. You can tell the size by the distance between his eyes. Not good to get too close.'

'Thank you for telling me that,' AxMan said. 'But you had me at crocodile.'

Once more AxMan felt very far from his tai chi studio. The swamp smell of rotten eggs grew stronger and animal cries echoed around the boat. AxMan's thoughts kept going back: Dania kidnapped… Micky dead… He couldn't stop replaying Micky's look of amazement, as the machete came towards him.

'I hope that counts as a funeral at sea,' AxMan muttered, as he leant over the rail, staring into the blackness of the forest. He wondered if he should say a prayer. He had no idea what Micky's official religion might have been. He only knew that Micky believed in thinking positive. The stout bullet-headed man must have been thinking more negative thoughts than he'd intended.

'What doesn't kill you makes you stronger,' he'd said. 'Yes, but that machete killed you,' said AxMan, under the puttering of the boat's engine. He couldn't think of any prayers that included the words "continuous realistic and positive improvement". So, he muttered a few of the catchier hymns from his childhood, in the hope they might help, although his memory of the Hebrew was weak.

AxMan ... but no, he couldn't think of himself as AxMan tonight. When he thought about the violence of his songs and the real violence he'd just seen, he shuddered. His songs were fake. He'd had no idea what he was calling for when he sang about rebellion and fighting The Man. *He* was a fake. He was just little Bennie Goldstein and always had been, and that's what he should be called.

After half an hour, the boats arrived at a makeshift wooden pier in the jungle. PanAm gave a low whistle and two armed men rose up from where they'd been keeping watch. She spoke briefly with them and waved the party ashore.

It was even hotter here, with an even stronger sulphurous smell, and when Jamie turned off the boat's headlamps the darkness was impenetrable. PanAm switched on a torch and led them along a boardwalk into a wider clearing. Oil and kerosene lamps flickered dimly under the trees. Wooden platforms stood on stilts over the swamp, connected by boardwalks. More groups of men and women in mixed semi-military clothes looked up from where they'd been cleaning weapons, stacking crates or chopping vegetables. People called to friends. People emerged from tents.

In the middle of the area, PanAm stopped by the entrance to a small camouflage tent, guarded by a large woman wearing a bandolier stuffed with bullets. She nodded them in, to find a little hunched man in olive fatigues. He had with a grey beard, rich dark skin and tired eyes. He glanced up from where he'd been peeling a yam and inspected them through thick glasses, frames held together by sellotape.

'Mr AxMan,' he said. 'I'm Jeremiah Peckerham, commander of the rebel army. Welcome.'

'Call me Bennie,' AxMan said.

'Well, Bennie. Welcome.' Then he stood up, opened his arms and gave him a large hug.

It seemed to AxMan/Bennie that it had been a long time since he'd last been welcomed. He'd been arrested, slagged off by his ex, disowned by his own country, kidnapped, beaten up, threatened, shot at, chased, lined up to be killed (twice) and watched his best friend have his head cut off – but welcomed? Even in England he was only generally welcomed by his most hardened fans. He mulled over these questions and realised that his brain was slowing down. He was, after the events of the last days, exhausted. So he plumped for standard rock etiquette and gave a double devil's horns.

'Yeah, dude,' he said. 'Delighted.'

Then collapsed.

# Track 5

# 44 Unfinished Business

AxMan woke slowly. Hot sunshine filtered through the mangrove trees. Insects and birds sang lustily in the branches. He was lying on some kind of wide wooden platform above the swamp and the young rebel officer PanAm sat next to him, taking apart a machine gun. Whoever else might have been sharing the platform during the night had gone, leaving scattered clothing.

'You're awake, Bennie,' PanAm said, not looking up from her work.

Bennie? He'd made some kind of resolution about his name, hadn't he? He sat up slowly. 'I'll tell you when I'm sure. Where are we?'

'Same place we were last night. Our main camp.' Before she could continue, three helicopters roared across, invisible above the trees. AxMan flinched and looked for somewhere to dive out of sight, but PanAm didn't shift. 'They can't see us – long as we don't leave the forest canopy.' She click-clacked her gun back together like it was Lego. 'You're a deep sleeper.'

'It depends on who's trying to kill me.' AxMan painfully pushed himself up to sitting. 'Talking of which, I'll be off now.'

'Off?'

'Before you saved us, we were on our way to Saint Donkey. If you take me to Freddie Forrester, I'm sure he'll want to leave the island too.'

PanAm stood. She was slight, looked like an undergraduate promoted beyond her years, but slung the heavy machine gun across her back, like it had no more weight than a Fender Strat. 'You'll need to speak to the Commander. But you should have something to eat.'

'I could handle that, as long as it's not pineapples or peppers. A little ganja wouldn't go amiss either. And can you direct me to the nearest loo?'

PanAm pointed AxMan towards a nearby row of wooden planks with holes over the swamp. 'And you can wash on the other side of the camp. The water may smell, but it is clean enough.' Then she disappeared.

By the time AxMan had sluiced himself with sulphurous water, she'd returned with a bowl of soup and a plate of fried plantains. Weed, she said apologetically, was not on the menu. Perhaps because AxMan was hungry, perhaps because he no longer itched, the food tasted better than he expected. Gradually, he returned to life and while he ate he looked at his surroundings.

Rebel soldiers moved around the walkways between the mangroves. They busied themselves training and repairing the skiffs moored alongside. Some were fighting, throwing each other with great shows of grunting. Others flung themselves flat on the ground, aimed their guns at targets and shouted, 'Bang!'

'Economy.' The lieutenant followed AxMan's gaze. 'We're short of bullets. The instructors look over their shoulders and tell them where they think the shots will hit.'

'It sounds a bit optimistic,' AxMan admitted.

She shrugged. 'Everything here is a bit optimistic.'

AxMan watched the soldiers in silence and PanAm asked if she'd said something wrong. 'No,' he said, scratching the back of his neck. 'You reminded me of someone. He always believed in being optimistic. But he died.'

'Did he die in an optimistic way?'

'I suppose he hoped optimistically he wasn't going to die when the pirates chopped his head off.'

'Oh dear, oh dear,' the commander said. And then, for good measure, 'Oh dear.'

* * *

When AxMan was ushered in with PanAm to see the rebel commander, he found Peckerham kneeling in the centre of his tent in full uniform – or at least in mismatching parts of uniforms. He appeared to be trying to fit together fragmentary maps of the island. Road maps, printouts from Google Earth and tourist guides with cartoons of beach umbrellas. He'd spread them over the ground like a toddler's jigsaw. 'Bennie, do you have any ideas?'

'Hey, man,' AxMan said. 'It all looks very cool.'

'You might not think it so cool once you know where you've come to.' The commander pointed to a splash of bright green in the extreme north of the island, with drawings of dangerous-looking reptiles. 'We're hiding in this swamp because the army's surrounding us. Soon the army will find where we are exactly then we'll all be about to be dead.'

AxMan exhaled. It had all seemed too good to be true. 'I've been declared about to be dead three times already, if I've been counting right. It's starting to seriously get on my tits.'

The leader tugged anxiously at his beard. He looked even smaller and frailer than he had the night before. 'It's good to have people with a fighting background. Our soldiers are always singing your rebel songs.' He searched among a pile of papers in a corner of the tent. 'I have the lyrics here somewhere. Killing and maiming. And battling The Man. It'll be excellent to have you on our side. For as long as we have one.'

AxMan hesitated. 'I don't know.'

'Of course you might not agree with our politics. I shouldn't take you for granted.'

'No, it's not that. Look, dude, I'm sorry to disappoint you, but those were just songs. I'm not a fighter, I'm a musician.'

'I know. Rebel metal. I've got some CDs too, though I think they might be bootleg—'

AxMan shook his head. 'I get angry and sing about things. It's not the same as doing them.'

'Ah.' Peckerham stood, took off his taped-up glasses, and waved them around, before putting them on again. 'That's a shame. I could have done with some tactical advice. You have to understand, I have no knowledge of military matters. I'm not really even a leader. That's why they chose me.'

AxMan had been glancing round the tent, which was full of things he wouldn't have expected – dictionaries in dozens of different languages, biographies of politicians from across the political spectrum, philosophy books – so he thought he must have misheard. 'I'm sorry? That's why they chose you?'

'In a way it's your fault.' Jeremiah's face worked with a strange unreadable emotion.

'My fault?'

'Not now. It's complicated and very sad. Anyway, we don't have a lot of call for musicians. Are you much good at cooking? Carpentry? Any medical experience?'

AxMan shook his head in confusion. 'I had a chef, an interior designer and an acupuncturist to do all that for me. Meanwhile, thank you for saving my life. If I can borrow your rebel navy flagship for a few hours, I'll continue my escape to that donkey island. I'm sure Freddie Forrester will want to come too.'

'Ah,' Peckerham said. And then, 'Oh.'

PanAm jumped in. 'The flagship has already gone to get supplies. He seemed to think he could get through army lines if he said he was running tourist cruises. Anyway, it's too dangerous to go during the day. You'll have to wait until the moon sets, which will be after midnight.'

'Well, if you're sure.'

'She's right,' Peckerham said. 'But if there's anything else you need…'

'What I do need, dude, is a phone.'

Peckerham looked surprised.

'You see, people think I'm an assassin and dead. It would be good to tell them I didn't kill that poor woman president and that I'm alive. While I still am.'

'We aren't allowed to turn phones on in the camp,' PanAm said. 'In case they give away our position.'

'You can't even get onto Twitter?' AxMan tried to get his head round a life without social media.

'There is a way,' Peckerham said. 'Sometimes we record a message and one of us tries to smuggle through enemy lines to send it.'

'Can someone do that?'

'I suppose so. It's very risky for the person who goes, but it's possible. PanAm will take you to the communications tent.'

'Well, man, if it's dangerous… I don't want to put anyone at risk.'

PanAm nodded. 'They're used to danger.'

'And in return,' Peckerham said, 'before you go tonight, you must entertain our troops. Some songs about killing and maiming might help. Even if you don't know how to do it yourself.'

# 45 First Past the Post

As AxMan followed PanAm along the boardwalks to the communications tent, they passed men and women happily occupied under the trees, bayoneting bags of hay, repairing gaps in the walkways or teaching the children in the camp to chant violent slogans.

Another army chopper flew overhead and again he ducked, instinctively. The children laughed and pointed at him. Many of the adults recognised AxMan and greeted him with smiles and devil's horns. He made devil's horns back at them. They strummed air guitars at him and he strummed air guitars in return. They called out choice lyrics from his songs. He was impressed but said nothing. Having faced real violence over the past four days, he wasn't sure he still wanted to sing about it.

F or thirty years, he'd been singing about fighting The Man. Yet after all that The Man was still in charge. These nice people were probably going to lose, as nice people did all over the world. It made him angry. People needed to love each other, not fight.

From today, he'd write only love songs.

He turned to PanAm. 'What's this about it being my fault he's the leader?'

She adjusted the rifle she was toting as they walked. 'You really want to know?'

'He said it was complicated and sad.'

'Our leader is really a professor of political linguistics. He worked for the last twenty-five years on how nouns cause all our wars and verbs will end them. I was one of his students.'

'Nouns? Verbs?'

'Yes, it involved a great deal of statistical analysis and a complex set of mathematical equations. I only understand less than half of it, but it's very clever…' She trailed off and shifted her gun to the other side. 'Take some of the things people disagree about: money, politics, art… If you say it like that, each becomes a thing. Fixed. Unchangeable. My politics says X. Yours says Y. Then we fight to see who's right. But if you make them into verbs, and ask questions like how to pay or earn, how might you do politics, how to make art, then you can discuss them. Negotiate. Change.'

AxMan asked if she had any relatives called Slapstone, because his head was beginning to hurt already.

'Anyway,' she continued regardless, 'one day the professor heard one of us playing your song *Fuck off Boss-Man*. There's this line you sang: *Screw you, the boss who wants it. Big up the boss who don't.*'

'Yeah, one of my favourites, but–'

'He said later he couldn't get it out of his mind. He went and wrote an article that proved the only people fit to be leaders are those who don't want to lead. It was published by an academic journal with a circulation of three men and a goat, but somehow President Bachman saw a copy. She took it as a personal insult and banned it. So of course everyone read it.'

PanAm took a sharp corner. 'We found all kinds of new people coming to his lectures at uni, scientists, literary undergraduates, people off the street. They began agitating for him to stand against Bachman for president. All the other candidates had been either caught embezzling party funds or having each other shot. He said no, of course. He had no political desires.

'We said that was exactly why they wanted him. He'd proved it in his own article. By not wanting to stand, he'd shown he was the very one who should. *Big up the boss who don't.* He said he hated politics. When she heard that, Bachman had him arrested for undermining the political system.'

They crossed a dilapidated bridge over the swamp. Below, AxMan was sure he spotted the shadow of a crocodile and stepped very carefully across the broken planks. 'I thought Bachman was one of the good people.'

'We'd had hopes, but she was the most dangerous kind of politician. A person who thought she was good. People who are sure they're on God's side, so anything they do must, by definition, be godly. They do bad things, for the best of reasons.

'Anyway, our professor was sentenced to ten years in jail, but a group of us students found him. We smuggled him out. We crossed the island, hiding him in sewers and cattle sheds. The police should have been able to smell us five miles off.

'Finally, we got here and started building this camp. All the time, we kept nagging him to be our leader. We said nobody wanted it less than him, and he finally agreed, but only – he insisted – if we ran everything as a democracy.'

AxMan walked on. On their way across the winding boardwalks between the platforms, they passed men, women and children of all ages, sizes and lack of abilities, but there was something almost endearing about the enthusiastic way they set about stabbing unfortunate mangrove trees with bayonets or leaping on each other with blood-chilling cries.

He didn't trust them to fight a mouse. The least of Freddie's crew could probably have finished them off in a few minutes, but AxMan felt strangely at ease here, in the dappled sunlight, among these wishful amateurs and misfits. He couldn't understand why.

'How good are these fighters?'

PanAm smiled. 'You don't expect to get out of this alive, do you?'

'It was kind of my intention.'

'We're hiding in this swamp because the army is surrounding us. It is true there are a few other pockets of rebels around the island, but they are having the same problem. We expect an attack any time now, then…'

She scuffed a trainer on the boardwalk under her feet, like an unhappy child. AxMan fell silent. PanAm asked what the matter was.

'What use am I? I can't fight, cook, build things or smuggle out memory cards…'

'A concert tonight would be good,' she said as they took a turning towards the centre of the camp. 'We don't have much entertainment.'

'Well, a concert was what I was supposed to come to the island for.'

They passed a group of older men and women making bombs by pouring petrol into olive oil bottles and chattering merrily.

'Everyone seems very happy,' AxMan said. 'Have you told them they are probably going to die?'

'Yes. We are a proper democracy. Everyone is told the truth about everything.'

'That doesn't much sound like the democracies I know. At home, the leaders try to tell people as little as possible. If a politician ever tells the truth, we assume the reality must be even worse. So they go back to telling us what we want to hear, so as to get re-elected. In any case, many of the most powerful people never have to stand for election at all. We don't elect bankers or business leaders and certainly not army commanders.'

PanAm shook her head. 'No, no, no. All the senior officers are elected in the proper way. First past the post, just like in your country.'

'First past the post?'

'And there's the post.' She pointed to a wooden pole sticking up out of the water. 'We all run and the first to reach the post wins the job. The proper way, yes?'

'It's one way. But I can't imagine Jeremiah Peckerham winning a race like that.'

'In his case, we all made sure to be slower.'

'And some of those officers over there, in charge of those squads. They look fatter than any of the people they're ordering around. How did they get first past the post?'

'They cheated.'

AxMan scratched his beard in thought. 'Maybe it is more like a normal democracy after all.'

# 46 Phone Home

They turned a corner and AxMan discovered a small tent in the shade of a mangrove tree. On the platform outside sat a young man and two women, one of whom crouched on her knees, repairing a broken tripod.

'These are our communications experts,' PanAm said.

The women introduced themselves as U-Haul, Sprite and Alberto. U-Haul was a stout, confident woman, wide as a tank. She was excited to have such a celebrity to post online. Alberto would film him. Then Sprite would upload it to a phone and trek undercover through the forest to a place that was safe to send from, hopefully avoiding the army that was encamped all around.

'You'll risk your life for me?' asked AxMan, whose greatest experience of dangerous communications involved texting his dealer.

'We all do what we can,' said Sprite, who was younger and slimmer than U-Haul but just as self-assured. 'Only women can get away with it, as we can make like we're peasant girls, foraging for jungle fruit. But sometimes they catch us even so.'

AxMan tried not to think about what might happen after the 'even so'.

Then they found a small patch of sunshine. Alberto, a skeletal young man with a dry manner, operated an elderly camcorder, while Sprite held a microphone and U-Haul directed. Alberto had said little up till now, but he and Sprite set about organising the shot with cool efficiency. U-Haul seemed happy to let them work without interference.

AxMan had starred in almost as many music videos as he'd owned Gibsons and found it confusing to work with a director who didn't throw a creative strop about the lighting, or confide every ten minutes that she was only doing this job to finance her big art-house movie about teenage domestic abuse in Glasgow.

Despite this lack of professionalism, before long Alberto nodded to U-Haul, to say he was ready.

AxMan addressed his fans. 'I'm pleased to like inform you, dudes,' he began, 'that I am neither dead… nor a murderer, yeah.' It felt odd, speaking straight to the camera without a song to sing. He felt more stage-fright recording this message than he ever had going on stage.

'I myself witnessed President Bachman being shot, didn't I? But not by me. Definitely not by me, man. She was killed by the man who's nicked her place. Lucky Strike Morton.' He gave devil's horns. 'He's The Man. Don't believe the stories he puts out. He hasn't got me yet.

'Thanks, Mum, for your support,' he went on. 'And thank you to the Orthodontists Association for putting on a memorial for me, even if I'm not quite deceased. Teeth have always been a big part of my life. Respect.' Then he sent a message of condolence to Micky Slapstone's family in Huddersfield.

'He died doing what he most loved – fighting The Man. Or, in this case, pirates.' AxMan cleared his throat. 'Perhaps the legacy he left behind was more important than any song.'

However, before he could continue, PanAm stiffened and put her finger to her lips. Alberto lowered his camera.

At first, all AxMan could hear was the yelps and trills of the birds, but then he heard the dark throb of a motor. It was different from the helicopters – lower, more surreptitious. At first a low growl, then louder. All around, he could hear rebels shouting to get into position, grabbing guns, calling urgently to each other. And the throb of the engine, growing closer.

# 47 Winners and Losers

Freddie heard the motor too. Just after he kicked Pontiac in the groin.

Earlier in the morning, he'd met Jeremiah Peckerham in his tent. He reckoned he'd give the rebel commander the respect he'd offer to any gangland leader until he had reason not to. Pontiac and Edsel were dragged in under armed guard. Edsel shook, though Pontiac stood tall and waited to hear his fate.

The little professor tugged his beard nervously. 'Mr Forrester, we must put your experience of thuggery and coercion to good use.'

'Maybe, but first you gotta whack these two,' Freddie said. 'They sold us out. You can't trust them.'

'This is not true,' said Pontiac with much waving of arms. 'You can trust us to fight for whoever pays us. I swear on my grandmother's grave, if I knew where it was. We're professionals. Give us guns and we'll fight for you too.'

'Like he said…' Edsel twitched uncontrollably. One short and needle-thin, the other large as a barrel. They looked like a TV comedy duo, but Freddie was not inclined to laugh.

'A firing squad,' he insisted. 'This gangster was my number one and he shafted me.'

The professor ran a hand over his hair. 'To be honest, Forrester, I believe you, but we're both short of bullets and of people who know how to shoot. To waste the former on removing two of the latter might be considered foolish.'

After more deliberation, he ordered that Pontiac and Edsel would stay alive but must help Freddie with training. He put them under Freddie's command so that he could keep an eye on them. Then Peckerham sent one of his sergeants along to ensure Freddie didn't kill them himself. Freddie had every intention of doing so as soon as he had a chance, but that didn't mean that he couldn't enjoy himself in the meantime.

'Fighting is not about being nice,' he'd said to his little squad, as they stood nervously around him. They looked soft and inexperienced.

He called Pontiac and Edsel out into the centre and demonstrated his point by punching Pontiac in the throat. The recruits gaped and the gangster doubled-up, choking in a very satisfying manner. 'This is about winning.' He poked Edsel in the eye. 'There are no rules.' He stamped on Pontiac's foot, pulled his head back and smacked him under the chin. 'Any way that works. Now you try,' he said to his squad.

This training lark was fun, Freddie decided, as he stood on the board-walk and watched his students launch into hitting each other in vulnerable places. If he ever got home, he'd consider running self-defence classes. It'd be a good way to launder money.

While the others trained, he grabbed Pontiac in a headlock. 'So what's with the National Football Stadium?' he whispered.

'It's where they play football, boss,' Pontiac croaked.

Freddie tightened his grip. 'On the boat, you said my folks might have been taken there.'

'I heard things.'

Freddie twisted Pontiac's ear. 'What things?'

'Don't know for sure. Lucky kind of hinted at it.'

Freddie let him go and kicked him in the balls, and it was then that they all heard something approaching. Seeing his lieutenant had hunched forwards in a perfect position for a rabbit-punch to the back of his neck, Freddie did that, before telling his students to stop freaking out.

'It's a single boat,' he said. 'If it was the army, you'd be dying in a hail of bullets by now.' Except they didn't listen. They snatched up their weapons and pointed them at the nearest mangrove trees. 'Put those fucking things down!' he bellowed. 'Before you shoot yourselves or shoot me.' Reluctantly, they obeyed and Freddie set off with them in the direction of the noise.

* * *

AxMan arrived at the rudimentary wooden pier at the same time as Freddie and found the rest of the rebel soldiers milling around excitedly, like punters at the opening of a new club. Rocking in the sunlight stood the fishing yacht – the Rebel Navy Flagship Jamie's Cruises. But someone had painted out "Jamie's Cruises" on the bridge. Now it read "Jamie's Logistics". The rebels jumped aboard, heaving crates and barrels onto the dock.

PanAm looked at the sky. Here, away from the tree cover, the boat would be seen by anyone who flew overhead. She shouted to the soldiers to move faster.

AxMan joined in and picked up a heavy crate of dried beans and green vegetables. Puffing, he carried it down the gangplank, before going back for another and surprised himself by enjoying the experience.

By this time, Jeremiah Peckerham had joined them and was thanking Jamie for his bravery in crossing enemy lines.

'No bravery,' Jamie said. 'Just bribery. Our new slogan: "Delivering Is Us".' He handed out business cards.

'Well, thank you. We can eat again,' said the leader. At which, Jamie presented him with a bill for services, the size of which seemed to take the rebel leader by surprise.

'I have a business to run,' Jamie said. 'More to the point, nobody else will do it for you.'

'Business ethics again?' AxMan struggled past with another crate. 'You sound like my dealer.'

'I'm honoured. Drug dealing is one of the purest forms of capitalism. I can only aspire to such heights.'

Reaching sadly into his jacket, Jeremiah brought out a wad of worn bank notes, counted out most of them.

'What about weapons and ammunition?' PanAm asked.

Jamie said, 'That's more difficult.'

AxMan dropped his crate. 'Jamie, don't you have another uncle or aunt who knows someone who knows someone?'

'It's true. I have a resourceful family.' Jamie took a list from PanAm and scanned it. 'You have the money to cover this? I speak on behalf of my Credit Division, Jamie's Finance.'

'You'll get the money,' PanAm said, 'when we win and take over the country on behalf of democracy.'

'Trouble is, Jamie's Finance has run a credit check. It suggests you'll lose.'

AxMan threw up his arms in frustration. 'But if you don't sell these guys what they need, dude, they'll definitely lose.'

Jamie began to untie the boat. 'This only proves the accuracy of our predictions.'

'What if we threatened to shoot you?' PanAm asked.

'If you shoot me, you certainly won't receive anything.' Jamie jumped back on board.

Freddie put his foot on the nearest rope as Jamie went to pick it up. 'You take credit cards now?'

'We take money in any way.'

'I thought so.' Freddie looked at AxMan. 'You got yours on you?'

AxMan felt in his gilet pocket. His cards were still there. 'But I don't know though,' he said. 'Buying guns for rebels. Doesn't that make me look even more like a terrorist?'

'Not much of a rebel after all then? I thought you invented rebel metal.'

'I told you, that was just songs. All that violence…'

Freddie held out his hand. 'Give.'

'I–'

Freddie waved a hand towards the rebel soldiers, watching. 'Look at this lot. They sing your songs about violence. They think you're a fucking hero. You want to let them know the truth?'

'Maybe they should know the truth.'

Freddie waited. AxMan pulled out his platinum card and handed it over. 'My lawyers might have maxed it out already. I kind of owe–'

Freddie gave the card to Jamie. 'You buy them what they need, then tonight you take us both to Sainte-Âne, as agreed.'

'Jamie's Logistics always sticks to its agreements. PIN please.' Jamie pulled out a Bluetooth card reader and slotted the card in. AxMan surprised himself by remembering his PIN. He tapped it in and waited. For a long minute nothing happened and he decided his lawyers had maxed the account after all.

Then Jamie grinned and started the boat's engine. 'All good. Jamie's Logistics is more than happy to take the money you earned from singing about violence. We're going to do good business together. Until the army kills everyone. But there can't be winners without losers. I learned that when I hacked into my online MBA course in Harvvard, Oregon, with two "v"s. That's life. Until, of course, it isn't.'

# 48 Give Chancy Peace

AxMan watched the RN Jamie's Logistics chug away, disappearing beyond the tall skein of mangrove roots.

'Man,' he said to Freddie. 'I'd feel almost guilty going tonight and not taking these guys with us.'

Freddie rubbed a trainer at a patch of slime on the boardwalk. 'Guilt is for making other people do what they don't want to do. You're not a fighter and I'm not a team player. He's back at midnight. The moon sets at one. We leave this fucking place after your inspirational gig.'

'I don't know about inspirational.' AxMan scratched his ear. 'Thing is, I need a guitar. I've never sung acapella.'

'You think they care? They want Winston Churchill not Leonard Cohen.'

'I care. I have my standards.'

AxMan turned away, walking heavily over the uneven boards. He never felt less like making music. He found himself a secluded spot away from the main camp. Here, he perched awkwardly on a tangle of tree roots, began running through his pre-gig vocal exercises. But his voice sounded wrong.

Time was strange. Before the last four days, he couldn't remember going a single day without playing – not since he'd been thirteen, learning chords in his bedroom to the backing track of dentist's drills. Now he was accompanied by jungle birds instead of root canal.

He tried singing the opening lyrics of *Stick It To The Man*. But his mind kept straying. Couldn't stop thinking about what would have happened to Dania after the pirates captured her. Everything he'd said seemed to bug her in some way, but she had a certain spice. Thinking about her, he realised he'd almost forgotten Cla-Rice, his muse. When he remembered, he felt momentarily guilty.

'But she left me,' he said out loud. And wondered if that might make the beginnings of a softer non-violent song. 'But she left me,' he crooned in various keys, but nothing seemed to follow. What rhymed with "me"? Twee... spree... flea...? He looked around the forest for inspiration – mangrove tree?

He gave up that idea and started humming through his back catalogue. However, now that he'd seen real fighting, his old songs revolted him with their cartoon aggression. Like an animated cat chasing an animated mouse.

He tried vamping on the idea of peace. "Give peace a chance" was good, but it had been done. He tried different variations in different keys: *Give a chance to peace. Peace-giving is chancy. Give chancy peace...* It had been so much simpler when all he had to do was imagine a kid with a gun and attitude. Peace wasn't so easy to sing to. It was so, well... peaceful.

He found himself remembering that strange town they'd stumbled on in the mountains. Closed power station and deserted roads. To his surprise, a new line of lyric came. He told himself this was no subject for singing about, but then another line arrived. Then another. A snatch of tune. A chorus. A bridge. Before long, he'd scraped together a song of sorts.

In that manner, the day passed. If any of the rebels came over to this side of the camp, they kept out of his way, unless to bring food or drink. That confused him. He wasn't used to respect when he was composing. It was usually the opposite.

As soon as he picked up a notepad at home, the door would bang open. Cla-Rice would urgently need his opinion on a new dress, a trending holiday destination or the latest restaurant to be seen in. More than once, he'd hid from her in desperation in their yurt, strumming his Les Paul unplugged.

* * *

Late afternoon, Freddie came to visit, bringing a teenage rebel soldier with bright red hair.

'Gunter told me about a raid he'd been on,' Freddie said.

'Oh, dude, I'm so up to here with fighting.'

'You'll want to hear this. Trust me.'

AxMan sighed. 'OK, though I don't trust you.'

Freddie told the teenager go fetch what they'd discussed. AxMan watched the kid run off, then said, 'Is it true what Pontiac told us, the charity gig was a scam?'

Freddie took a while. 'Yeah.'

'I don't believe you're saying this, man. I mean, I fell for your story. I dragged Micky here and Micky got his head chopped off for it.'

'It was more egg-sucking complicated than that.'

'How complicated can it fucking be? You didn't give a shit about peace or world hunger. You just wanted the charities and the money. And, yeah, I fell for it and here I am and now Micky's dead, all because I believed you… I shitting believed in it.'

AxMan pushed leaves into the swamp with his foot. 'It would have been such a good thing to do. Help people. Men, women, children. For real.'

'That's why it was such a great scam. You don't make scams out of bad ideas. You need good ideas to fool the mark with.' Freddie spat at the foot of a tree that had done him no harm.

'So I was the mark.'

'Don't feel bad about it. It wasn't just you.'

AxMan said nothing as Gunter came back clutching an odd-shaped canvas bag, which he opened to take out an old acoustic guitar, spotted with mould. He held it out. 'An honour.'

AxMan stared at the instrument, dumbfounded. 'Is this yours?'

The kid hesitated and repeated, 'It's an honour.'

AxMan noticed a bullet hole in the neck. 'Where did you get it?'

'Take the thing,' Freddie said. 'Stop making things difficult.'

AxMan took it. 'Thank you,' he said to the teenager, who said, 'AxMan!' sat down and made devil's horns.

AxMan tried tuning the guitar but gave up. The old battered instrument had never been concert-quality and was warped by the damp air. Still, it felt good holding an instrument again. He tried his most famous riff.

*BLAM BAM*

*BAM BAM-KRAM*

*BAM-BLAM*

Only it came out more like

*PLINK TWANG*

*TWANG TWANG-PING*

*PING-TWANG*

Nevertheless, Gunter was delighted. AxMan played the rest of *Stick It* to Gunter's greater excitement. After the kid had run off, AxMan sang Freddie the new ballad about the deserted town.

'Three Mountains A,' Freddie said.

'Right. But what do you think of the song?'

'I liked your older ones better.'

'You too?' AxMan strummed a random chord.

Freddie appeared about to go, but instead he jabbed a finger on AxMan's forehead. 'Stick with playing your biggest hits.'

'So now you're a music producer?'

'I know what people want. That's my job.'

'Fuck what people want. I want to play something different for once.'

'I might like to not bury rivals in the foundations of buildings, but we don't always get the choice.'

'Would you? Would you like to do something different?'

Freddie toyed with a low mangrove branch. 'Probably not. I like my job. It fits well with my skillset. I once did this online careers questionnaire, didn't I? And that's what it said.'

'It said to be a gangster?'

'Not exactly. It said tobacco salesman or oil company boss. But it comes to the same thing.'

# 49 Assassin

Before AxMan's farewell gig, each squad was sitting eating on their wooden platforms. He felt more nervous than he ever had at Glastonbury or Donnington Park. It felt eerily like a Young Zionist summer camp his parents had sent him on when he was twelve, to learn about nature. What he'd really learned: how to be bullied, heavy petting and how to roll a joint.

He ate with PanAm and her squad. Sprite, U-Haul and Alberto joined them, bubbling with excitement. Once they'd managed a few mouthfuls, U-Haul told how Sprite had dressed as a local fisherwoman, rowed a skiff down channels to the edge of the mangrove forest, dodging army patrols. There she could log on to the internet.

'I uploaded your video, Bennie.' Sprite wiped a sliver of plantain round her bowl. 'Stayed as long as I dared to see if there were any reactions.'

She pulled an old laptop from her shoulder bag and showed him what she'd saved. 'Twitter is mostly delighted you're alive, except for those who still insist you're an assassin. On Facebook, your government is pleased you survived and is taking away your citizenship because you've been with us – a proscribed terrorist group. If you try to go back, you'll be deported. On Instagram, your ex-girlfriend is overjoyed you're not dead and is writing a new song about your failings called "Rancid Love".'

Rancid Love! Only a short time ago, this would have struck at AxMan's heart, but now he felt numb. No feelings. That surprised him. Probably, he concluded, he was suffering from some kind of PTSD.

'PanAm, I have one more question,' he said. 'Although I hope I still have the brain power to understand the answer.'

'Go ahead. We've a little time before the concert.'

'Why do you rebels still call yourselves after brand names like so many other people in this country? What's going on? Why do it? You say you're fighting The Man, but your own names are against you.'

'Not everybody is named after a brand,' PanAm snapped. 'I know many people who are called ordinary names like Maria, Oreo and New York Times.'

'Those last two are brand names.'

'Are they?'

'Most definitely. You see, man, you've made my point there. And look at you. Named after an old airline. And you can't deny that U-Haul and Sprite are products, can you? And Pontiac and Edsel, the gangsters who betrayed us? Even the president calls himself after sticks of tobacco that give you cancer.'

PanAm agreed that these were brand names, though she'd never really thought much about it. She'd just accepted it, like he apparently accepted many things in her life – being orphaned, being beaten up by police officers and joining an armed revolt. She was a slim, self-effacing young woman with a pleasant manner and relaxed appearance, who could hardly have been less like AxMan's mental image of a freedom fighter, but she was also not one for thinking deeply about matters.

After contemplating the name thing for a minute, she conceded that there did seem to be some kind of pattern here and that possibly people wanted to honour their children so much that they christened them with the names of their favourite products. But for the children to change their names later in life would in turn mean dishonouring their parents and guardians. It was indeed something to puzzle over.

By now it was almost fully night and rebel troops gathered for AxMan's set. They brought crates to sit on and rucksacks for pillows. PanAm ordered her unit to build a stage out of ammo boxes. AxMan wondered whether he should ask if they were empty, but in the end said nothing. The rebels lit up the swamp with torches, kerosene lamps, burning branches – glowing jewels under the trees. Alberto lined up the video camera with U-Haul. PanAm found herself a place to sit, her arm round Sprite's waist.

Pontiac and Edsel volunteered to be stage managers. It warmed AxMan's heart. As Micky would have said, there's good in everyone. Only Freddie scowled at them as he settled himself at the very far end of the walkway, his back against the stump of a mangrove tree.

And so it was that, as the night grew thicker, Jeremiah Peckerham emerged from his tent into the flickering amber circle of light to introduce the headline act, indeed the only act.

AxMan stood to one side, next to a box of mortar bombs. Here he was in a real rebel camp, about to sing to real rebels who were really going to fight The Man.

The little professor wouldn't normally have been AxMan's idea of a warm-up act, but he addressed his troops like he was Wellington before Waterloo. His hair might fly in a halo and AxMan could see at least three leaves in his beard, but he waved his arms, tugged his nose and got the troops hooting and cheering.

'We may not be many–' he began. At this, the troops cheered less. 'We may not have planes and tanks–' The cheers faded entirely. 'But we can fight.' The rebels shouted full volume again. They called AxMan's name, made devil's horns and shot in the air, bringing down branches and threatening to reduce troop numbers even further.

Jeremiah beckoned to AxMan. He strode onto the wooden platform. Took a breath, plucked a figure on the warped untuneable acoustic guitar, announced his new anti-war song. The rebel soldiers fell quiet. Even Alberto took his eye from his camcorder.

'I wrote it this afternoon,' AxMan said. 'It's about how violence doesn't solve anything.'

There was a shocked silence.

A voice called out, 'But it does.'

'Violence makes more violence, dude,' he shouted back.

'Sing *Stick It To The Man*.'

'This is a peace song–'

'*Wiv a gun in your han'*,' called another.

He sang them his new Three Mountains number. Sweet and soft, it evoked the mystery of the deserted town and the futility of war. But the rebel soldiers didn't seem impressed. They wanted war, futile or not. He followed up with the other two new songs, *She Left Me* and *A Chance of Peace*. But love and peace left them cold as yesterday's boiled plantain. It was just like at Midlands Metal Hell. Did nothing ever change?

With a heavy heart, he stopped on the line *Heaven without an AK-47*, put one foot up on a crate of grenades and played seven notes.

At the opening riff of his biggest hit, the rebel soldiers roared again. What was it with his fans? Why did they have to lock him into the past? But look, he was a pro. He knew his job. He pushed the beat, marching up and down on the makeshift stage of ammo boxes, waving gun-fingers.

Two younger rebels ran onto the stage and thrust an assault rifle into his hands. Irritably, he tried to give it back, but they just waved and cheered. He looked for one of his stage managers to pass it on to, but to his annoyance both Pontiac and Edsel had deserted their posts.

So AxMan waved the gun half-heartedly. It was nothing like the props he'd used at gigs – shorter but heavier. He pointed it at various people. He posed dramatically and squeezed the trigger…

Unfortunately, it seemed no-one had thought to check if it was loaded. It fired.

The audience yelled. The soldiers at the front leapt for cover. Bullets ricocheted off the mangroves.

The jolt of the assault rifle took AxMan entirely by surprise. He lurched backwards, shooting up into the jungle canopy. Monkeys screamed.

He brought the gun down, but now he was firing at his audience. They tried to flatten themselves behind the ammo boxes. Aghast, he tried to stop shooting but the heat of the firing mechanism had swollen his fingers, jamming them inside the trigger guard. It was like the worst of nightmares, except AxMan never had nightmares about shooting rebels, only of appearing on stage with no clothes on.

He turned for help to Freddie, who promptly disappeared behind a crate of avocados. AxMan turned the other way and saw PanAm and Sprite drop behind a small shrub. He wrestled the gun, but it fought back, veering left and right, like a dog chasing rabbits, like it too renounced all songs about love or peace.

Finally, silence fell. AxMan would have sworn on the Bible that the gun fired for at least fifteen minutes, though when he watched Alberto's video later, the magazine had in fact emptied in ten seconds. The rebel army slowly reappeared from their hiding places. A spicy smell of smoky cordite filled the air.

Still shaking, AxMan turned to apologise to the leader.

But to his horror Peckerham's body lay motionless on the boardwalk.

AxMan stared in anguish, unable to speak. Freddie leapt up from behind the avocado crate, brushing avocado salad from his clothes and sprinted across. PanAm and her squad ran from the other direction.

AxMan told himself this hadn't happened. He hadn't killed the rebel leader. It wasn't possible. It was like the day he and his best friend Danny had tried smoking dental novocaine stolen from his mother's drugs cupboard and Danny had turned white and floppy and had to be rushed to A&E. But this time it truly wasn't AxMan's fault. He never wanted a real gun in the first place, had tried to give it back. He wasn't a real gun kind of person.

Then Jeremiah Peckerham opened his eyes. To AxMan's relief, he moved. Shakily, the little professor pushed himself to his feet, pale with shock. He stared at AxMan.

AxMan was about to speak, to explain, when the rebel leader hissed one word at him.

'Assassin.'

# 50 People are Trying to Kill Us

AxMan threw down the automatic rifle. Backed away, his hands raised in defence. But the professor repeated himself.

'Assassin!'

'Assassin!' the rebels shouted, aiming their guns at him.

'No,' AxMan screamed in terror.

Alberto was still filming, panning from the mob of soldiers to AxMan and back again. Freddie had drawn his pistol.

'It was the gun!' AxMan pointed to where it lay on the deck. 'My fingers—'

But then AxMan noticed Peckerham wasn't looking at him at all. 'Assassins, assassins,' the leader said, ever the linguist. 'Plural!'

On either side of the commander lay Pontiac and Edsel. From the way they had fallen, they must have been moving towards him, under cover of the music. Each clutching a revolver, face down in their own shiny dark pools of blood, like they'd accidentally fallen into puddles of paint and were too ashamed to get up. Peckerham tugged his beard. A flurry of splinters fell from it. 'The singer saved my life.'

There was a long silence, then one man cheered, followed by another. Soon the whole assembly was shouting AxMan's name and applauding. Some had been grazed from the rounds he'd fired. One had lost a finger but it was only a little finger and nobody seemed to care terribly.

They continued to whistle and call out even as they patched up their wounds: AxMan was here with them. AxMan was on their side – no matter how much he tried to explain that violence never solved anything – AxMan was as mean as ever. AxMan was taking no hostages. AxMan was their man, man!

But while everyone celebrated around them, AxMan noticed Freddie didn't join in. He was examining Pontiac and Edsel. AxMan went over, but then wavered and sat awkwardly on the boardwalk – his legs had given way.

'I shot two men,' he said. 'I mean, like not on purpose, but…'

Freddie shrugged. 'What's done is done.'

AxMan couldn't look away from the two dead men. Like they'd hypnotised him. There was even an ethereal glow that came from under Pontiac's body. Then AxMan realised what he was seeing.

'Hey, man,' he said, 'I think his phone's on.'

Freddie rolled the body over and pulled out Pontiac's mobile. 'Maybe I should have been even more negative than I thought.'

'So Lucky Strike now knows where we are.' Peckerham beckoned to PanAm.

PanAm examined the screen. 'Then why hasn't he attacked us?' She paused as the realisation hit her and AxMan at the same time. She turned to shout to the nearest troops.

But even as she spoke, there was a roar of helicopters. Searchlights flared down through the mangrove canopy. Bombs exploded in plumes of swamp water.

The rebels stopped in mid-celebration. AxMan grew angry again. He'd just saved the rebel leader's life. Was it all going to be for nothing? He snatched up his gun and pulled the trigger, then remembered it was empty.

PanAm shouted to take cover, but no-one was listening. Trees caught fire. Rebel soldiers fell. The dark shapes of government soldiers and motorboats moved towards them beyond the flames.

Jeremiah Peckerham turned pale, tugged his beard. 'It's all over,' he declared to anyone near. 'I've failed everyone. Give in! Save your lives!'

AxMan was impressed at the way PanAm and the other officers ignored their leader. They ordered those with the heaviest machine guns to aim through the tree tops at the helicopters. Others were sent to build up barricades to hold off the army as long as they could. Yet others were instructed to throw whatever essentials they could grab into the boats, skiffs and rafts.

'You go here,' PanAm called in the chaos, pushing AxMan into a round-bottomed skiff that was being filled with boxes. Freddie pulled a machine gun off one of the dead rebels and fired at the shapes AxMan could see advancing through the mangroves. PanAm ordered Freddie to join him.

'I can fight too!' AxMan shouted, with his new-found discovery.

'You have to guard the munitions!' she shouted back. She heaved more crates into the boat, narrowly missing him.

AxMan stared at the boxes in concern. 'Might they explode?'

'Yeah. If they're hit,' Freddie said. 'That's why they call them explosives.'

AxMan tried to scramble out of the boat, but Freddie caught him by the scruff of his gilet and dragged him back in. 'Terrorists take orders.'

All around them, men and women were shooting and being shot. Boats collided with each other as they abandoned the camp. With the flickering flames, the sweeping searchlights, the dazzling lights and shifting shadows, the scene was almost poetic, AxMan felt, if it hadn't been real.

PanAm sent over a young female soldier called Alia, who started the motor and the boat moved off through the flying bullets.

AxMan had forgotten he was still holding the machine gun he'd been given, till Freddie gently pushed the barrel away from him. 'You might want to try shooting towards the enemy – on purpose this time.'

AxMan stared at his gun unhappily. 'Do you know how to refill it?'

Freddie unlatched the magazine, grabbed a loaded magazine from one of the crates and clicked it into place. 'Try aiming before you fire. You'll be amazed at the difference.'

AxMan fired at things he could hardly see and thought he heard a splash of something falling into the swamp.

'Did I hit someone?' he shouted over the noise.

'You scared a few trees!' Freddie yelled back.

More explosions lit up the swamp as Alia adeptly wove in and out through the tangled roots. She looked like one of the youngest of the rebels, with plaited hair and a long studious face. She smiled shily at AxMan when she saw him watching her steering. 'Holiday jobs in the resorts. Teaching water sports. Good training, yes?'

But they seemed to be leaving most of the gunfire and explosions behind them. Before long, they were travelling alone in the dark. The flickering and noise grew fainter and fainter behind them, the fade at the end of a record.

Alia cut the engine so as not to attract attention and they drifted in the blackness. AxMan's ears still rang, but now he heard a scrabbling at his feet. He felt an oar thrust into his hand.

'Row,' Alia said. And they began rowing away from the camp as fast as they could.

# 51 AxMan's New Best Friend

AxMan took turns at the oars throughout the night. At times, they heard the shouting of army troops close by, shipped their oars and floated silently until the voices moved away. By dawn they found themselves on a wide slow-moving river. No more swamp. The vague grey shapes of tall trees rose on either side, like smoke from old funeral pyres.

'We're lost?' AxMan twisted round from where he sat in the bow of the little skiff.

Freddie had been taking his turn to row. He stopped and left the boat to drift. 'No, I know this river. Upstream, we reach a small town. Pipilla. They call it the Pineapple Capital of Benkuda. If we get there, I can see if my old contacts are still alive.'

'I suppose we can forget about the boat to the Donkey island.'

'Change of plan, you could say. Your tour just got more gigs.'

Alia examined her hands. Like AxMan's they were red and blistered. 'I wouldn't go to that town with these.' She nodded towards the crates of bullets, grenades and mortar bombs.

'Why not?' Freddie asked. 'I could find a few willing buyers.'

'They aren't yours to sell. We have a place arranged for rendezvous in case of emergency like this.' Despite being not much older than a kid, she spoke with determination. 'And if the police catch us with them, we'll be dead.'

'She's got a point,' AxMan said.

Freddie grunted. 'She hasn't a point.'

'They don't belong to us.'

Freddie slapped his leg angrily. 'Oh, spare me! You know they haven't a sodding hope of winning and even if they did, what are they going to gain? One stinking government replaced by another. Democracy? Another lot pretending they know the will of the people. And what do *I* gain? No more corrupt police to help me. No more preference from political parties for getting in the vote. For all I know, they'll go and legalise drugs then I'm truly fucked. Who's going to look after what I need, if not me?'

'The explosives belong to us rebels.' The girl reached for her pistol.

Too late. Freddie had moved faster and his machine gun was already pointing at her head. 'You think these few boxes will make any difference? A proper rebellion needs a million. But with these, I can get a crew together and find my family.'

Alia shot a nervous glance at AxMan.

He shrugged. 'I don't know, dude.'

'Yes, you do.' She thrust out her lower lip in a show of confidence, which made her look even more afraid.

AxMan scratched his beard. 'I'm trying to think what Micky would say: "A butterfly's wings can make a hurricane." It's one of his quotes from someone or other, though I can't remember who.' He picked up his machine gun. 'I know how to use this now, Freddie.'

Freddie kept his gun pointed at Alia. 'You don't get it, rock singer, do you? Who gives an egg-sucker about butterflies? I'm interested in my life and the life of my family. That's fucking all… Killing her would be like treading on a snail. I just wipe the mess off my shoe…' He looked at AxMan's gun. 'And you won't shoot me.'

'Because I haven't the balls?'

'No, because the safety catch is on.'

AxMan looked at his gun in confusion, trying to work out where the safety catch might be. 'I don't think it is.'

Freddie knocked the barrel aside, drew his pistol from the back of his belt and held it to AxMan's temple, keeping his machine gun pointing at Alia. 'You're right, I lied. Never believe a gangster. Now, give me that AK-47 of yours before a spotter plane sees us. It's your turn to row.'

\* \* \*

It was midday before they reached the town Freddie had spoken about. The sun shone hot. Slum huts rose up from the banks like a giant had thrown handfuls of corrugated iron onto the hillsides in a drunken game of knucklebones. Women washed their clothes in the brown water and children played cricket on the mudflats with balls of crumpled tinfoil.

They passed quaysides, where AxMan could see cops checking IDs.

One police squad was dragging a family into an unmarked van. AxMan shivered.

Freddie had made them stash the munitions in a creek a short distance from the town. Now he told AxMan and Alia to row as far past the cops as they could. They tied up the skiff at a broken-down concrete wharf.

'You really want to stop here?' Alia asked.

'Just follow me,' Freddie said sharply. 'You don't speak, you don't answer questions. I know these people. They'd sell us to the government for a bag of chips.'

AxMan climbed out of the boat, behind Alia. 'Do you believe him?' he asked her quietly. 'These people don't look dangerous.'

'No, he's right. There are army spies everywhere.'

'No chit-chat.' Freddie hurried them towards a steep path from the river, past piles of rubbish where pigs rooted for food. AxMan squinted at a small child as they passed, one of many scavenging with older men. The child seemed harmless, but the men had an evil look.

The child glanced up and shouted, 'AxMan!'

AxMan waved the child away. At this, three others joined in, chanting, 'AxMan! AxMan!' and started making devil's horns. 'When's the gig?'

'Not AxMan,' he hissed. 'I'm not AxMan.'

But as they went, more people emerged from flimsy huts to call Ax-Man's name and shout his lyrics.

'Shut them up,' Freddie said.

'Like, this is not helpful, dudes,' AxMan said to the growing crowd.

But to his consternation he found himself surrounded in a narrow alleyway. '*AxMan*,' they chanted. '*Wiv a gun in your han'*.'

Freddie pulled out his two guns and ordered them to get out of their way. They all laughed. '*AxMan's friend*,' they chanted, '*Wiv two guns in his han'*.'

'He means it,' AxMan shouted, but without warning a middle-aged woman grabbed him by the arm and tugged him into her tiny shack. Freddie dashed after them, pushing Alia in front of him. Others crammed their way in behind. The rest pressed their faces up against the windows. The woman pointed to three polished wooden seats.

'Sit!' she said. 'Stay!'

AxMan sat. Stayed. The interior of the shantytown hut seemed impressively clean. A cheap TV sat on a bamboo bookcase, above a shelf of books and magazines. A floral-patterned rug covered the wooden floor. Even the woman's clothes were new, a stylish blouse and skirt with block heel sandals. AxMan raised his eyebrows.

'This is a slum?' he said to Freddie, while the woman ran out of the room. 'I came here to save starving children and they've got TVs and the latest fashions.'

'Get on with it.' Freddie checked his watch. 'They may be poor, but they have their pride. To buy that blouse, she probably didn't eat for a day. Take whatever she gives you and get out before someone calls the pigs.'

The woman came back with a tray of cacao tea in glasses that didn't match, followed by a small girl and boy, who did. The twins hung back behind her legs, watching the strangers with suspicion.

The woman smiled. 'Bang-bang. Virus.'

AxMan didn't understand. Was she ill? But she shook her head and pulled out her phone. There was a wobbly picture of AxMan desperately trying to control his assault rifle as rebels dived for cover.

'Oh, shit.' AxMan held his hands out. 'Look, man, the gun. I didn't mean to–'

The woman nodded furiously and repeated, 'Virus. Hero. AxMan. *Stick it to The Man!*'

In the background, he could just make out Pontiac and Edsel aiming their pistol at Peckerham, before being cut down by a hail of bullets.

Everyone inside and outside the hut cheered. 'Hero. AxMan. *Stick it!*' they repeated.

She patted him proudly on the knee. 'You saved the professor.'

'*Saved the prof!*' came from the faces at the window.

Freddie drained his cacao tea and stood up. 'OK, you're a viral hero. Show's over. Let's get going.' He prodded Alia to her feet.

'A viral hero?' AxMan stayed sitting down.

'Yes, we'll get you a Nobel prize. Shift!'

'No,' AxMan said firmly. 'It was *me* she invited. *Me* she saw on You-Tube. Not you.'

Their host thrust a plate of sweet biscuits at them. 'AxMan. AxMan's friend,' she said firmly. 'Eat. Come. Stick it to The Man!'

Freddie pushed them away. 'Stick it to The Man in your dreams. We're off before The Man sticks it to us.' He dragged AxMan to his feet.

Just then, they heard a commotion outside. Someone was trying to push their way through the mass of onlookers.

Freddie pulled his gun. 'You called the cops?'

The woman backed away, waving her hands and screaming. 'No! Not me!'

'Don't kill her!' AxMan shouted.

Freddie tugged him towards the door. But as they reached it, there was a rippling of someone pushing the other way. PanAm appeared, a rifle over her shoulder, followed by four of her squad. She looked drawn and tired, but grinned with pleasure when she saw the three of them.

'You made it,' she said, hugging Alia. 'I wasn't sure you'd remember the place.'

'We remembered,' Alia glanced towards Freddie and AxMan.

'And the boxes?'

'They're safely stored in a creek down the river a bit,' she said, toying with her plait.

AxMan looked at Freddie. 'Freddie made sure…'

Freddie started to say something, but seemed to think better of it.

PanAm glanced at his gun. 'You can put that away now.' She sat and took a sip of tea. 'It's good to be back together, isn't it? Back in the fight.'

Freddie nodded. 'Sticking it to The Man.'

# Track 6

# 52 Shoot the Locals

Meredith found President Lucky Strike amusing himself in the presidential-sized jacuzzi with three naked female interns and a rum and soda.

'Fuck it!' he said. 'Can't a man work in peace?'

But Meredith had already pushed past the PA who was trying to stop her. 'We have to talk.'

'Take off that ridiculous suit and join us all,' Lucky said, flapping a soapy hand towards the interns. 'I can find you a man of your own. I've got a personal guard for you with great abs. You look like you need it.'

'I need you to listen.' Meredith put her briefcase down with a thump.

Lucky Strike made a face. 'Listen, listen, listen. That wasn't why I became president.'

Meredith eyeballed him hard. 'Head office is hacked off. There are clips of this AxMan pop singer all over the internet like herpes. All that devil-worshipping heavy-metal so-called music. The rebels have turned him into an online recruiting sergeant, singing about democracy and how he saw you kill Bachman.'

'Us,' Lucky Strike said. 'I didn't see you trying to throw your body in the way of the bullet.'

She sat stiffly on a plastic chair. 'You really want to make an enemy of me right now? You've lost the north and are starting to lose towns in the north east. All because of this supposed artiste. The people are sabotaging police stations, helping the raiding parties, hiding rebel soldiers from the army. Talking of which, your army is about as much use as a torn condom.'

Lucky Strike punched the tiles. 'I'm not going to get beaten by a mob of underfed farmers and slum-dwellers from the swamps.' He gestured at the nearest intern to pass the soap. 'It pisses me off that this AxMan egg-sucker got involved with it all. But look, even your own government don't give a shit about him. I had your Trade Secretary on the phone this morning.

The prick's desperate to sell us a load of fighter planes and tanks to bomb the rebs with.'

Meredith snapped her head up and Lucky Strike felt the full force of those eyes. 'You bought?'

'Of course not. Not before we haggle.'

She pulled up her sleeve, reached into the water and grabbed him by the balls. He tried to wriggle away, but she had a firm grasp. 'You'll have remembered of course that Gropius-Plante has an exclusive binding agreement with you to supply all planes and armoured vehicles, as well as police restraint, interrogation and torture equipment.'

Lucky Strike squeaked, 'I never said we didn't.' The three female interns stared from their side of the hot tub in concern.

Meredith let go and shook the suds off her fingers. 'And when it comes to killing people, be clever, Mr President. You can do what you like in the soccer stadium, where nobody's looking, but you've heard what happened in Yattacha?'

'Yattacha? Yattacha?' Lucky Strike widened his legs tentatively, checking everything was still in order. 'The crummy town up in the north where you persuaded Bachman to pay for a hydro-electric dam that drowned three villages and never worked? It used to be one of my best areas for coke.'

'They had a demonstration this morning.'

Lucky Strike frowned.

Meredith tapped the side of the tub. 'A hundred local farmers and shopkeepers decided to march on the town hall to complain about the government taking their food. They threw stones at the mayoral facade. Unfortunately, at the time the mayor was sitting in his mayoral office, right behind the mayoral facade. He hid under the mayoral table and had to be coaxed out by one of his cleaning staff, at great loss of dignity.'

'More fool him. Better he stayed there.'

'At this point he called in all the favours he was owed by his chief of police. After the smoke dispersed, twenty-three civilians were dead, including twelve school children walking past on an outing. A hundred pictures and videos uploaded to Twitter, sparking riots in other cities, including here in the capital. It doesn't play well.'

Lucky waved a hand. 'Stop worrying. It'll all be sorted.' Meredith eyeballed him again and he swiftly closed his legs. 'People,' he said, bending forward with care, so that the nearest intern could massage his back. 'Why don't they just leave governing to the professionals?'

'It's time you wiped these bastards out properly.'

'You think I don't want to? It's not been so easy. The rebel units keep moving. One moment they're hiding in the villages, next they're hiding on the farms.'

Meredith slid a small bundle of papers from her briefcase. 'Then we'll napalm the crops of anyone found supporting them. Burn down their houses. Soon enough the peasants will realise their Satanist pop star can't grow pineapples for them.' She stood. 'And we'll send in battle-hardened troops and air support. As many as you need. Bomb the hell out of the rebels. Kill every last one of them.'

'You can get the British army to do that?'

'For fuck's sake!' She wiped a few soap splashes from her tropical suit. 'Not officially. From our Gropius-Plante security subsidiary. We call them non-combatant military advisers. They're real bastards and they hate gangsters and musicians. We'll lend you the money to cover it.'

Lucky Strike drained his glass of rum and soda and held out the glass to an intern for a refill. 'Usual rates, I suppose?'

Meredith handed him the sheaf of papers. 'Just sign your name. You can manage that, yes?'

# 53 A Very Ethical Stock

The army post lay deserted. Instead of the gunfire of the night before, sunrise brought loud bird whistles from the jungle on all sides. AxMan posed with a Sterling sub-machine gun in one hand, a Browning pistol in the other and one foot on a box of live cartridges.

U-Haul held the battered camcorder in a large fist and squatted down for a dramatic angle as AxMan thought about an appropriate expression. Micky would have told him to visualise victory. Sprite asked him to stop smirking.

'I'm not smirking,' he said. 'I'm doing "victorious".'

'Either way,' she peered over her sunglasses, 'stop it.'

Dania would have told him to get angry. He tried that.

'Are you feeling OK?' Alberto was standing to one side, holding a large piece of tin to reflect a forceful light on AxMan's face.

'Perfectly.'

'It's just that you look like you ate something bad.'

AxMan gave up trying to think and let his mind go blank. If he had to stay with them, he wanted to do more for his fellow rebels than pose for Instagram. Was that all he was: a figurehead? The army had recently increased the bombing of towns and villages that supported the insurgents. Rebel raiding parties came back with fewer survivors and AxMan felt guilty for not playing his full violent part.

* * *

'Forget it,' Freddie said that evening as they sat eating grilled roots in hills near the centre of the island. 'It's not easy, this violence thing. It takes years of practice.'

'I've had years of practice, mate. Practice is all I've had. It's OK for you. You go out and do it for real.'

Freddie speared a piece of burnt plantain. 'Yes, and it's so real that one day I might not come back. How will that help anyone?'

AxMan was mulling this over when PanAm joined them outside their tent under the trees. The young officer toyed with her food, but didn't eat.

'As bad as that?' he said.

'Worse,' she said. 'The other side is fighting differently. There are proper soldiers now. With the latest weapons.'

'No, not soldiers,' Freddie said, without looking up. 'Non-combatant military advisers.'

'Non-combatant military advisers who combat,' PanAm said. 'And half our rifles jam.'

Next thing, they heard shouting. They followed down the hill to find a convoy of trucks parked on a gravel track below. Rebel soldiers rushed to carry the crates before government drones spotted them, barging against each other, bargain-hunters in a January sale.

Jamie J Johnson was the traffic policeman, directing from the bonnet of his new Porsche Panamera, as his crew of twenty men and women in dark green J Inc uniforms passed food and weapons out of the trucks.

'Ax, Fred, Pan,' Jamie called out merrily. He bounced off the bonnet, waving pieces of paper. 'Great news. We have three new sub-divisions. Jamie's Munitions, which is here supplying you with guns and ammo. There is also Jamie's Events Staging, for the president's rallies, and Jamie's Birthday Parties. That last was my girlfriend's idea. She said the brand needed something touchy-feely. She's right. It's taken off like a champagne cork. Our stock launch goes live next week.'

He handed them each a handsomely decorated certificate. 'I've allocated you all shares. My personal gift for helping me reach this capitalist milestone.'

'I don't know, mate,' AxMan said. 'Me and stock markets.'

Jamie fluttered a dismissive hand. 'These shares are very ethical. You know me.'

Freddie opened up a crate of M16s and Sten guns. 'Screw shares. What about some weapons that work?'

'All my weapons work. They are under my personal guarantee.'

'Fine.' PanAm presented him with a list written on the back of an old map. 'Here's a hundred faulty guns ready for you to replace.'

'I'd really love to,' Jamie said pleasantly. 'But I can't.'

AxMan took a step forward. 'I thought you said they had your personal guarantee.'

Jamie stepped back. 'What were your people using them for?'

'Fighting,' Freddie said, 'it might surprise you.'

'There you go. Violation of guarantee conditions.' Jamie folded up the list, with a nervous glance at the sky. 'Got to get going now.'

'Guarantee conditions?' AxMan grabbed his throat, but Jamie didn't seem at all perturbed.

'Haven't you read the terms and conditions?'

'Come on, dude,' AxMan said. 'Nobody ever reads the terms and conditions. They just tick the box. Don't you?'

'All the time.' Jamie's smile never wavered. 'But I'm not the one that's trying to claim on my guarantee. See Section 7, subsection 42: "Purchase does not include permission to kill, maim or otherwise reduce quality of life."'

'But what else would you use a sodding weapon for, if not to kill, maim or reduce the quality of life?'

'Search me.' Jamie shook himself free. 'But that's not my problem. Guns don't harm, you know. Humans do that – and animals of course,' he added thoughtfully. 'But not with guns.' He took out his mobile phone. 'I'll message my legal department. You're in violation of contract and I'm going to insist on the confiscation of all weapons I've sold you, without refund, along with the ammunition.'

PanAm pointed out most of the bullets couldn't be returned as they were now inside people.

'You're in a fix then, aren't you. Is there anything more? I have to sell a load of mortars to the government and extra AK47s to the international security advisers, who of course are only advising.'

Freddie had been turning away, but now he stopped. 'Hold on. You sell to them too?'

'Of course. Jamie's Munitions can't show preference to one side over the other.'

AxMan pointed towards the south. 'You've seen what they do. They burn villages, take their food, make men, women and children disappear.'

'A fair point, Mr AxMan.' Jamie climbed into the back of his car. 'But even if I wanted to stop, it would ruin my flotation plans. You wouldn't believe how much a military dictatorship needs. And not only weapons. My girlfriend was right. All the colonels have kids with birthdays.'

'What about your teachers at Harvvard with two "v"s? Don't they teach morality?'

'Of course.' Jamie tapped his chauffeur on the shoulder, ready to go. 'Would you prefer if we decided only to sell to the government?'

'Of course not.'

'And would the government be happy if we only sold to you?'

AxMan thought about this and said sadly, 'I don't imagine so.'

'There you are. Everyone's happy.'

# 54 I Know Where The Safety Catch Is

Before dawn the next day, AxMan watched PanAm leave on a raid to retake a town they'd recently lost. Freddie led his personal squad into a far-off clearing for training. AxMan felt a mixture of anger and relief. Anger he was kept in bubble-wrap in case the rebels' talisman might get hurt. And relief he was kept in bubble-wrap so as not to get hurt.

The latest camp hid among the sparse trees and shallow caves that dominated the plateau in the centre of Benkuda, with leaves and branches spread over tents as camouflage, and AxMan spent the morning meandering through the surrounding hills without purpose, clutching his machine gun, half-hoping he might accidentally meet an army patrol.

He returned at midday in time to watch some of PanAm's raiding party straggle back, but PanAm wasn't among them.

'Don't fret,' Freddie said. 'No-one's more of a natural survivor.'

AxMan fretted and Jeremiah Peckerham wandered around, muttering unhappily, asking everyone from the squad when they last saw her. Finally, she slipped into camp, an hour after the rest of her unit, spattered with blood. For once, AxMan thought she looked what she was – a teenager, dispirited and out of her depth. Grown up too quickly.

The leader called an urgent council meeting in his tent. They sat on whatever boxes and crates they could find and worked out how many men and women they were down.

'Fewer recruits every day,' said the little professor. 'Low on guns, half don't work, but anyway hardly any ammunition to put in them. The non-combatant military advisers are growing more combatant.'

'They were waiting for us at the edge of town,' PanAm said.

'We're losing the battle of minds.' Peckerham wiped his wire-rimmed glasses. 'People who used to give us shelter, food and money are scared to help. That's how Lucky Strike gets away with what he does. It's always how men and women like him get away with it. Face reality. Bad guys always win. Time to wave the white flag.'

'No!' shouted a younger rebel wearing stolen army fatigues.

'We must take that town back,' said another, and there followed a loud argument in which nobody could hear what anybody was saying and everybody was convinced they were right. AxMan noticed Freddie stayed silent the whole time.

\* \* \*

But after the meeting, PanAm beckoned to AxMan and Freddie to join her outside. She sat down heavily with her back to a rock, seemed to AxMan like she was losing heart.

PanAm stared at the ground for a minute, then roused herself. 'We found your place.'

'My place?' AxMan wasn't sure he had a place round here.

'This is the Three Mountains A you sang about? To the north of us.' She brought up a photo on her phone. It had been taken from the cliff above, looking down at the strange power station. 'Where your economic adviser built her useless town with the billions she lent us. Just like your song said, except…'

She flipped through more photos, all taken under cover of the trees. Three Mountains was no longer empty. It bristled with jeeps, prefab huts and a surprising number of battered shipping containers. Men and women in uniform. Others more like servants.

'The combatant non-combatants have set up a base here.' She zoomed in to a Gropius-Plante logo on a hut. 'They have burger bars, a bowling alley, a brothel – all the home comforts a mercenary would want while he was away killing people. They even have slaves to do the menial work. Political prisoners, farmers, men and women who got in the government's way. We managed to talk to a few through the fence. They call themselves the Disappeareds. You should sing about *them*.'

She showed them video clips of the Disappeareds. Some wore battered jeans or shorts, others were dressed like waiters, cooks or ancillary staff.

'Look, I'm sorry for them,' AxMan said. 'But an artist doesn't write songs to order, mate. These things can't be–' But then, 'Stop!' He squinted at the screen. 'Go back. There. Can you make that bigger?'

It was a blurred figure – little more than a blob of pixels, but something about it was unmistakable. The urgent strut. The bullet head. Even the faded Muse T-shirt. 'When did you take this?'

'This morning.'

'Nah, not possible.'

PanAm looked confused.

'That's my friend. That's him, dude. That's Micky.'

'The one who had his head cut off?'

AxMan snatched the mobile from her. 'It's him. Not a single doubt. The way he's ordering those people around.'

'He's dead,' Freddie said irritably.

'Maybe he's not.'

'We saw his head fall into the sea. People don't tend to survive that.'

'I don't understand it. But—' AxMan turned to Freddie.

'Not with me you're not,' Freddie said.

'I haven't asked anything.'

'You're about to.'

AxMan twisted his hands together. 'If it's him... I don't know. He might be an annoying twat, but I mean...We can't leave him there.'

'I knew it!' Freddie's tone suggested he could indeed leave him there.

'And it's not just Micky, dude,' AxMan said. 'It's all the Disappeareds. Free them, film them, tell everyone what's going on.'

'He's got a point,' PanAm said, though she sounded exhausted. 'It'd be more fighters for us too.'

Freddie kicked at a rock by his feet. 'You're both seriously mad. That lot with guns there aren't the rural police, who have to say the words out loud when they read. That's mercenaries. They know how to shoot straight.'

'When did you get scared of being shot at?'

Freddie shook his head. 'I've always been scared of being shot at. That's why I had a gang to get shot for me.'

'I'm talking about a friend.'

'I'm talking about not getting perforated.'

AxMan grabbed Freddie's arm. 'You obviously don't have many friends.'

Freddie shook him off.

'You know,' PanAm examined the photos again. 'Most of the guards are at the front gates. Not guarding the Disappeareds. At night with a small squad, in the back and out fast—'

AxMan slapped her on the shoulder. 'You won't regret it.'

'I haven't said yes yet.' She looked at Freddie. 'And we can't tell the leader.'

'Fuck you both,' Freddie said, but he spoke more slowly this time.

'Go for it,' AxMan said. 'Let's fight The Man for real. I'm ready. I've killed two men. I know where the safety catch is now.'

# 55 Three Mountains Revisited

AxMan had talked lightly of killing, but felt heavier in the late afternoon when they set off – separately, so as not to alert Peckerham – AxMan, Pa-nAm, Freddie and five of Freddie's most trusted young men and women, carrying an odd assortment of guns, rocket launchers and wire-cutters, looking more like scrap merchants than soldiers.

For all his bravado, AxMan couldn't forget the two lives he'd taken. It was different in a song. Whatever they'd done, even though they'd tried to kill him, Pontiac and Edsel had been real live people. Until they weren't.

PanAm said she'd film the Disappeareds on her phone, but as they joined up in the hills above the camp, U-Haul, Alberto and Sprite arrived with their ancient digicorder.

'We don't trust you to hold your phone steady,' U-Haul said with a jab of a thick finger when PanAm tried to send her back.

It was a murky sticky afternoon and in the scrubby woods only a gloomy grey light filtered down through the branches above. The squad made little noise as they worked their way out of the trees and took a steep winding path over stony ground beyond.

They could see more easily, but could more easily be seen. The barren landscape was lunar. Grey outcrops pushed up around them, frozen volcanos.

PanAm took point. Freddie the rear. AxMan trudged in front of him, looking around nervously. He was telling himself to relax when PanAm held up her hand and they all stopped.

AxMan clutched his gun, peered about for enemy soldiers. He saw a movement under a boulder and hissed at Freddie. Freddie hissed at him to shut up. Then he was sure he heard the click of a gun to his left and spun round, gun at the ready, but there was nothing but bare rock. Freddie kicked him on the ankle.

After a minute, PanAm waved the little raiding party on and they crept forwards more carefully, trying to make even less sound with their worn-out boots and trainers.

They reached the edge of the plateau. Far beneath them lay a river, almost dried up, a narrow stream that ran through a burnt-out village. The mercenaries couldn't have been long gone. Smoke still rose from the remains of the houses, which stood out like the ribs of burnt animals, blackened and foreboding. AxMan spotted what looked like a doll's dress, fluttering on the edge of the water.

They paused in thought, then silently continued on.

* * *

Dusk was falling when the unofficial raiding party reached Three Mountains A. PanAm led them to a vantage point where they'd be hidden by thick trees. Below, the empty town AxMan remembered from before now bustled with military vehicles, soldiers in grey and black uniforms, and other more tattered men and women. The Disappeareds. Guards patrolled the main gate. Lights were coming on. Security cameras scanned.

AxMan borrowed a set of army field glasses, captured in one of the raids. He searched across the slaves that he could see, but they were already being rounded up for the night, herded into the rusty shipping containers lined up at the back of the power station.

He nudged PanAm and pointed. She frowned at first, not understanding, and he mouthed 'containers' and counted them on his fingers – ten. Micky, he was sure, would be locked into one of them.

The smell of the evening's cooking rose from the base, meaty and rich. Up above, Alberto handed out ration tins of bread and cold plantain, with an apologetic shrug. AxMan took his and sat on the ground, thinking about the celebrity restaurants he used to eat at in London and New York.

By midnight nobody was out of their huts except the armed guards. As PanAm had predicted, most of the guards stayed by the front gate, though units of three made regular circuits of the perimeter fence. She timed the latest patrol and gave a hand signal – twenty-five minutes to get in and out.

The raiding party split into three and AxMan followed her with Freddie and U-Haul down a path just visible in the lights from the garrison. U-Haul seemed in her element, sashaying like she was going to the pub with friends.

Closer. AxMan could hear music. Third-rate dance-floor numbers. Did these soldiers have no sense of style? It was bad enough getting defeated by mercenaries without doing it to Baccara. PanAm took them to where the forest had grown close to the fence.

'The fourth wire up is live,' she whispered. 'You can touch any of the others, but touch that one and you don't come back.'

Then she squirmed forwards across the damp earth, cut the bottom three strands and beckoned.

U-Haul wriggled past her with difficulty, but got through. Freddie was next. AxMan followed, desperately trying to hold in his belly, which had grown a little smaller over the past few weeks, but not so much as he'd have liked. He felt the back of his mismatching jacket snag briefly on a wire. Held his breath. Nothing happened. He slid on past. On the other side, they waited for PanAm, then ran to the nearest container.

PanAm pulled a bolt cutter from her shoulder pack, but before she could cut the padlock, a door opened twenty yards away. Flashing light spilled out, along with loud disco music. AxMan froze in the light – caught clutching his gun like a plastic Action Man. Freddie grabbed him by the back of the gilet and yanked him into the shadows.

'Fuck!' AxMan said. 'That hurt.' Freddie motioned to him to shut up.

There was scattered applause from inside the disco prefab. Then abruptly everything stopped. Lights turned off. Men and women came out talking stridently and dispersed.

PanAm cut the padlock to the container. AxMan put his head inside. The interior was dark, with shapes huddled into shabby bedding, like piles of discarded washing.

'Micky?' he whispered. Then again, a little louder.

Three faces peered from under torn sheets. A man with a moustache said, 'Who the hell?'

Another pointed and whispered, 'Hey, is AxMan!'

'*Wiv a gun*,' said the third, smiling. The rest of the men were waking and asking what was going on.

'Shit,' Freddie said. 'Is he there?'

'I don't think so.'

AxMan swiftly closed the door, but it opened again and a gaggle of excited men and women appeared, making devil's horns.

'Get back in, dudes,' AxMan whispered, pointing his semi-automatic at them for emphasis.

U-Haul had already opened the next shipping container. AxMan

looked inside and quietly called Micky's name. However, he only woke
another half dozen fans. These came out to join the first, muttering to each
other in delight.

They hissed AxMan's lyrics. AxMan told them to shut up before they
got everyone killed. So they shushed each other earnestly, and excitedly
watched the rebels progress to the next container.

At the third container, PanAm was still trying to cut a difficult bolt.
Freddie suggested she might like to hurry before AxMan's fan club attracted a different audience.

The hasp finally snapped. As with the previous two, the smell inside
was pungent with unwashed bodies and other private odours, but this time
AxMan stopped and inhaled like a wine connoisseur. There was an aroma
he recognised from a hundred tour buses.

'Micky!' he said excitedly, sniffing to locate the source of the smell. He
stepped on something soft.

'Fuck off,' it said.

'Micky,' AxMan whispered joyfully. 'Wake up. It's me, AxMan.'

'And I'm trying to sleep.'

AxMan bent down. 'You're alive! We've come to find you.'

'Great, I'm alive. Now piss off and leave me alone.'

AxMan was confused. By now, the other men in the container were sitting up, shouting, complaining and pointing. PanAm and U-Haul pleaded
with them to stay quiet.

'We've come to save you,' AxMan said, reaching down. It was definitely
Micky Slapstone, head attached and all.

'I don't want to be saved.'

'Of course you want to be fucking saved,' Freddie said. 'You're a slave,
living in a container!'

He grabbed him, tried to haul him to his feet. But Micky fought him
off, flailing his arms, catching him on his nose. Instinctively, Freddie
smacked him around the face.

'Hey, that's Micky you're slapping,' AxMan said.

'Then tell him to move!'

AxMan pulled on Micky's other arm. 'Come on! Whatever doesn't kill
you makes you stronger.'

'I gave that up.' Micky tried to crawl back into his bedding.

'This isn't you talking, Micky. They've brainwashed you.'

'No, I've started thinking negative. It's the best decision I ever made.'
Micky pushed them away, but AxMan ignored him. He picked up his
friend and pulled him to the door.

'Help!' Micky shouted.

'Shut up,' AxMan snapped. 'You'll get us killed.'

'We all die in the end. Help! Over here!'

Shouting came from the guard house.

'Help!' Micky repeated. 'I'm being kidnapped by people who think positive.'

Freddie punched him on the side of the head and knocked him out. 'That's a positive,' he said.

AxMan took an arm and, with U-Haul and PanAm taking other limbs, they lugged Micky's unconscious body out of the container. The assembled AxMan fans applauded, made AxMan gun-shapes with their fingers.

An alarm horn sounded. Bright lights came on all over the base. Taking fright, the Disappeareds disappeared back into their containers. The rest of the rescue party ran over and they sprinted as fast as they could down an alley between the huts. Then stopped. They'd only reached a dead end. AxMan could hear guards yelling on all sides.

# 56 Screw Invisible

PanAm kicked at the nearest door and broke it open.

'Who's in here?' she shouted, pointing her gun through the doorway. Nobody answered.

AxMan dragged Micky inside, the other rebels piling in after them. PanAm slammed the door shut. The place was pitch dark and smelt of sweat and cigarettes. Then someone hit a switch and the room filled with dazzlingly bright flashing lights.

They were in the disco. Fag-ends and half-empty beer glasses lay all around. The prefab walls still glistened with damp. Alberto was standing with his hand on the switch.

'Turn those fucking lights off!' Freddie hissed. Alberto turned them off and the interior plunged into darkness again.

'Do you think they saw us?' AxMan said.

'Even if not, they'll search every hut.' PanAm's voice came from near the door. 'And then we're dead.'

'So we run for the wire,' U-Haul said.

'Only if you have an invisibility hat,' Freddie said.

'We fight.'

'We'd be fighting the whole garrison,' PanAm said.

'Invisibility hat?' AxMan said thoughtfully.

'It was a joke.'

'Has anyone got a torch? Or a cigarette lighter or something?'

A phone flashlight came on. It was U-Haul's, her face illuminated dramatically from below. The rest of the raiding party stood pale in the dim glow, guns ready, but AxMan moved down to the far end of the dance floor to the DJ's console. He stooped inside. Pulled out a tangle of wires. He'd had an idea and it scared him shitless. 'That phone?' he asked. 'Does it have any of my songs on it?'

Freddie rolled his eyes. 'For once, can you forget your fan base?'

'I mean it.'

U-Haul tapped the screen. 'There's a couple of the old ones.'

AxMan took it and plugged it into the disco.

'You know what you are doing, I hope,' Freddie said.

'Trust me.' AxMan reached up and flipped the main switch. 'Invisibility is so last century.'

The coloured lights burst on again and AxMan's music blasted through the speakers. It was like jumping from a high cliff into the sea. Once you stepped off, there was nothing to do but hope. He picked up a mic and stepped off.

'*Open the doors!*' he boomed. The others looked at him as if he was mad. '*I mean it!*' He reached under the DJ's mix desk and turned the volume up full. '*Screw invisible. Let's be visible!*'

The others braced themselves against the walls of the disco, fingers on the triggers of their semi-automatics. PanAm pulled open the door.

'*It's time!*' AxMan announced over the music. '*It's time to fight The Man!*'

There was a collective roar from the streets nearby. He hoped the Disappeared would take the challenge. But he might be wrong.

'*Fight The Man!*' he thundered. '*Fight for your freedom!*'

Voices shouted back at him from outside. '*Fight The Man! Fight for your freedom!*'

'*This is AxMan!*' AxMan roared into the mic, like he was on stage. Though it might be the last stage he'd play on. '*The cause needs you.*'

'*The cause needs you,*' the voices echoed.

The passageway in front of the disco began to fill with Disappeareds. Men and women shouted and waved. AxMan dropped the mic and ran over to where Freddie was still standing guard over Micky's unconscious body.

'Let's go,' AxMan said and pulled Micky up in a fireman's lift.

The rebels moved out, guns ready. He could hear the mercenaries shouting over the music, but more and more slave workers were arriving from all over the site, chanting lyrics, blocking the alleys.

'This way,' PanAm shouted.

AxMan looked back. The mercenaries were fighting through the crowd. The crowd danced to the music. Beyond, he could see a woman in among the guards, waving her arms, ordering them to fight the crowd. A woman with a blonde bob. Meredith Heel. She saw him and smacked a soldier next to her, pointing. The mercenary raised his rifle and shot. AxMan ducked. Other mercenaries fired into the crowd.

Some of the Disappeareds screamed and ran. But others turned and faced the enemy. They brandished chairs, mops and metal buckets from their work. AxMan had never felt prouder. His fans! His Axers! But also never more scared for them. He wanted to fire back, but he couldn't drop Micky.

Freddie shouted at him to egg-sucking move. Meredith glared at AxMan from the distance. Shouted at the guards either side of her and they aimed at him through the crowd of workers. He turned and ran as best he could, ducking and weaving, carrying Micky's body.

The rebels sprinted for the gaps they'd cut in the electric fence. Most of the raiding party reached the fence before him and scrambled through. AxMan bundled Micky under, dragged him through, trying desperately to keep him from touching the live wire.

U-Haul was already through and laying down covering fire. As AxMan reached the other side, he looked back and saw PanAm leading a group of the Disappeareds towards the wire. She stopped to fire back at the mercenaries. Yelled at the Disappeareds to keep their heads down as they went through.

Freddie shouted to AxMan to carry Micky to the top of the path, but AxMan ignored him and fired repeatedly at the guards on the other side.

'Did you see?' he shouted. 'They were shooting the Disappeareds.' He fired again, more furious than he remembered ever feeling before.

Freddie slapped his face. 'Stop. You're the one who sings about peace.'

'Did you see?' AxMan shouted over the gunfire.

'It's not personal.'

AxMan found he was crying. Freddie slapped him again and told him to take Micky up the hill.

At the top, they reloaded their guns. PanAm counted numbers. All the rebels were back – three rebels and five Disappeareds wounded, but none seriously. They waited in the darkness for the mercenaries to counterattack.

AxMan was sure Meredith would want to come after him, but down below the mercenaries were busy beating the remaining slaves, forcing them back into their containers. Other guards milled around the perimeter, repairing the wire. Nobody came up the path after the rebels. They seemed to accept the loss of a few workers. Like they'd written them off in annual accounts. Natural wastage.

The raiding party set off back to camp. Soon the strange mercenary base was left far behind. The rebels and their rescued slaves walked silently. PanAm led the way without speaking, a slim figure, hardly visible in the night. The other rebel soldiers took turns to carry Micky and help the injured.

When they emerged from the forest onto the stretch of barren rock, the moon had set and the sky filled with more stars than AxMan had ever seen before, glittering in silver clusters, uncountable sequins. Better than any rock concert light show. He filled with awe at their beauty. How small was humanity in the face of this enormous dazzling universe.

He thought back over the fighting and was shocked at how easily the mercenaries shot at the slaves who worked for them. And how fiercely he'd wanted to kill mercenaries in return. It scared him. This wasn't him, or was it the real him? Micky would say a positive man takes action. Except Micky seemed to have changed his mind.

# 57 Mr Negativity

By the time they got back to camp, people were already up and working in the pre-dawn darkness. Shapes moved between the tents. AxMan slumped down by a fire outside the cave they'd been sleeping in. He couldn't look at the others, so he stared away, towards the slowly lightening horizon. It reminded him of his childhood, climbing out of his bed on winter mornings to find his father and mother already drilling teeth in their adjoining rooms.

It started to piss with rain.

One of the youngest rebels had started a pot of coffee and now wordlessly poured the watery black coffee into metal mugs. PanAm and Freddie brought Micky's unconscious body over to the fire and tried to place him carefully on the stony ground, but they were so exhausted that he slipped and his head knocked against a rock.

'Shit!' he said, coming to. 'That hurt.'

'Micky,' AxMan said. 'You're safe.'

'I'm here.'

AxMan hugged him then leant back. 'What the hell? I saw you beheaded. I saw your head fall into the water. I mean–' He peered at Micky's neck, like it might have stitches all round, like some kind of Frankenstein's monster, but it looked unscathed. 'It's a miracle.'

'So why aren't you dead then?' Freddie asked, nursing his mug. 'And I don't believe in miracles.'

'Aikido saved my life,' Micky said.

'Aikido?' AxMan said.

'The martial art. You remember I studied it once.'

'Yes. You gave up after one lesson. The sensei corrected you and you said he didn't appreciate your individuality.'

Micky shrugged. 'Yeah, exactly: I studied it *once*. Anyway, before I

walked out he taught us this neat defensive move. When I saw that pirate
was about to swing his machete at me, I tried it.'

'And it worked!'

'No. I tripped on a boat-hook and fell face-first into a load of bilge
water. Stank like hell. Anyway, as I fell, the machete went over my head
and cut the head off the pirate behind me. So, there it is – Aikido saved
my life.'

'That's what we saw? It was his head that went into the sea and we
thought it was yours?'

'It was an illusion,' Micky said. 'Everything's an illusion. That assault
rifle Freddie's holding is an illusion: just atoms. Atoms are mostly empty
space, so that gun is mostly empty space. The smell of this coffee… also
just atoms that make you think of breakfast.'

AxMan sat back and laughed. 'There's no doubt now you must be the
real Micky. I'm getting a headache already.'

'And my sister?' Freddie broke in. 'What happened to her?'

Micky gave a sigh. 'The pirates took her below deck.'

AxMan didn't want to know more, but Micky went on. 'Mind you,
from what I heard she landed few punches while she was down there. Then
next day, while we docked at some town, she managed to grab hold of a
machete and cut at least two of them on their arms before they got it off
her again.'

'That's my pacifist sister.'

'Then they sold us. I heard she got taken to the presidential palace.'

Freddie leant forwards. 'The palace? Not the national stadium?'

'Who knows?' Micky closed his eyes and rubbed the top of his bullet
head. 'People went to both. Fuck, you hit me hard.'

'Here you are, dude,' AxMan said, 'Even when I thought you were
dead, I never let myself stop thinking positively. Isn't that what you always
said? And to prove it, we saved you. Just like Tim Tiggler and all those
others taught.'

'No,' Micky said calmly. 'When I saw that pirate's headless body fall
into the sea, I realised the books are crap. The lectures are crap. The world
is total crap. They've been lying to us all this time, Ax – it was pure luck
that the other guy got chopped and not me.'

He clicked his neck left and right. 'Nothing makes a difference. You
think you can make a difference? You still die in the end. Everyone will
eventually die. Even the earth will die, burned up by the sun and everyone
will be forgotten. You, me, the self-help gurus, Gandhi, Jesus, Shakespeare,
Geldof, Bono, *Tom Toggler* … Everyone.

'We get born in pain, we get all the pain the universe throws at us then we die and turn back into manure. Into shit. Literally. Negative thinking is the only way that makes sense.'

AxMan stared at him blankly. 'But all this time I thought you were dead, I've been surviving by remembering your sayings. "Feel the fear." "Stand on the shoulders of giants." All of that. Like you always said: Continuous Realistic and Positive Improvement.'

'Much good it did any of us. From what I heard in Three Mountains, you rebels are losing. In a few days or weeks, they'll catch up with you and we'll all be tortured, imprisoned or shot. At least back there, I had food and a bed. And if I focused hard on all the bad things that were likely to happen, I was rarely disappointed.'

He lay back and closed his eyes. 'Now I need to rest. Even remembering I once had positive thoughts makes me tired. It's not worth the effort.'

AxMan didn't know how to reply to this. He looked at Freddie, who gave a shrug. 'He said it, not me.'

# 58 We Have Clowns

'No more guns. No more food. No more business,' Jamie said on the phone from the capital.

'Is it my credit cards?' said AxMan in despair. He'd already burned through three and was afraid of maxing out the last.

He was calling on Sprite's mobile from high in the hills, far from the camp. The early morning rain had cleared and the afternoon was hot with the smell of damp earth and the caw of a palm crow, calling, '*You failed, you failed, you failed…*'

Jamie cut in. 'It's not the credit cards, guys.' Jamie's Munitions had recently set up in a new warehouse in Benkuda City and AxMan could hear a buzz of activity behind him. Jamie's worker bees. 'It's that Meredith Heel that's advising Lucky Strike. She doesn't like us dealing with you.'

Freddie had been standing in the shade of an olive tree, listening in. He bent towards the phone. 'Tell her to go impregnate herself.'

Jamie's voice faded and came back. 'I'm not sure self-inseminating advice would be the best move. She says I'm a traitor to capitalism. This is of course totally unfair. Capitalism is selling to everyone you can. I told her, but she didn't understand. Even when I quoted the Harvvard online business school: "A true entrepreneur never takes sides." She said I could insert the Harvvard business school somewhere anatomically impossible. I don't think she's as well-educated as she makes out.'

AxMan grimaced. There was a long and ominous pause at the other end. 'It's worse, isn't it?'

'Yes,' Jamie replied mournfully. 'They're forcing me to accept a takeover by Gropius-Plante.'

'Shit, man. This is not good. Shit, shit, shit–'

'I'm sorry,' Jamie was saying. 'It's at a knock-down price too.'

'Then sell us food and bullets while you still can. We've hardly enough for a week at this rate. And the mercenaries are getting closer.'

'No can do.' Jamie dropped his voice. He told them to hold on and AxMan heard footsteps and a door being closed. Jamie came back. 'She's got accountants crawling over everything that comes in and goes out, like slugs in the rain. If she suspects anything wrong, she said something about chopping small pieces off me and feeding them to a nearby poultry farm.

'You should see her in full flow. She's amazing. She could run the UN single-handed, given a chance, and invade China in her spare time. I've never known anyone like her. She even scares Lucky. But it didn't sound like good capitalist free market trading to me. Or good food hygiene.'

'Listen,' AxMan said. 'We understand. You don't have any choice.'

'Of course he has a choice,' Freddie snapped. 'Everybody has a choice.'

AxMan wasn't sure, but Jamie agreed. He had a choice and he chose not to have body parts turned into chicken feed.

Freddie took a deep breath. 'What if we came down there and fed you to the animals ourselves?'

'Well,' Jamie said, 'given that you are far away and she's here in Benkuda City, I think that's a risk I'll have to take.' But then his voice brightened up. 'Of course if you have any other requirements that don't involve feeding or killing people – a trip to the seaside in a limousine? Or Jamie's Events for that special birthday? We have clowns, balloons, Game of Thrones-themed inflatable ball pools–'

\* \* \*

Freddie had been in danger of liking these guys and it worried him. The call with Jamie sealed it. The time had come.

After they'd rescued the Disappeareds, Freddie had made a point of quietly speaking to as many as he could, as they queued under the trees, to be given breakfast, blankets and a place to shelter. He asked each in turn if they'd seen Dania, his parents or cousins.

They all had their stories: there were families whose businesses Lucky Strike had stolen, criminals who insisted on their innocence, political opponents and women from abroad who'd been offered jobs in hairdressing salons and found themselves in a Gropius-Plante military brothel.

There was always a rumour mill, but when it came to news of his family the gossip was contradictory. Some said they'd been shot in the football stadium. Some said they'd seen them working as slaves in the presidential palace.

Freddie shuddered. How many had already been Disappeared for good? Was he already too late? But however much he wheedled, cajoled or threatened, it seemed nobody had been to the national stadium or the palace to see for themselves.

He found Micky sitting by the cave the rebels were using to store their weapons and ammunition, happily telling some of the younger Disappeareds that the pro-democracy rebel army had less chance of surviving the next few weeks than a grasshopper in winter. And anyway, democracy was no better than anything else. People lied and pretended to care about what they didn't really care about. And the politicians weren't much better.

Micky had slept for an hour, then bounced up and insisted to anyone within earshot that he was ready to work. For the rest of the morning, he'd been buzzing around the camp, helping distribute food, suggesting which of the rescued slaves might make good fighters.

For all the little guitar tech's new-found negativity, Freddie had never seen Micky so happy. All the time he'd been preaching positive thinking, he'd always looked gloomy and upset. Now that he believed life was beyond redemption, he went around grinning like a maniac, handing out weak coffee and thin plantain stew, with a merry laugh and a quip about how they were all doomed. It was baffling.

Freddie tapped him on the shoulder. 'You said you thought Dania had been sent to the presidential palace.'

'That's what some of the guys said. That or the football stadium.'

'Which?'

'People said different things.'

'I haven't found a single one who says they saw her at either place.'

'They're lying.'

Freddie gave a cold smile. 'Or you were?'

'Come with me, mate.'

Micky trotted deliberately away from the others, until they were out of earshot. He explained that some of the Disappeareds had only survived by making up accusations about their neighbours. If you were at the stadium or palace and came out alive, people assumed you'd shopped someone. Bad for the CV.

Freddie exhaled. Were there no depths that humans wouldn't sink to? 'I'll give them their CV. I'll push their CV so far down their throat that they'll need an MRI scan to read it.'

'I don't think violence will do it. I can take you to someone I know was in the stadium for sure, but you have to promise not to ruin his oesophagus. Trust me.'

Freddie agreed reluctantly that violence might be better held in reserve and Micky led him across to the camp's makeshift hospital tents. He beckoned to a small thin man in his fifties, who was waiting to be examined.

'You were in the fucking soccer stadium?' Freddie said. 'You lied to me?'

Micky coughed. 'Freddie's OK. Tell me what you told me before.'

'I just need to know about my family,' Freddie said more gently. Gentle didn't come naturally to him. It took an effort. 'The Forrester family. My relations. I'm worried sick about them.'

The man, who introduced himself as Sergio from Gran Canaria, nodded and shook his head. He had short grey hair and a hooked nose that curved round to meet his chin, like a caricature of the moon and thought about things for a long time, until Freddie decided he must have some kind of learning difficulty.

'Not in the stadium,' he said finally.

Freddie restrained himself, as he'd promised, but not easily. 'Micky here says you're lying.'

'I was in stadium.' Sergio's head agitated faster by the second. 'Forrester family only early…' He ran out of words.

'You saw them? You saw my parents? My cousins?'

Sergio reached deep into his vocabulary. 'I was in but Forrester family finished.'

'How "finished"? Whacked? Killed? What do you mean "finished"?'

Trying to get his meaning across, Sergio joined battle with the English language, which was clearly not his best friend. But he was a fighter. He punched his verbs, pummelled his nouns, fragments of adjectives and adverbs flew through the air like shrapnel.

Finally, as the dust settled, it became clear that many in the stadium didn't survive. He'd been tortured. Many were shot. The pitch had been drenched with the blood of adults and children. But, it seemed, the Forrester family were taken away.

'Taken away?' Freddie asked.

'Presidential palace,' Sergio said, with an effort.

It seemed, after more verbal pugilism, that a large work camp had indeed been established in the palace grounds, by the aviary. At the mention of the aviary, Freddie shivered, remembering what Bachman had promised would take place there. And knew that Lucky Strike would remember it too.

# 59 A Special Dawn Raid

Freddie went back to his tent to consider matters, but before he could consider for more than a few minutes, Peckerham called a democratic council of war in the centre of the camp for all the senior rebels. Freddie ducked out, saying he'd caught a fever.

While they talked, he nicked a map from Peckerham's tent. He took his squad training and laid out twigs and branches on the ground to represent streets and buildings for them to train with. He told them to be prepared for a covert exercise. Then he sat on the hard earth with his back against a rock and made a list of essentials they would need to steal as they left.

That night, Freddie got up two hours before dawn and wished he hadn't. Rain had swept in again overnight and now poured miserably off the branches above, leaked through holes in the tents and flooded over the ground. At least, he said to himself, it would mask any sound.

It was only a hundred yards to the cave where the guns and ammo got stashed. As far as he could tell, peering out through a tent opening, no-one was awake. AxMan and Micky lay behind him, muttering in their sleep, no doubt dreaming of recording studios and groupies.

Freddie felt guilty about leaving them to their certain deaths then shook off the feeling. Guilt was a useless emotion. Guilt about AxMan, guilt about Micky, guilt about the rebels, who'd trusted him. What a waste of energy!

He shoved his sympathies to one side, like he might a persistent hooker in the street. Whatever he felt about these rebels wasn't important. Empathy was death. The moment you gave in to your emotions, you were vulnerable. It was one thing using other people's emotions to manipulate them, quite another to get emotional himself. It was like a dealer who shot up with his own gear.

Freddie had hung onto Sprite's phone and she hadn't yet asked for it back. Now he turned on the torch app, shading it with his hand, and went around rousing his squad with a sharp knock on the shoulder. He told his two lieutenants it was a special exercise. They were going to test the guards at the munitions cave. He turned off the torch app. Waited for the men and women to assemble silently in the darkness, pulled his rucksack onto his back, picked up his gun. It was time to be his own man again.

There was no visible movement from the munitions store as they approached it, the cave's opening a smudge in the darkness. Freddie crouched and motioned to the nearest men: they were to deal with the guard on the right of the entrance while he prepared to lead the others towards the left. Held his finger to his lips. Radio silence.

Someone said 'Pssst!' behind him and he turned, ready to get angry. But it wasn't one of his squad. It was AxMan, clutching his gun.

'Get the hell away,' Freddie whispered.

'You're planning a raid? I want in.'

'This is not for you.'

'Me too, mate,' said Micky. 'We might as well be all doomed together.'

'For fuck's sake, not you too.'

'We're fighting The Man with you,' AxMan said. 'Democracy forever!'

'Shut up!' Freddie clamped a hand over AxMan's mouth. 'I'm not fighting The Man. I don't give a flying fuck about The Man. Or your egg-sucking democracy.'

Just then, he heard a clicking. A dozen safety catches snapped off. A dozen torches found him with his hand still clamped over AxMan's mouth and the rest of his squad hunched down, guns at the ready. A dozen rifles pointed at them.

Freddie tried to squint into the sudden light. A child again, caught scrumping for apples.

'PanAm?' he said. But he already knew the answer.

\* \* \*

'When did you know?' Freddie asked Peckerham.

Morning had come, but AxMan had hardly noticed. Rain still hammered on the canvas roof, running down the insides of the torn canvas walls of the leader's tent, onto mugs of cold coffee, onto sodden books and onto the floor, with its soaking carpet of ill-assorted maps.

In Peckerham's hand, a drenched tourist map, covered in cartoon pictures of golfers, surfers and women in tiny fuck-me bikinis. And on it, Freddie's scribbled plans for breaking into the palace grounds. PanAm and her squad held AxMan, Freddie and Micky at knifepoint.

'PanAm came to me yesterday evening with her suspicions.' Peckerham sat on a folding canvas chair, a picture of despondency. Rivulets dribbled down his goatee, but he seemed oblivious to them. 'I didn't believe her until I saw you just now though – I thought I knew human nature.'

'Don't do yourself down,' Freddie said. 'I've cheated better men than you.'

'Execute the three of them,' said U-Haul.

AxMan jerked in alarm. 'Hey, I didn't have anything to do with it. I just wanted to go on another raid.'

She tightened her grip on her knife. 'You were with them. We caught you.'

'No, no, no, man. I'm on your side. Tell them, Micky.'

Micky rubbed his ear. 'Whatever. Democracy. Dictatorship. We all die in the end.'

'That's not helpful. PanAm, you believe me.'

She stared at the ground. Peckerham raised his eyes far enough to examine the pencil sketch that Freddie had made of the palace surroundings. 'You were attempting to steal our guns and ammunition, you don't deny that?'

Freddie nodded. 'I was doing you a favour. Most of you are more likely to shoot each other in the butt than hit the enemy.'

AxMan glared at him. 'Because they're just villagers and farmers?'

'No, because these klutzes are being used, like amateurs are always used. For fuck's sake, you're just a singer. And he's, well, a...' He looked at Micky.

'PA, guitar tech, dogsbody and gofer.' Micky beamed. 'And proud of it.'

'None of you know how to do violence properly.'

'Sod off.' AxMan stabbed Freddie in the chest with his finger. 'This is all your fault. I didn't ask you to make up that concert scam. I didn't ask to spend the last I don't know how many days wandering around this benighted banana republic trying to stay alive eating plantains. And, go on, call me a pop singer. Yes, I'm a singer. If I could sing those mercenaries to death, I would.'

Peckerham gazed blankly at them, like someone had taken out his batteries.

AxMan felt sorry for him, but the rest of the rebel council grew angrier, pointed their knives at the three of them and said it was time to make examples of traitors. They poked, punched and prodded them, and finally pushed them out into the pouring rain to be stabbed to death without waste of bullets.

AxMan noticed PanAm held a machete which had been left by the pirates. It trembled slightly in her hand, but whether from anger or sadness, he couldn't tell.

'Kill me, if you want!' Freddie shouted over the hubbub. 'But not these two. They didn't have a fucking idea what was going on, as usual.'

'Hey!' AxMan said.

'We can't trust any of them!' U-Haul yelled back. 'We were OK in the swamp till they came.'

'Thank you,' AxMan said to Freddie. 'You tried.'

Once again, the three of them found themselves preparing to be executed.

'That's life.' Rain bounced off Micky's shaved head. 'The band plays. Then it ends.'

'You know,' AxMan said. 'I preferred you when you were naively positive. When you were managing gigs…' He stopped.

'That's–' Freddie began.

'Shut up!' AxMan blurted. Freddie looked surprised and AxMan realised that people rarely, if ever, dared tell him to shut up.

'According to the voting rules–' Peckerham said.

AxMan wiped rain from his eyes. 'You shut up too!'

Peckerham tugged at his sodden goatee and rocked to and fro on his feet.

'Just decapitate the three of them and get it over with,' U-Haul said.

'For God's sake!' AxMan turned to Micky. 'What were you saying before?'

'Before what?'

'Before them lot decided to blunt their knives on us.'

Micky frowned. 'Something like, "That's life. The band plays…"'

'That's it. Now shut up and let me think!'

AxMan stared at the ground. The rain poured in torrents over them all, soaking them in their mixed-up uniforms.

PanAm was about to speak… but AxMan held up a hand.

U-Haul was going to break in… but AxMan stopped her.

Then he turned and hugged Freddie and Micky, much to their surprise.

'I came for a concert?' he said.

'Yeah,' Freddie said. 'To help save the starving children. But like I said, it was all a con.'

'Forget that con. This is a much better con.' AxMan faced Peckerham. 'I've got an idea.'

'Too late for ideas,' PanAm said, readying her machete.

'Trust me, dude, this is the best idea I've ever had. And anyway if it doesn't work you won't have to cut off my head. We'll be dead anyway.'

# Track 7

# 60 Counterinsurgency

Day by day, Meredith Heel received news of how the rebels were losing. They were losing to her non-combatant military advisers, who were winning all the combats that they weren't officially having. It was about time, because she was afraid Martin Plante was losing faith in her.

The history of Gropius-Plante was littered with the skeletons of staff members who'd fallen out of favour. A corporate Death Valley. Meredith couldn't imagine how she'd keep up her lifestyle if she was handed the Gropius-Plante blackspot. Not least the payments her ex screwed out of her in court; she'd be lucky to get a job in the City cleaning sewers.

She was deeply relieved when her spy, embedded in the rebel camp, messaged her that many insurgents were starting to desert. That Forrester guy was turning out to be useful to her after all. All good intel in exchange for made up info about his family. Shame she'd have to have him shot in the end.

It didn't surprise her the rebellion was falling apart. A singer, a gangster and a middle-aged lecturer in political science should never be able to break a powerful dictator backed by a western military security contractor (even if officially it wasn't).

For all this, something continued to niggle at her, but she couldn't put her finger on it. She sat at her desk, poring over intelligence reports, trying to work out what the remaining pro-democracy fighters might be up to. Even as she strolled down to the burger bar near the presidential palace, she went over the puzzle in her mind, like a challenging crossword.

She sat at her usual table in the sunshine, ordered a diet Lucky Strike Burger and observed the city, busy at its work. Builders were adding gold plate to the palace gates, in the name of Making Lucky Strike's Ego Great Again.

An outdoor concert was being set up in the square, as indeed were many across the city in anticipation of some national holiday Meredith hadn't kept track of. Massive speakers were being winched into place by willing hands. It was good to see the locals so keen to break sweat for less than the minimum wage.

It was the threat of poverty that did it. Lucky Strike had been a good choice to lead the country into the future – from poverty with a few rich people to more poverty with a few richer people. So some children starved? They'd have starved anyway.

Even over the last few days, the city had swollen with poor farmers and itinerants looking for jobs – manual labour that Meredith's new factories would need: poor people tried harder if they were hungry. But still she felt something was up.

After lunch, she shared her apprehensions with Lucky Strike in the presidential office. The president told her to stop bitching.

'Bullets always win. When we torture the rebs we've captured, they tell us they've only got supplies for three more days,' he said from the floor, sweating through his daily crunches, his large feet squeezed under the desk. 'You should exercise more. It removes poisons from the liver and helps you see straight.'

Meredith believed in exercise about as much as she believed in the tooth fairy. She'd grown up in the backwoods of Essex – an insecure nerd in a school system which venerated footballers with their brains in their feet and WAGS with their brains in their mammaries.

If crunches and Zumba steps were so good for the mind, the jocks and camp-followers would have been solving Fermat's last theorem, instead of pulling on expensive replica kit and short skirts and humping each other against a wall behind the pub.

'Anyway,' Lucky Strike continued, 'didn't your informer tell you they had some clever idea for a last desperate push in the north? You had me send all those troops to defend Three Mountains. Maybe I should bring them back and deduct the cost from what I pay your boss.'

'I don't know. I just have this feeling.'

He lay back, breathing heavily. 'Or maybe Bachman was right. I should cancel the repayments. Those power stations were a con from the start.'

Meredith placed a stiletto heel on his throat. 'Remember what happened to Isobel Bachman. It wouldn't take more than a phone call.'

'Piss off,' croaked Lucky Strike. 'You need me as much as I need you.'

She pressed a little harder, just so he got the message, then lifted off.

Lucky Strike rubbed his Adam's apple. 'You're a hard one,' he said. Then rolled onto his stomach and started a set of tricep push-ups.

'We have to have more support,' he said between gulps of breath. 'I want to exterminate this lot completely before I host next month's annual meeting of the Association of Caribbean Islands. When's the British army coming?'

Meredith was getting pissed off. These islanders were like midges at summer camp. They never stopped. Lucky Strike was as bad as the rebels – constantly demanding the impossible. She smiled though and said, 'The prime minister sends his best wishes and suggests that it would be counterproductive to actively involve his troops openly. Military contractors are better.'

'Screw contractors. Get onto the Pentagon. The Brits never do anything without them anyway.'

Meredith clicked open her briefcase. He was like a child, always wanting the next toy. Well, she could supply toys. 'Most clients get best satisfaction from upgrading their package. We have some great new counterinsurgency deals. I recommend the Davos Extra. Or better still, Global Supreme: with full air-support and forest destruction.'

She placed the latest Gropius-Plante counterterrorism brochure on the floor in front of Lucky Strike's nose. A cockroach was crawling towards his ear, unseen by him. She contemplated leaving it to go its merry way into the inviting pink cave, but the urge to kill it was too strong. She ground down on it with her heel and was rewarded by a soft crunch.

\* \* \*

Meredith should have felt happy. Plante would be pleased at the new sale. Capitalism worked. But she returned to her office with a migraine, which she self-medicated with a double espresso and paracetamol. Then she opened her emails. Her inbox was packed. Different arms of Gropius-Plante were coming back to her with advanced plans for making more profit out of the island.

There was a hydro-electric scheme in the north-east that would mean flooding a couple of villages that nobody cared about, except a few liberal snowflakes. The extra electricity was not needed any more than it had been at Three Mountains, but another part of the corporation wanted it so they could build a factory with cheap labour to make plastic toys to sell in the US and Europe.

Capitalism worked.

Talking of which, the takeover of Jamie Incorporated was going more smoothly than she'd expected. Men from Jamie's Munitions had even arrived that afternoon – without being asked – to check they hadn't inadvertently supplied the palace guards with faulty weapons. They'd brought crates of new guns at no extra charge so that they could take away the old to be serviced.

Capitalism worked.

She closed down her computer with a satisfied sigh, as the sun set in a dazzle of red over the aviary. Returning home to her large empty house in the ambassadors' quarter, she cracked open a beer and sat alone for an hour in her empty TV room, in front of a TV talent show. The audience sparkled with smiling faces, while the celebrity judges only showed how a small amount of talent could yield a lifestyle that was the envy of the world.

She toasted the day. The money scorecard looked good. The rebels were about to be defeated and that gangster and singer would finally be killed. A spider scuttled across the floor in front of her and this time she let it go. Look how considerate she could be, preserving an innocent creature that had done her no harm. It was a shame she had no-one to share her compassion with, but she'd change that soon. There was always Tinder.

Capitalism worked.

# 61 The Final Gig

That night, even nature took a break. The stars disappeared behind cloud. The ocean lay as flat as stainless steel. People noted how few cars there seemed to be on the streets of Benkuda City, but made nothing of it. Tourists had fled the turnip-shaped island weeks ago.

Most of the inhabitants went to sleep, but some didn't. These included the ex-farmers and unemployed workers who'd silently entered the capital over the last few days and joined up with the slum dwellers who were already there. They stayed awake, though they remained quiet.

At the edge of town, Army Private Paul Lever was furiously counting the minutes until the end of his duty. It was an hour before dawn and the countryside around the small military vehicle depot extended black and silent in all directions. He was a city boy and not used to such places. He clutched his rifle and yearned for a soft breast to lean on and a glass of something with rum in it.

Then he tensed. He thought he'd heard a footstep crunch nearby. He raised his rifle.

Nothing.

He called, 'Who the fuck's there?'

No-one. Then a quiet cough.

Before he could fire, a blast of noise cut through the night, bore down on him like a freight train.

'*Screw them turncoats. Screw them pigs! This is for real!*' AxMan's voice came at him from all sides. Lever could see nothing to shoot at, but shot anyway.

The music pounded, heavy riffs filled the air. '*Stick it to The Man. Stick it to The Man!*' They all but drowned out the sound of his own gunfire. Something moved in the darkness. It looked – he didn't believe it – like a loud-speaker stack. Trundling towards him like Godzilla.

Flashes in front of him. Was he being fired at?

*'Save yourself. Save yo' people. Save the world!'*

Private Paul Lever needed no more invitation. He ran. But in front, he saw more dark shapes advancing.

He tripped and fell, scraping hands and knees on the gravel. Lay, half-dazed, the four/four chords thumping over his head. Three shadows came out of the night. One tall, one medium and one short, they held guns and bolt cutters.

The shadows shouted over the music. 'Careful, I thought I saw someone, dude.'

'Can't see nothing. Sod it! I was looking forward to someone to kill.'

'You know, Freddie, you're a glass-half-empty man, isn't that what you used to say, Micky?'

'A half-empty glass is just on its way to being completely empty.'

'Well, yeah, thank you, that helps enormously.'

The three shadows passed Lever without seeing him and moved on towards the depot.

* * *

Private Lever wasn't the only one. At precisely the same time, the new stacks of speakers that Jamie's Events had placed throughout Benkuda City came to life. Full volume: AxMan's biggest anthems.

Buildings shook. Car alarms shrieked. Jamie had pulled favours from every audio hire shop on the island. Then, when they ran out, every media company in the Caribbean. He'd mounted speakers on low-loaders and arranged for cousins to drive them.

Those who were asleep woke to the signal. Those who were already awake snatched up placards. The predawn streets of the capital began to fill with marchers.

Sprite posted videos of the Disappeareds online – to the sound track of AxMan's Three Mountains song. The population woke up to the sight of their fellow islanders working as slaves.

As he prepared to break into the army transport depot, AxMan could feel his adrenalin rising. This was the biggest gig he'd ever played. He never thought it would all end this way. But better to die on stage than in a Zimmer frame. Mind you, right now a Zimmer frame felt quite tempting.

Freddie had done his best by sending false intelligence to Meredith

Heel. As a result, he'd got five battalions sent north. But too many troops and mercenaries had stayed in the city, stationed between them and the palace. And he'd reckoned, it would take the rest of the army no more than two hours to get back.

It was a shame. AxMan had grown to like being alive, but he was only too aware his plan was insane. Having said that, given who called themselves sane in this world, maybe insanity was right.

A suicide mission, yes. But at least it was a mission. He dedicated his last minutes to his fans and cut the bolt on the transport depot door.

\* \* \*

Meredith Heel leapt from her bed at the noise, incensed that a neighbour should be partying at five in the morning. Her phone rang. Her senior security commander informed her the capital was being besieged by AxMan's backlist.

'Get the power turned off,' Meredith snapped. Really, did she have to think of everything?

This however turned out to be a bad idea. The commander phoned again.

'The speaker stacks are running off generators, ma'am. The songs haven't stopped but the street lights have. In the dark, the reb' forces seem larger. The army's getting spooked about being outnumbered.'

'Who's sodding counting?' Meredith said.

'Take a look at the internet, ma'am.'

She looked on her phone. To her horror, dissidents had been uploading videos of themselves marching, laughing and singing. Sleep-deprived journalists had dragged themselves from their hotel bedrooms and were sending real-time reports. All the social media channels buzzed with what they were already calling "AxMan's Bloodless Revolution".

'Screw bloodless,' Meredith said to her commander, her mobile jammed under her ear as she struggled to tug on jogging bottoms in the dark. 'How long to get the army back from Three Mountains?'

'They're already loading the planes. Ninety minutes tops. The helicopters sooner.'

'However fast, I want them faster. Meanwhile, I want every man you've got in the streets, protecting ordinary innocent people from these extremists and their communist songs. And turn the fucking lights on again.'

She ran downstairs to where a Gropius-Plante Land Rover waited to speed her to the nearest military post, outside the Benkuda national bank. There, she found army recruits behind sandbags and mercenaries unloading the crates of replacement weapons delivered by Jamie's Munitions the previous day. They ran to defend the dictatorship with the passion that only money could buy.

Crowds marched towards them, chanting AxMan's lyrics. She ordered the nearest officer to have his men fire. However, no shots rang out. The new machine guns jammed, the replaced rifles failed, the restocked grenades bounced without exploding.

Their state-of-the-art rocket launcher produced the most attractive roman candle, flaming green and pink, before subsiding to something that sounded rather like a soft fart.

As the crowd surged closer, the army recruits threw down their guns. Against Meredith's advice, Lucky Strike had reduced pay for the lower ranks to buy a new presidential helicopter. Now they tore off their army jackets and melted into the crowd.

'Come back and fight, you anarchistic unpatriotic bastards,' Meredith shouted. 'Fight for the people's president.'

'*Stick it to The Man!*' came back at her. '*Wiv a gun in your han'.*'

The lieutenant in charge of the post carried a pistol. Ordering him to give it to her, Meredith fired at the deserters. One young soldier fell and lay still.

'That's what you get for supporting socialists!' Meredith yelled.

Just then a low-loader appeared at the far end of the street, pulled by a farm tractor. Speakers hammered out AxMan's deafening music and on the platform danced an unmistakable figure, making devil's horns to the crowd.

Meredith checked her gun was still loaded. This was her chance.

Leaving the military advisers crouched behind their sandbags, she quietly slipped out of the emplacement and melted into the mob. She danced, so as not to stand out, though she had always danced awkwardly, like a scarecrow, her father had said. She even began chanting, '*Stick it to The Man! Wiv a gun in your hand.*' though the words stuck in her craw.

The people around her chanted back excitedly. '*Wiv a gun... Wiv a gun...*'

AxMan's low-loader moved slowly towards her. She could make him out through the smoke, beard, gilet and jeans unmistakable, striding back and forth as if he was headlining at Glastonbury. He flung up an arm,

Travolta-style. 'Revolution, now!' Got an excited shout from the crowd in return.

Meredith had to admire him. He was a star. She took up position by a no-entry sign. Patiently, she waited for her moment. It was as if all time, all her life, had come down to this.

Finally, the tractor moved within range. At last, she had the fucking pop singer where she wanted him. Meredith raised her gun and steadied it against the side of the signpost.

It was like when she was eight and pushed her best friend into the swimming pool at school sports day, seconds before the starting pistol. After all, was it fair that Shona always won, just because she was a better swimmer? It was the only race that Meredith ever won, and she was proud of it.

As she aimed, AxMan surprised her by turning and looking straight at her. Their eyes met through the smoke and gloom. Almost romantic. It was as if he knew. Had always known. Realised that this was his fate. To die on stage.

But he didn't stop performing. Like a machine that had only one programme. She noticed a single bead of sweat glinting above his left eyebrow. Slowly, it began to trickle down. She had him at her mercy. She clenched her teeth and squeezed the trigger.

The singer stopped in shock. For a second, he looked just like eight-year-old Shona in the swimming pool.

Meredith fired twice more. Blood spurted through AxMan's leather gilet. He toppled off the low-loader onto the ground.

Meredith ran forwards and pumped three more caps into his head and body. She gave a giggle and put her hand to her mouth, in awe of what she'd done. He lay still. Eyes open. No more songs. No more seven-note riffs. No more Bennie Goldstein.

A horrified gasp from those on either side. The oxygen sucked out of the street. A backing-away in anguish. The rock singer was dead.

# 62 Don't Worry. It'll Get Worse

Meredith had never personally shot a man before tonight and now she'd killed two. The deserter and now AxMan. It felt good. Like the old days, shooting pigeons with an airgun in her parents' back garden.

She had to admit there was something moving about this tragic ending. Like the end of an opera she'd once been forced to watch. Violins swelling to a crescendo. AxMan, the hero dying in a flurry of arpeggios. He'd known. Resigned to his death. And finally it was over. Maybe she'd missed out on something by hating the arts.

'There's your hero!' she yelled over the music, which was still playing. 'That's what happens. You can't win. This is too big for you.'

She stamped her foot in victory.

As she spoke, another flatbed truck appeared at the far end of the street. Also playing AxMan music. Clinging to the speaker stack, to her horror, a familiar figure, beard, black gilet and jeans. He sang and waved and made devil's horns, punched the air. A second AxMan.

At that moment, the electricity came on again – all the street lights, traffic lights, shop-fronts. Neon signs flashed. Alarms wailed.

Meredith looked down at the man she'd killed. On closer inspection, he didn't seem much like AxMan at all – thicker hair and a narrower head.

The crowd saw the new AxMan approaching and roared. AxMan lived. They turned to advance on Meredith, who aimed her gun at them in panic.

'Woke snowflakes!' she shouted. 'You don't understand. We represent the true will of the people!'

But they laughed and chanted, '*Woke snowflakes!*'

She shot a few men, women and children as she backed into the nearest side street, then sprinted for her life.

* * *

Meanwhile, the real AxMan headed towards the centre of Benkuda City in the turret of one of the armoured cars they'd stolen from the depot. Freddie navigated and Jeremiah Peckerham drove. Micky sat in the back and told them how it was all going to go wrong.

AxMan was having a blast. Around him marched, danced and chanted rebel soldiers and citizens, impervious to the danger. As they progressed, more cars and trucks joined them, bristling with banners and loudspeakers. Fireworks went off overhead in a rattle of detonations. The familiar chords young Bennie Goldstein had composed in his bedroom decades before thumped across the city.

Jamie J Johnson could be seen in the turret of a second armoured car following them, tapping on his laptop, co-ordinating a dozen flatbeds as they criss-crossed the city, each with its AxMan clone. AxMan watched them when they got close. They attracted bigger crowds than he ever had. He didn't know how to take this. They were doing a better job of being him than him.

In response, he climbed up onto the top of the turret. Yelled out his song lyrics, like he was double-tracking. There was a loud cheer from all round and Jamie J gave him a thumbs-up. AxMan signed him a devil's horns in return.

Still the crowds came. The population of the island named after a turnip turned out not to be the passive root vegetables everyone made them out to be.

'Look at them!' AxMan waved his phone and shouted down to Micky.

Micky grinned happily up at him. 'Don't worry, it'll get worse.'

The first serious gunfire came from the cops outside the national TV station. As the crowds approached, they raked them with bullets. Fearful for the first time, AxMan jumped down into the turret. But for no apparent reason the police stopped firing and retreated. Rebel soldiers rushed into the TV station to take over. AxMan shook his head in surprise and they moved on.

To the parliament building. Again, there were gunshots, but again the troops fell back.

'It's too easy,' Freddie shouted up.

'We're winning.'

'No, this is Meredith Heel's doing. Lucky Strike would retreat as willingly as a rottweiler with its teeth in your leg. She's dropping back to draw us on. The army's on its way from Three Mountains. She wants to catch us between the two.'

'An ambush?'

'Fucking-A.'

'We have to stop everyone before they're killed.'

'Good luck with that. You started it.'

AxMan turned in the turret and tried to wave people back. They just laughed and made devil's horns at him. He gave up in desperation. Stopping the torrent of protesters would be like trying to dam the Atlantic.

All the time, Jeremiah Peckerham steered the armoured car through the crowds towards the palace and towards danger. AxMan could hear more sustained gunfire ahead. It was growing closer. They turned a corner. In front of them stood the palace square and beyond the palace, its gates gleaming with fresh gold plate in the growing dawn light.

Over the past week, AxMan and Freddie had arranged for two of Jamie's largest fixed loudspeaker stacks to be placed on the great square. These were already blasting out a medley of AxMan songs. All the trucks were converging, following AxMan's plan. As he watched, three more low-loaders with AxMan tribute acts entered the square and took up positions on either side. Behind them danced a thousand protesters. More. Filling the square. Chanting AxMan's lyrics.

But Freddie had been right. Deep lines of mercenaries were waiting for them, dug in behind the palace railings, protected by concrete blocks and razor wire. Others ranged along the roofs of government buildings on either side. The first of the returning army helicopters appeared. It hovered low over the palace square.

This was the real enemy – Meredith Heel's elite military contractors, together with Lucky Strike's palace guard, well-trained and well-prepared. These guns worked. To prove it, they shot into the crowd. The helicopter started firing rockets at the loudspeakers, silencing them, one by one.

AxMan ducked down inside the turret and slammed shut the hatch. The armoured car filled with engine fumes and the body odours of four frightened men. In the front, Freddie gazed through the visor with a rigid jaw.

'Not so fucking bloodless now,' he said.

'Shit. How many of these people are going to die?'

'Probably most of 'em… Most of us.'

AxMan wrung his hands. 'But we can't let it happen.'

'It was their choice,' Freddie said. 'We didn't tell them they had to join us.'

'We kind of did.'

'If they'd thought negatively,' Micky added from the back, 'they'd have had the sense to stay at home.'

# 63 Continual Something-Something Improvement

Jeremiah Peckerham sighed and took his hands off the steering wheel. 'Do you want to turn back?' They could hear rounds hitting the outside of the hull.

Freddie looked at AxMan. 'This was your idea.'

Micky nodded. 'Yeah, and I told you we probably wouldn't bloody survive. That's the trouble with you optimists. You always imagine you'll be the exception. Well, mate, here we are.'

For all his bravado, AxMan felt numb. All his anger had gone. Did he want to turn back? 'What, and leave all the others?'

'You always have a choice,' Micky said.

Freddie slapped the inner wall of the armoured car. 'There, I told you before! Everyone has a choice.'

'You mean like I chose to believe in your scam concert?' AxMan said.

'Exactly. Nobody tells the fish to bite the worm.'

'What did you ever choose? Aside from you?'

'Enough, children!' Peckerham gave another sigh. 'No bickering. So we tried and we lost. They've won. They always win. I give in. You do all remember, I never wanted to be a leader. That was never *my* choice.'

AxMan swallowed. Yes, he could run. Go back to being a stage hero, singing about rebellion. Selling a few albums less every year. Maybe Cla-Rice would take him back. If not, there'd be groupies to keep him warm as he grew older. Probably also fewer every year. Would death actually be any worse?

He didn't like the thought he was having, but he had it anyway. Fuck it! He reached over and pushed Peckerham out of the way.

Jammed his foot on the throttle.

The armoured car accelerated forwards at full speed across the square.

'Well, this is my fucking choice!' AxMan shouted over the whine of the engine.

Peckerham tried to stop him but he didn't have the strength. The ancient armoured car jolted over the cobbles. Freddie yelled he was mad. Micky laughed. The palace gates loomed through the view slit. Palace guards dived out of the way. Metal crashed against metal.

AxMan whacked his head against the armoured visor. The car came to a grinding halt and all went dark.

For a moment, nothing moved. He could see nothing. Hear nothing. Was he dead? Then he realised. The visor had slammed shut.

Tentatively, he opened the turret hatch and looked out. The sun rose low over the far side of the square. The palace gates hung at skewed angles- the thin layer of Lucky-Strike-ego-boosting-make-the-island-great-again gold plate blistered like torn banana skin.

The presidential guard kept firing at the rebels. The rebels kept firing at the palace guard. The mob continued to chant.

Forgetting where he was for a moment, AxMan made devil's horns and waved. People waved back. He climbed out and made a fist and they all made fists in return.

'Get the fuck back in,' Freddie called.

'It's not that different from a mosh pit,' AxMan shouted down.

He called out to Lucky Strike to give himself up. Of course nobody could hear him.

He climbed out and stood on the roof of the armoured car, ignoring Freddie, who yelled to him to stay under cover.

'It's not a gig,' Freddie called up. 'And that's not a mosh pit.'

A fresh burst of fire spattered the hull of the armoured car, inches away from AxMan's feet. Mosh pits weren't normally so dangerous. He turned to clamber back.

But then, as if in answer to him, there was a noise from the presidential palace.

AxMan stopped. Shouting came from the building – a great deal of shouting – growing louder, like a flood of people rushing towards them. It sounded like more fighting was taking place inside the palace than outside.

At first he couldn't hear distinctly, but then he started to make out phrases. '*Think positive,*' and '*Continual something-something Improvement.*'

But they couldn't be.

'Look!' Freddie shouted. AxMan peered over the top of the turret. The presidential guard was retreating. Seeing the guards retreat, the mercenaries also started moving back into the palace. The snipers disappeared from the rooftops.

AxMan jumped down to join the mob, chanting and making devil's horns, like a child at a party, and Micky joined him.

'No,' Freddie shouted. 'It's a trap.'

'No, it's CRAPI!' AxMan followed the mob up the same entrance steps he'd been swept up only a few weeks earlier during the prison riot.

Inside, Gropius-Plante troops sprinted from office to office, shredding documents and smashing hard drives. He ran after them, ready to fight anyone who turned on him, but no-one did. Indeed, they were more preoccupied with the shouting coming from the other direction.

Men and women were running through from the rear of the palace. They looked very much like the slave labour at Three Mountains, some wearing servants' liveries, others in tatters, and yet others in boxer shorts or torn T-shirts.

Outnumbering the military advisers and armed guards, they fought with makeshift weapons, lumps of wood, sharpened metal table legs. They shouldn't have had a hope against guns and trained fighters, but no-one had told them this.

And all the time they shouted '*Think positive*' and '*Continuous Realistic and Positive Improvement.*'

AxMan found himself joined by Freddie, Jeremiah Peckerham and Micky.

'Did you teach them that?' he asked Micky.

'Not me, mate.' Micky gazed at them in consternation. 'I told you, I decided all that was bollocks. I told all the other slaves they'd do best to give up and prepare to die.'

'Did you make many friends?' AxMan rubbed his ear thoughtfully.

'No. But I didn't expect to. Friends are—'

'Just an illusion,' Freddie said, 'distracting us from the fact that life is shit.'

'Something like that.'

They followed as the military contractors retreated into the encampment behind the palace. There, the remaining advisers ran from hut to hut, snatching up their belongings, pursued by the implacable mob of Disappeareds, like some weird, unstoppable zombie movie. Freddie raised his gun, but then lowered it again.

'It'd be like shooting sheep,' he said morosely, like this soft-heartedness worried him.

Land Rovers, trucks and Humvees left at speed, laden with mercenaries and their weapons.

AxMan found a worker's mop and swung it wildly – a ninja staff – yelping as he chased mercenaries.

'This isn't a bloody game,' Freddie called, but AxMan yelped louder.

As they advanced, he made out a tall woman with long unwashed hair and stylish but grubby jeans, hitting out with a garden spade. One of the forced labourers threw a stone at the soldiers and missed. The stone bounced off the metal side of a hut and hit the woman squarely on the head.

'Hell!' she shouted.

'Dania!' AxMan called.

'Dania!' Freddie yelled, next to him.

Dania turned round and squinted in their direction. 'It's the gangster and the pop star!'

She was hardly recognisable, face scarred, hair scraped back. Freddie ran over and hugged her. Then she hugged AxMan, who said he'd never mind being called a pop star again.

'The family?' Freddie held his sister's arms. AxMan hardly dared listen to the answer.

'Mostly alive,' she said. 'Parents, aunts, uncles and almost all the cousins. We dodged the aviary.'

As she spoke, the presidential helicopter suddenly roared up from beside the palace, 'Lucky Strike 1' in bright red and blue letters on its side, closely followed by a Gropius-Plante helicopter gunship, in one of whose windows AxMan was sure he could see a face with a blonde bob, gazing down at him.

The gunship turned in the air, spraying the mob with machine gun fire, to show that Meredith Heel remained to the very end an enemy of all socialists, anti-capitalists, pro-democracy environmentalists, Greens, rebels, wokes, snowflakes and especially singers.

AxMan grabbed Freddie's machine gun. He fired back. He knew there was no hope of hitting anything from that distance, but he felt he had to do something. He fired until he'd used up all the bullets in the magazine.

A minute later, the two machines wheeled away across the city and disappeared out over the sea.

# 64 Absent Friends

It was impossible. Ridiculous. As Micky said, the good guys never win in real life. But they had. They'd won. As the news spread, Lucky Strike's supporters realised that backing the president had been a silly misunderstanding – in fact, they'd not actually been supporters at all. It turned out that nobody in the country had actually been in favour of this murderous upstart. Even the army. They simply hadn't got around to saying so.

As for ex-President Lucky Strike Morton himself, he headed straight for his Cayman Islands bank account and a future with his wife, broken only by endless games of golf. It would be punishment enough.

In the minutes of euphoria after taking the presidential palace, Freddie and Dania had discovered their parents in the palace grounds. Freddie's mother was chasing passing mercenaries with a broom, while his father sat on the ground and told her crossly that she'd get hurt. Then they'd searched together for any further relatives who'd stayed alive and found many of them, including Sid, the idiot cousin who'd been scared by Bachman's SWAT team into calling Freddie to the marketplace ambush just six weeks before.

Celebrations went on all around and involved such timeless rituals as destroying priceless paintings and looting the remaining computers. Some things, thought AxMan, never change.

Later he stood with Dania, Freddie and Micky in the first-floor reception room, behind tall French windows that led to the palace balcony. Together, they watched PanAm drag Jeremiah Peckerham onto the balcony in the sunshine and shove a microphone into his hands. Cheers rose from the crowd below: '*Long Live The President!*'

'I am not the president,' the little professor said, once the noise had died down. 'Nor do I want to be. I want only to spend more time with my books and my family. Nobody has asked if I minded being president, and if they had asked I'd have told them I did mind, very much.'

He tried to go back inside, but PanAm held fast onto his arm. 'If you mind then that seals it,' she said. 'You wrote the book.'

Then PanAm beckoned AxMan onto the balcony to join the celebrations.

'No, no, no!' AxMan turned to Freddie. 'Mind you, would it be so much different from the peace concert we never had?'

He grabbed Freddie by the arm and told him he should come too.

But Freddie held back. 'Too much publicity is not so good in my line of work.'

So AxMan joined the new President Peckerham and led the crowd in singing the Three Mountains song. The morning sun shone bright on the rebel soldiers and supporters waving and singing in the palace square below.

* * *

It was utopia. It was paradise with an AxMan soundtrack. Throughout the rest of the day, the cafés and bars played his music. People bought him drinks and asked to share selfies. Many shops owned by The Man were looted and vital items liberated for the people: trainers, iPhones, designer handbags. There was much dancing. Many little Benkudans would be conceived in the nights that followed.

Jeremiah Peckerham announced his first cabinet. The little professor stood by his principles and drew on people who least wanted to govern, including some rebels but also a number of moderates and even a few farmers and slum-dwellers.

PanAm became Secretary of State, U-Haul Culture and Media, and Jamie J Johnson got Finance, with the blessing of his teachers on the online course at Harvvard with two vs. He promptly and unilaterally announced the cancellation of all the island's debts.

To everyone's surprise, the new president offered Dania Forrester the Ministry of Social Security and Justice, on the basis of her long experience watching Freddie at work. She'd refused, of course. Peckerham replied that, if he wasn't allowed to refuse on the grounds of not wanting it, neither was she.

Meanwhile, out in the wider world, the videos and photos that PanAm had taken of Three Mountains played heavily on the BBC and CNN. More stories emerged of the slave workers and the dying fish. Gropius-Plante denied all knowledge and, in the spirit of transparency, blamed a rogue employee. Meredith Heel was swiftly reassigned, sent to revive the economy of Uzbekistan. Without a return ticket.

That first afternoon, AxMan and Micky finally entered the penthouse suite Dania had booked for him all those weeks before, in what used to be the Isobel Bachman Ocean View Hotel – then renamed the Lucky Strike Continental Deluxe, now the Prof J Peckerham International – and were reunited with their suitcases. Micky went a strange colour when he saw them sitting on the floor.

'You know,' AxMan said, 'I wonder how all this would have turned out if that Meredith Heel hadn't had drugs planted on me.'

'Ah,' Micky said. 'You know we said we'd always be honest with each other?'

AxMan closed his eyes in resignation. 'Shit, you didn't.'

'I thought you might want something on the trip. Sorry.'

'Yeah, so am I.'

'I was only thinking of your needs, Ax.' Micky spread his arms wide. 'Though I didn't think I'd put in quite so much.'

AxMan tried to aim for forgiveness. 'I knew it was you really. I just didn't want to embarrass you.'

Reassured, Micky left for his room, saying he could sleep for a month.

Once he was gone, AxMan remembered he hadn't asked him to rebook their flights home, then resolved to do it himself and was stunned to find how easy it was. Then he felt he needed a nap and when he woke in the mid-afternoon his email inbox was full. Every TV channel wanted to interview him.

Pissoff Entertainment sent enthusiastic congratulations and said all that talk of not paying what they owed him was invented by the newspapers.

His mother told him how proud she was. The synagogue and the Orthodontic Society had asked her to send their best wishes. She was looking forward to talking to him about the new root canal treatment she was developing.

And there were congratulatory messages from Kylie, Paul, Ringo, Madge, Phil, KT, Dave, Annie, Bruce, Roger and Mick.

# 65 Thinking About You

AxMan saw the message on Twitter. She was ready on Skype, she said, if he was online and wanted to speak. AxMan logged on and saw Cla-Rice's pixilated face. It was the first time they'd spoken in person since he'd messaged about dumping her clothes.

She was wearing a low-cut halter-neck top and bright red lipstick and seemed nervous. 'I've left The Font, haven't I. It was always a mistake. He came over like a hero, but all he did was a few charity gigs, just to show off.'

She adjusted a bra strap. 'I totally get that you probably can't forgive me, baby.'

AxMan noticed her lips seemed fuller than before. Her cheeks were smoother and higher and appeared to move less.

She continued. 'I totally get that. Just because he was good in bed, didn't mean anything. Even when he was on top of me, I was thinking about you. You know how to make a woman feel good. I miss you. I'm wearing the red bra and thong you bought me. OK, if you want to tell me to piss off, I understand fully. Go on, say it. I'm ready.'

She held up her hands in submission and braced herself for the onslaught, lips half open.

'I don't know,' AxMan said into the tiny microphone. His own picture appeared low down on the right, squashed tiny next to her bouncing left breast. 'It hurt me when you went.'

'I'll never forgive myself. I didn't know what I was doing. He so took me in with his leather trousers and promises that I'd have my own songs with his new producer. But he's not gone viral like you. Not that that matters. Who needs him? Listen, baby, we're soulmates, us. We've got something special. Do you want to do internet sex?'

AxMan sat up straight. 'What?'

'Just a thought. Like we used to when you were on the road. I can talk you through it.' She loosened the halter-neck to reveal a large blotchy nipple.

'No!' said AxMan. 'Not now. It's been heavy these last weeks. I can wait till I get home.'

'Can't be too soon, sweetie-babe.' She complacently readjusted her top and blew a large kiss. 'I can't wait for us to be photographed together – and not just photographs, big boy,' she added in a husky tone, then rapidly became brisker. 'Can't talk too long. I'm about to be picked up for a spot on Graham Norton. I know, all this publicity stuff is bore-o-rama, but his people just kept asking me to talk about you. Anyway, when will you be flying back? I've got a bit of a gap next week.'

'They need me here for a little longer, girl.' AxMan could still hear the crowds on the promenade outside.

'What the fuck do they need you for?'

'This is politics, yeah. You don't just storm the palace, people have to decide what to do next. Like make laws and stuff.'

'Yeah, well, whatever. Are you making laws with that woman?'

'Woman?'

'The gangster's sister. Whatshername, yeah? Is she part of it?'

'Dania? Not really.'

'The famous Dania,' Cla-Rice said with a raucous laugh. 'I saw her pictures. She should do something about her lips. They look thin. I could help her with that. And she's more scarred than I expected. I suppose that's some kind of ritual they have out there.'

'No.' AxMan shook his head. 'That's from when she saved my life. Among other things. You should come here and meet her and see the sights.'

'You know me, babe, I've never been much interested in sights. I'm a people person. Look, the car from the BBC will be here any minute.' Cla-Rice was already turning away from the camera as she cut off the call. Her picture vanished like it had never been there.

AxMan sat for a minute staring at the laptop screen, lost in thought.

# 66 Evening Drinks

As evening approached, AxMan sat with Freddie, Micky and Dania outside one of the city's dockside bars. He'd heard it said that happiness doesn't come from getting what you wish for, but what he'd mostly wished for was to stay alive and he was content to settle for that, for the time being. Along with saving a small bit of the world from The Man.

AxMan asked Freddie for his plans. Did he think he'd work with Peckerham behind the scenes?

Freddie was holding up his vodka so that the setting sun glinted off it. 'I've seen governments come and go,' he said. 'For the moment, I'm one of the heroes. Soon, politicians will start worrying about votes and that means speeches about law and order. Finally, they'll come looking for someone to make an example of. My plan is not to be that example when it happens.'

Dania took a drag and blew her smoke away from the table. 'So, Mr Viral Rock Star. You must be looking forward to going home to London and to your girlfriend with the expandable tits, yes?'

'Of course.' AxMan didn't add any more.

'All that rain and cold weather.'

'It doesn't rain that much.'

'And no doubt you've already booked your plane ticket.'

'Yeah, but I came to try to save the starving children. I'm not sure I've done much of that.'

'We'll work on it.'

Micky happily relayed the more recent predictions of imminent disaster for Benkuda. 'Either an economic crash or a counterrevolution. Or both.'

AxMan shook his head. 'I don't get it. As long as I can remember, you've told me to focus on what I want to achieve. Now we've achieved all this. Meredith Heel has gone. Lucky Strike's gone. They've got a new president who might actually make things better. And all you talk about is how bad everything's going to be.'

'I for one haven't changed my opinion.' Dania drained her glass and signalled to the waitress for another. 'The pirates gang-banged me in their boat. Then they sold me. I thought I'd be shot, but instead I was forced to work in one of the brothels behind the palace.

'And now, here I am. If I'd expected good things to happen, I'd be disappointed to have ended up battered and scarred and aching in every limb, but I sit in this glorious sunset and think how lucky I am to have this wine and this nice dress and my brother and two good friends. While expecting the worst, I'm still happy.'

AxMan sat back and frowned at her. 'But I still don't understand. All those Disappeareds in the palace. It must have been you who had them chanting "Think positive" and "CRAPI" and all that?'

'Continuous Realistic and Positive Improvement,' Dania said. 'Micky told me about it after we were captured. It's rubbish. Nobody improves. We just get better at pretending. But it makes a great slogan, doesn't it. It got them all fighting.'

AxMan finished his drink. 'You know, I believed all that positivity stuff. When I thought Micky was dead, I kept trying to think positive in his memory.'

'But were you happy? Are you happy now?'

'I was until we had this conversation. Now I'm just confused.'

'Maybe confused is the most sane way to be.'

AxMan said nothing. But he noticed that Dania had put her hand on his knee. He also noticed, strangely, that he was indeed happy. There was no problem to fix. The sun sank into the sea. The vodka was good. He liked the people he was with. And for the time being he actually felt chill.

\* \* \*

AxMan tried to be negative and think of all the bad things that might happen. Then he tried to be positive and thought about all the good things that could result instead.

Finally, that night he gave up thinking, ripped up his return ticket and decided to stay and organise a charity concert. For real this time. With all his new best friends... including Paul and Madge and Dave and Eric and Kylie and KT and Mick.

Freddie and Jamie J offered to provide the flights, hotel rooms, security guards, SUVs, drugs and Portaloos. At a price.

Dania and Micky cheerfully informed him it would be a disaster.

And so, for the time being, happiness reigned over the people of the island that a passing privateer had once named after a turnip and declared his favourite in the entire world.

And who would begrudge them that?

# Author's note

We all hobble painfully up onto the shoulders of giants. Many great books and helpful people inspired me to write this little one. Voltaire's *Candide*, for one. Joseph Heller's *Catch 22* for another. If you haven't read them, I urge you to. Those who have will spot that Jamie J is a not very veiled tribute to Heller's Milo Minderbinder.

While the island of Benkuda, Midlands Metal Hell, Fruitcancorp and all the characters in this novel are made-up, people like the fictional Meredith Heel do exist and have for some time. Their job is to lead countries like Benkuda into debt, whatever lies and false promises it takes, and make money out of them. If you want to explore more, read John Perkins' controversial *Confessions of an Economic Hit Man* (New York, Plume. 2004). You can find online arguments over his claims, but few deny that rich nations and their corporations have made obscene amounts of money from locking developing countries into debt from which they struggle to escape.

When it comes to Benkuda, you may find some distant resemblances to the Dominican Republic, where I filmed my BBC2 satirical documentary *Sex, Drugs and Dinner*. It was there that I saw agribusinesses like Fruitcancorp grow food for the rich and impoverish the poor. I never joined a rebellion, but I could have been tempted. This film, in turn, was inspired by Colin Tudge's eye-opening *The Famine Business* (Faber and Faber, London 1977). You might like to check out his work.

I also nicked the Dominican quirk of naming children after their favourite brands.

Writing a book is not unlike making a film, as it happens. So many people help it on its way, credited and uncredited. There are more than I have space to mention and some prefer to remain anonymous.

I would particularly like to thank Mike Forde for invaluable insights into guerrilla warfare. I'm grateful to Duncan Green of Oxfam, Sarah Marsh and Mike Noyes of CAFOD, Tim Lang of the Centre for Food Policy and Jana Phillips, who went out of their way to share their knowledge of world hunger, charities, gangs and working in developing countries. Asher Kenton, Peter Gilmour, Richard Hennerley, Dante Bonutto, Sumerah Srivastav and Bjorn Billgren gave irreplaceable advice on the world of heavy metal, but none more than Simon Cann, who has constantly kept me honest when it comes to the musical facts. Special thanks, too, to my fellow writers, Simon (again), Jan Woolf, Eve Richings and Charlie Hopkinson, who read and re-read my many drafts, going beyond the call of duty; to Morgen Bailey for her editing skills; and to Jane Dixon-Smith for her brilliant cover, as ever.

Finally, I have to thank my wife Elaine for coping so gracefully with living under the same roof as an author.

They all helped create the good parts. Any cock-ups are all my own.

# Thank You from the Publisher

Thank you for reading this book. Do consider leaving a review on Amazon. It really does help readers find the books that are right for them.

If you enjoyed *Play Me!* then try Charles Harris' bestseller, *The Breaking of Liam Glass* - the award-shortlisted satire of tabloid sleaze and corruption.

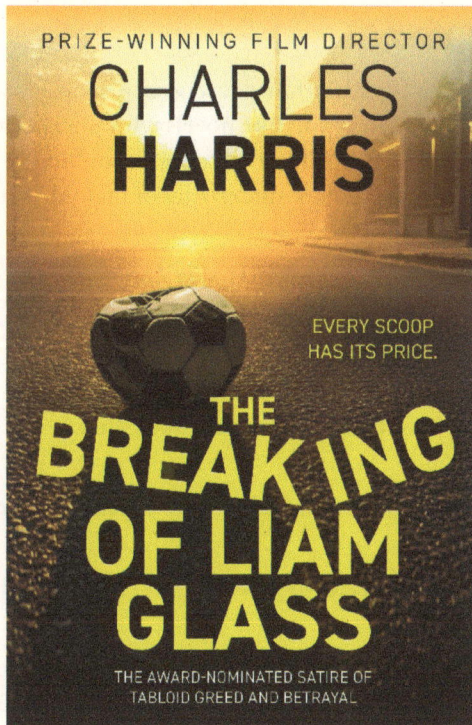

PRIZE-WINNING FILM DIRECTOR

## CHARLES HARRIS

EVERY SCOOP HAS ITS PRICE.

### THE BREAKING OF LIAM GLASS

THE AWARD-NOMINATED SATIRE OF TABLOID GREED AND BETRAYAL

**EVERY SCOOP HAS ITS PRICE**

It's Jason Crowthorne's twenty-ninth birthday and he's desperate. When he won Young Journalist of the Year, he landed the job in newspapers that he always dreamt of, but since then his career has been stagnating. Now he learns he's to be replaced by a cheaper hack. But then he uncovers the biggest scoop of his life.

Teenager Liam Glass lies in a coma after a mugging. Jason chases down tantalising rumours that the boy is the secret love-child of one of the Premier League's top strikers. A story he could sell for big money to the tabloids and spark a career-boosting campaign against knife-crime. Only, try as he might, he can't prove it.

A chance call from a sleazy footballing agent hands Jason an unexpected way to sex up the story. All he has to do is tell a little lie.

But to Jason's horror, that lie puts Liam's life at risk…

Sucked into a whirlpool of greed and moral corruption, can Jason find a way to save the boy's life, or has he lost his soul to chasing headlines?

*The Breaking of Liam Glass* is a fast-paced urban satire by award-winning film-maker Charles Harris. If you like novels with unexpected twists, vivid characters and an unlikely anti-hero who keeps bobbing to the top, you'll love this gripping tale of the dark underbelly of tabloid journalism.

Break open *The Breaking of Liam Glass* to
dive into a cut-throat world today!

Go to https://mybook.to/BOLG or order a
copy from your local bookshop.

**#1 Bestseller Amazon Hot New Releases – Satire**

**#1 Amazon category bestseller – Mass Media**

Nominated for the Eyelands International Novel Awards 2018
Nominated for the Wishing Shelf Book Awards 2017